COLLAPSE

OF SOCIETY ACCORDING TO DICK AND JANE

GRACE BUDRYS

COLLAPSE OF SOCIETY ACCORDING TO DICK AND JANE

PROMINENT
BOOKS
EDGE

5830 E 2nd St, Ste 7000 #9983
Casper, WY 82609
USA

FOREWORD

Dick and Jane play a central role in the story presented in this book. They serve much the same purpose here as they did in 1930 when they first appeared in children's books. Their assignment then was to teach children to read. Here, their purpose is to educate adults about the sociopolitical changes taking place around them and the belief system that fosters those changes. The story is set ten years into the future, meaning that the story interweaves facts and fiction. Written in 2021, it offers some historical perspective on the issues Dick and Jane were concerned about before the Trump II administration introduced new ones.

We follow along as Jane and Dick proceed to organize a small discussion group to share their concerns. The group includes two investigative reporters engaged in tracking the transfer of public goods and services to the private sector. They report finding a steady increase in the volume of such transfers, which the group considers troubling. They find the extent to which the transfers are being consolidated even more distressing. Members of the group determine that the unrelenting corporate takeover of public goods and services is causing society to lose control over its resources, restricting its ability to carry out essential responsibilities. They conclude that they are witnessing the collapse of society.

ONE

It was Saturday morning. Dick was checking his email because he hadn't had a chance to do that yesterday. He had been tied up in his lab all day. The lab was under pressure to come up with a vaccine for the latest virus, SARS-12, to hit the country. It was a coronavirus in the same family as COVID-19. It was just starting to spread. No one knew whether things would get as bad as they had been a decade ago. But funding agencies were now readier to start supporting research leading to a vaccine much more rapidly than they were back in 2020. The COVID-19 experience was still reasonably fresh in people's minds.

Dick was putting in ten-and twelve-hour days on it. It was a good thing that he had longish hair so that it didn't look like he was overdue for a haircut. It just looked like it always looked because it got curlier as it got longer, making it look just as short. His mop of dark curly hair looked attractive whether it was shorter or longer. When he looked at himself in the mirror, he thought he looked pale. He was spending too many hours indoors. His muscles felt stiff. He would have to spend some time outdoors. He needed some sun. Maybe he'd go for a run. That would help him think that he was doing something about looking unhealthy. It would keep him from thinking he not only felt out of shape but looked it. Which, of course, he didn't after only a few weeks on this regimen. He didn't look much like a nerd who spent all his time in a lab, even though that was closer to his identity than his athletic good looks would suggest.

Nevertheless, when someone puts in that many hours on a project that requires so much concentration, a person does get worn out. And, Dick was certainly ready for a couple of days' break.

Although vaccine development was not the focus of Dick's research, he was the person in charge of vaccine research currently being done at Abacus Labs. The lab was established about eight years ago in a partnership between Franklin University and a spinoff company established by scientists at the university. At the time, he was a biochemistry professor at the university who, working in collaboration with colleagues, identified a molecule that he expected to lead to a new drug for treating people with high cholesterol. That is exactly what happened. The drug, which turned out to be very successful, became a big seller. All the scientists associated with the research were richly rewarded. The university patented the molecule. The scientists received company shares. The university's portfolio became fatter.

Dick and the two other researchers he was working with at Abacus, Adam and Mark, both biophysicists, had suddenly been drawn into the search for a vaccine. The lab was using the new anti-viral platform developed in response to the COVID-19 virus, the messenger RNA approach. Everyone in the lab was pretty excited about having the opportunity to participate in a project that would employ this novel approach in creating a vaccine.

They were at the first stage of research. Their task was to isolate a non-infectious protein segment from the SARS-CoV-2 viral cell. The vaccine was designed to alert immune cells to replicate part of the protein and then carry out instructions to create antibodies that would eliminate the protein. The research was going well. Dick and his team were ready to take a break. The next step was to test the vaccine on lab mice to check for efficacy and side effects.

So anyway, here he was at home on Saturday morning, taking the weekend off, which he hadn't done for a while, and looking through piles of e-mail messages. The message that caught his attention was the one from the water department. It said the water to his house would be cut off for nonpayment of a past-due bill. The account was listed in both their names. His e-mail was on the bill, but his wife paid it out of her account.

"Hey Jane," he called out, "didn't you pay the water bill last month?"

"Yes," she said. "I'll look at my credit card statement. It gets deducted automatically. It's obviously a mistake. That happened once before, remember?"

"Yeah, I remember. It was right after the water department became a private-public partnership. Just after the city leased out the water treatment operation and it became the American Sanitary Water Works company, the ASWW. I remember it all well because we tried to stop the move. I remember going out and marching in protest. It got pretty rowdy. I think that there were just too many different kinds of national protests at the time for this one to get enough attention to have any effect. The protests against police brutality were attracting the most attention. That did make some difference. Some cities shifted funds going to the police and put the money into community services."

"True," Jane said. "In the meantime, people aren't paying attention to the fact that the government has been selling off all kinds of things. That began to happen so regularly that people became numb to it. They just haven't been protesting those kinds of things very much. But I think that may be changing. At least, I'm hoping that's the case. The people we know are paying more attention again and registering their opinion on the streets once again. We'll be remembering the more recent protests that we've been participating in for a long time."

Dick had half a smile on his face. He said, "Remember how we got sprayed with some kind of liquid during the anti-ASWW protests? They still haven't revealed what was in it. Remember, we had red, sore eyes for a few days and headaches on and off, but it wore off. I hope we don't discover that it caused lasting damage that won't show up for years, and suddenly we'll get diagnosed with some mysterious illness. Maybe we'll be lucky. Maybe it was just something like a household cleanser and not rat poison."

"Don't kid around about stuff like that," said Jane. "It could still do a lot of harm if it got absorbed into our sinuses through our eyes or if we inhaled enough of it to create some damage in our lungs. I was pretty angry about it at the time, especially because they refused to say what it was. The idea that the company that the police department got it from could get away with claiming the stuff was a product they created, and patented, is ridiculous. The company argued that the ingredients were a matter of intellectual property. What horseshit. I remember that we all thought it was probably a watered-down version of one of the standard household cleaning products that they put some green dye into. I remember that we had green streaks on our clothes that didn't wash out."

Jane was looking stern, which she had worked to achieve until it came naturally. She wore very little make-up, only a little mascara, wore her chestnut brown hair in a twist, and stood with her back straight. It was when she smiled that you could see that she was very pretty and was making an effort to set aside the image of a good-looking woman who got her job based on her looks. She had grown accustomed to making an effort to appear as someone who should be taken seriously.

"Yeah, I remember. I still have a t-shirt with green steaks in it," Dick said. I plan to wear it to other protests in the hopes of seeing other people with similar shirts. But for now, I want to know what we're going to do about the letter saying that we didn't pay last month's bill. I know that I can call the company and have the robot tell me that they don't accept phone calls. I can respond to the email, but it will be returned as undeliverable. We've been around this block before. I can write a letter and send it by registered mail, but that's a lot of trouble and no reason to think that anyone will read it. Besides, I would have to drive to the outskirts of town to get to the only post office that's left in the area to mail it. I had to do that for something else. It took me over a half hour to get there, another twenty-five minutes to wait in line, a half-hour to get back, and then we never knew if the damn letter actually got there. Fortunately, there was a follow-up letter that time. I think it was about our automobile insurance payment, telling us that they had made a mistake and that they did receive the payment. Somehow, I don't believe that the water company will do that."

He shook his head, looking defeated. "We've spent too much time on this. I don't want to get into it today. I don't have the energy to complain about watching so many organizations and institutions getting so screwed up."

"Why don't we just send a check to the water company and assume that if we overpaid, they'll credit us?"

"I'll go along with that," was Dick's response. "But unlike you, I don't have any hope of being credited for the overpayment. As far as I can see, this company did what every other company in the private sector does when they take over a public agency. They fired all the experienced workers to cut their payroll costs and hired inexperienced people desperate for a job and willing to work for low wages. And they didn't bother training them. If the new employees don't figure out the job on their own, the company just gets rid of them and gets new untrained workers. I don't believe the company cares if they don't fix the error and credit us. They don't care if we get pissed off. What can we do about it? There is no alternative water company. It's ASWW or no water. Yes, we had no alternative source of water before it was sold off, but the organization was more responsive to its customers. People who worked there knew their jobs. You could reach an actual person when you phoned. I know that because so many people have moved here to work in our lab over the years, who needed to set up the water service. They called, and it got done. I heard about the good and bad experiences connected to moving here, not just the water company experience."

Jane nodded and said, "I guess we should be thankful that they didn't fire the engineers in charge of managing the quality of the water. Of course, if they did and the new owners are giving those jobs to their relatives who have no scientific background and training, we wouldn't know about it until enough people contracted some dread disease."

Then she added, "I know we should stop talking about it because we've both complained about this before. But it bothers me. Have you noticed that what they charge for the water service has been steadily increasing? It has increased every couple of years since the company has been in existence. The increase in charges is far more than was projected. The excuse is a familiar one – that they needed to upgrade the plant. Maybe. But we're not getting information on how much is going for the upgrade and how much is going to that murky terrain, administrative expenses. The committee in charge of the deal testified about that when the deal was being considered by the city council. The representatives of what would be the newly formed enterprise said that "administrative expenses" included a variety of operating costs, such as maintenance and replacement of office equipment and utility bills through to costs associated with monitoring water quality, calculating water usage, sending out bills, and expenses, which everyone knows do not increase much on an annual basis. And they don't increase at anywhere close to the rate at which our bills are increasing. That leaves increases in executive salaries and perks, which are not reported separately and instead are buried somewhere in the murkiness."

"Yeah," Dick looked like he was ready to get into it now. "What makes Jimmy Burnett qualified to head up ASWW? The fact that he's the First Ward Representative's cousin? I guess it must be because his ward uses a lot of water, right? No, I guess it's because he headed up the group that did the study that ended up advocating privatization."

Pausing a moment before going on, Dick sounded like Jane had just criticized him. He said, "I know, I know. I should try to take advantage of my time off and do something enjoyable this weekend rather than going over all the stuff that drives both of us nuts. Want to drive up to the Rocky Cliffs State Forest and rent a paddle boat? It's only about a 40-minute drive. Paddling around is relaxing. And it's a beautiful day. What do you say?"

"Okay. That sounds like something I'm more than ready for. Did you add money to the toll road account? I think we got stopped at the toll booth for lack of funds the last time we drove in that direction. I know you don't need to hear this, but the tolls have probably gone up since the last time we were on that section of the road. That was about three months ago. As far as I could see, there hadn't been any improvements on the road. Only increased charges that I assume are benefiting the investors of the organization to whom the county leased that part of the Wisconsin highway system for the next one hundred years. As I recall, it's an international conglomerate, right?"

"Yeah, I think it is," said Dick. "I'll add to the account. I'll have to do it sooner or later anyway."

"I won't bother packing anything to eat. I remember the nice snack bar there that serves great hot dogs. It's a neat place. It's been in business for three-quarters of a century. The family that owns it kept it open for take-out throughout the pandemic. I haven't had a hot dog with all the fixings in ages. I like eating hot dogs when we're outdoors. It's easier to wipe off mustard and relish smears on your face and let the excess drop on the ground when you're outdoors. A lot messier when you're indoors."

Dick and Jane changed into shorts and T-shirts, packed sunscreen, hats, threw in some bug spray, and they were ready to roll. Once they left the city, it was a pleasant drive as they passed neatly kept farms interrupted by stands of oaks and maples. June was the perfect month for this kind of trip.

Just as they expected, the highway toll charge had gone up another fifty cents since they were on this leg of the state highway a few months ago. The road wasn't in bad repair. But it wasn't in better shape than parts of the road still owned by the state.

When they got to the Rocky Cliffs parking lot, they weren't prepared for what they were seeing. "Oh no." They said in unison. Jane said, "Oh my god, it's turned into a McDonald's, golden arches and everything. I'm so disappointed. I won't get my hot dog. But more than that, the place looks so commercialized now. The snack bar stand was such a nice, small-scale, family-friendly kind of place. It had those old-fashioned outdoor tables and umbrellas. Those are gone. This thing stands there representing everything we've come to the park to get away from – the city and all noise, the crowds, and everything."

"Remember, dear, that it's being here means that we don't have to have an increase in taxes to support the state park system. Because this place is surely paying the state for the right to set up shop here. You have to look at the important financial benefits to the state of Wisconsin."

"Oh, shut up, Dick. Don't say things like that. I know you don't mean it. It's just so sad to see something else that we enjoyed disappearing. Let's rent the paddleboat and try to ignore the arches. I know that we'll get hungry. Maybe we can come back later and find something to eat that isn't all fat and calories, and make up for it with a nice dinner. I hope that the boat concession hasn't been sold off to a private franchise of some sort."

As they walked further, they could see that the park was more crowded than they expected. Well, that was okay because from what they could see, there still weren't that many people on the lake. No one seemed to be registering the fact that the country might be experiencing a new virus. Maybe they were trying to get in their fun before everyone got locked down. After all, that's at least part of why Dick and Jane came out here. They could see families sitting at picnic tables, relaxing, watching the kids play ball, chase each other, and throw stuff for their dogs to retrieve. It was a Norman Rockwell scene until they walked a little further.

Dick was first to see the sign. "Crap. The boat concession has been renamed. You'll see it in a moment. It's now called Rocky Cliffs Boats, and in smaller print, under that, it says in partnership between the Rocky Cliffs State Park and Walterman Enterprises. Do you think the former governor is the owner? I don't want to think about how this deal was put together. Maybe it's not him, but it sure sounds like it could be the former governor or someone in his family. Whatever. It's depressing. Everywhere you turn, state and city properties are being leased out or sold off. That goes along with what's been happening to small businesses for quite a while. The ones that don't just close up shop are being bought out by big chains."

"It's just like all the sports stadiums that have been relabeled with the name of some corporation on a humongous new outdoor sign. Cities have been doing that for a couple of decades. It'd be interesting to find out when that trend started."

"At least the rental prices for the boats haven't gone up, but I wouldn't count on it staying that way. The buyers wouldn't be buying the boat concession unless they thought they would profit."

Dick and Jane paddled out to the middle of the lake. They agreed to face away from the McDonalds and the boat concession while they paddled. The sounds from the shore became more muted.

They talked about short trips they might take over the summer if the virus turned not to be as virulent as the COVID-19 virus had been. They still had the masks they bought then. Cities and states weren't telling people to observe any of the precautions instituted then. They just said to use good health practices like hand washing and covering one's mouth when coughing.

TWO

It was now Monday, the beginning of the week, and Dick and Jane were back to their routines. Dick expected to put in another long day. He and his colleagues were ready for the next stage of research, vaccinating the mice. But he didn't know when he would be able to begin doing that. He had had to order a new supply of mice. The mice commonly used in most lab research were not susceptible to coronaviruses. The lab would need to get a supply of genetically modified mice that had a human feature added to their lung cells, making those lung cells susceptible. Since every other lab doing vaccine research would be trying to get the mice, he couldn't be sure they would get there by the middle of the week when they were scheduled to arrive. The non-profit organization that breeds mice for such purposes went into high gear a month ago in the expectation that there would be a huge demand for the mice. Mice reproduce in about three weeks, but it would take a while to produce enough of them to meet the sudden demand. The researchers at Abacus had ordered the mice right away. If everything went as expected, they would get the mice in a few more days.

Once Dick and his colleagues, who had also turned into virologists for the duration of the search for a vaccine, established that the vaccine they were developing would produce an immune response when injected into the mice, it would be turned over to a pharmaceutical company to start testing on human subjects. Because things were moving at an accelerated rate, this time, a vaccine could be ready for dissemination by October. Public health officials were beginning to say that this version of the virus looked like it might turn out to be mild and mutate out of existence by the time the vaccine was ready for mass production. No one at Dick's lab was predicting another pandemic. Still, the work of creating a vaccine had to be done just in case, to avoid a possible disaster.

Jane was watching the emergence of the virus closely as well. She was an epidemiologist working at the Mintaka Department of Public Health responsible for tracking morbidity and mortality rates from all causes of disease and death in the city and the greater Mintaka area. While she hadn't seen much evidence that the virus was spreading, she knew that if it did start to spread, it was certain to cause illness among those who were always the first to be affected, people with chronic illnesses, especially those who were poor.

Everyone at the public health department was still on high alert because if the virus were to evolve into an epidemic, then the fear was that sick people who had no insurance would not get tested or treated, since they couldn't afford it. And that would contribute to the spread of the disease. The head of the department, Doctor Emmet, released a statement to the media, reminding people of what was at stake if the virus did take off, given the disorganized state of the health care system.

People will pass on the virus to anyone and everyone they come into contact with. Eventually, some of them will get sick enough to go to the emergency room. Because hospitals are required to treat everyone who comes to the ER, the ERs will become too crowded. They will be forced to admit some of those patients to the hospital even if they have no way to pay for the hospital stay. Hospitals will sustain financial losses. It's a familiar pattern. Hospitals will have to find a way to make up for the loss of income. They will charge those with insurance coverage more. Ultimately, those who have private insurance will end up paying higher premiums. Of course, the pain of finding that one has to pay a lot more for insurance is nothing compared to the troubles associated with having the illness. The politicians in this state have made it perfectly clear that they believe that

> *people who don't have health insurance don't deserve*
> *health care. Why the politicians don't recognize that*
> *they are foisting an increased financial burden onto*
> *people who have private health insurance isn't at all*
> *apparent to those of us in the public health commu-*
> *nity. It would cost so much less to treat people at an*
> *early stage of illness than treating people who get sick*
> *enough to have to go to the ER. ER care is the most*
> *expensive form of care.*

Of course, Doctor Emmet had said all this before, and it didn't convince members of the state legislature to revise their commitment to restricting eligibility to Medicaid. Jane didn't think it would be any different this time around either.

Jane was on the governor's task force dedicated to addressing health care reform in the state. The fact that the governor was a liberal and the majority of the members of the legislature were conservatives meant that the governor's task force was not likely to get anything it recommended passed. The split had existed over the last three electoral cycles. Before that, the governors were conservatives too.

Both Jane and Dick repeatedly asked each other the same question: "how it was that residents of the state could so easily ignore the fact that they were paying more for their private health insurance than people in other states precisely because hospitals were forced to treat so many people who couldn't pay their bills?" The answer was always the same: "the commitment to keeping state taxes low was a driving principle, and that was not about to change." They always ended up with the same question for which they hadn't come up with a good answer: what is it about taxes that makes people so passionate?

This evening, after coming home from work, Dick seemed more discouraged than usual. He said, "I was listening to the news on the car radio on my way home. There's a new group tweeting and posting messages all over the place, accusing people who want to expand Medicaid of being paid by the Chinese government to upset the political order in this country. They're saying Medicaid is inspired by Chinese communists. Can you believe that? Any conspiracy will do. But these people are armed and ready to fight Chinese communists on our soil. They have already targeted some of the governor's advisors on NEXT. You've heard about that? It's the newest opposition group. It has a very active media site developed by people who left Fox News because they thought it was becoming soft. These people are not soft."

Jane was working at home, like she did two or three days of the week, and had not listened to the news. "I've heard of NEXT, but I didn't know exactly what it was. I knew it was a politically conservative group, but I didn't know it was that extreme."

"Well, it's using the tactics used to attack Hillary Clinton. One of the messages on the site accused Tim Harrington, you know, the state senator from Madison leading the Medicaid expansion cause, of being a pedophile who is being blackmailed by the Chinese and being forced to work for them at the risk of having photographs of him molesting small boys released. He responded to the message by saying that there can't be any pictures because he was never engaged in that kind of behavior. The group released one photo that was grainy, but you could see his face and the face of a little kid who was nude, wearing a red scarf with a star on it around his neck, and looking scared in the photo. The picture was obviously photoshopped. I know people who have known Tim since college, and they say that he has kids of his own and would never in a thousand years do anything like that. And that this is a vicious smear. I believe them."

"Damn," said Jane. "Poor Tim. What he says about the benefits of extending Medicaid is so logical and reasonable. But these days, you have to be really courageous to head up a movement like Health for All in this state. If the NEXT people are ready to smear someone like Tim, there is no way to know how far they will go to attack people who they think oppose their views. They could get around to attacking us."

"No, we're not that important," was Dick's reaction. "I think we're safe."

"Now that they've started to attack people I respect, I'm going to follow what they do. I'm not as sure as you are that we're not possible targets. But that isn't going to stop me from working on Medicaid expansion in this state. There are too many people suffering who could get so much help if they qualified for Medicaid. And it wouldn't cost that much because the federal government pays for such a big share of it. That will continue because the Republicans still haven't managed to overturn the law that pays for that."

"They – the NEXT People – say," Dick went on, "that they are committed to protecting individual freedom. They're suspicious of the medical establishment. They say that people are getting entirely too much medical treatment and drugs. They continue to argue, against all evidence, that vaccines produce autism in children and cause premature dementia in adults. They say that Medicaid is just another scam created by doctors and hospitals. And that the people on Medicaid are taking advantage of it just because it's free. If people want to have health insurance and doctor's visits, they should pay for it. The government shouldn't be paying for it."

"Yes," said Jane. "I know, the conservatives have consistently argued that hard-working people shouldn't have to pay for lazy people to sit around, buy fancy cars, eat steak, and not work for it. You have to have a vivid but unhinged imagination to concoct that scenario. I'd like to see them live a life of luxury while being unemployed. More likely, they'd be stressed out enough to develop any number of chronic diseases. The only luxurious living sick people without insurance have a good chance of enjoying is whatever the hospital provides once they are admitted via the emergency room."

She went on. "Thank goodness that there have been a few changes in our health insurance arrangements over the last decade. Nothing dramatic, but no one expected big changes given the gridlock in Congress. The fact that everyone under 21 years of age is covered by the Children's Health Insurance Plan is good. The public option is good. But I worry about how we're handling the Medicare Trust fund, which has been depleted and has to have its funding renewed on an annual basis. It's not about to become more secure because so many people are unemployed and aren't contributing to it through payroll. That means that talk about privatizing Medicare keeps cropping up. Conservatives are constantly advocating turning it over to the private insurance companies that sell Medicare Advantage. Why isn't anyone pointing out that the only reason Medicare Advantage plans can offer so many services in addition to what traditional Medicare offers is because the federal government is subsidizing them? No, don't tell me that I keep harping on this. I know. It's just that it drives me around the bend that no one seems to object to that kind of thing. No one is bothering to object to the Medicare Advantage ads that paint such a rosy picture of what they provide without explaining the difference between HMOs and PPOs. Don't worry. I know you know the difference. I won't go over that once again. The pandemic did open up people's eyes to the idea that private insurance is superior to something like Medicare because it gives people choice. When so many people lost their jobs and their insurance at the same time and couldn't afford to buy insurance on their own, where was the choice? Losing insurance wasn't their choice. It was someone else's choice."

Dick shook his head and was about to say something, then thought better of it. Instead, he said, "Let's have a nice quiet dinner and read something uplifting for the rest of the evening, and go to bed. I'm tired. I know that the health insurance situation in this country is a never-ending source of frustration to you, but it's late, and I don't want to keep talking about it before we go to bed. You won't sleep, and you'll be wasted tomorrow."

"You're right. I'm reading a thriller mystery that is sure to provide a good escape."

THREE

The next day, Jane came home from her office later than usual. Dick was already at home. She said, "The head of my department called a meeting unexpectedly at 4 o'clock. There were only eight of us there. The others had to be linked in via video conferencing. He said he had just participated in a virtual meeting with folks in the mayor's office. It seems that the mayor's team is considering turning over the fire department to a private company. The mayor made the announcement herself. She said that her staff had considered every option for raising enough money to cover the costs of standing commitments – the biggest budget items being the public schools, teachers' pensions, safety net clinics, Medicaid, and the police. There just weren't any easy ways to raise the funds needed to cover these costs. They can't hand over any more roads to private owners. No one wants to see them installing tolls and creating huge traffic jams. The options they considered were either privatizing the police force or privatizing the fire department. People on the mayor's team agreed that it should be the fire department because it's a less politically charged entity. The mayor's team agreed to cut the police department budget as well, but neither she nor her advisors want to cut it too drastically without more money going to agencies that handle the kinds of problems the police would no longer be expected to deal with – mental health crises, sexual abuse, overdosing, stuff like that. The amount of money that leasing out the fire department would bring was not clear, but the mayor's spokesman said they were expecting it to be enough to cover the city's budget shortfall for years. How many years was not specified. They made it sound like it was an infinite number of years."

Dick was taking out wine glasses and pouring out some nuts into a dish. "Do you want a glass of wine, or would you like something stronger? I think I'm going to have a stiff gin and tonic."

"I'll be good with a glass of wine."

"Well, I'd much prefer to have the fire department privatized than the police department," was Dick's reaction. "Can you imagine if the police department were privatized? I'm afraid that it would go the way of prison privatization. That happened years ago, and things just got worse. The company that got the contract to run the state prison fired the guards who had been there a long time and hired all those untrained but enthusiastic recruits who couldn't wait to mete out physical punishment to prisoners who they were sure deserved it. You remember how much money and effort those companies invested in campaigning for the "three strikes, and you're out" legislation. That brought them loads of new prisoners, each one of whom represented an income stream coming from the state government coffers. Some of those prisoners had engaged in very minor offenses like being caught with pot or unpaid parking tickets. Even jay-walking. I know that's hard to believe. Can you imagine? Of course, there were also those convicted of violent crimes. No one seems to be thinking about the effects of throwing all of these people together. After all, the nonviolent prisoners come out of prison after a few years. No one seemed to be interested in knowing about the violence they would undoubtedly experience in prison and how their attitudes about society would change because of that experience. It's clearly a fertile training ground for antisocial attitudes and resentment against a society that abandoned them. So now we have a lot of men, mostly men, who haven't been able to get jobs because of their prison records. A lot of angry men, a disproportionate number of minorities, a fact that is reported over and over. All with loads of time on their hands and no steady source of income because they can't get a job. Great success story!"

"And now," Jane picked up on the whole issue of privatization, "we can watch efficiency measures being introduced in the fire department. Somehow, I think that more people will be interested in what happens in this case than they have been about private companies running prisons. After all, don't most people assume that everyone who is imprisoned is guilty and deserves the treatment they are getting? You know, I would be willing to lay down big bucks on a bet that whatever company turns out to have gotten the fire department lease will institute added charges requiring people to pay extra for some services. What I'm not sure about is which services will be on the added fees list and how long it will take before people start to complain about the cost of those services. Who knows, maybe people will just get used to paying for services and console themselves in the thought that it's better to pay more in fees to efficient – in quotes – businesses than it is to pay taxes to the government, which they keep repeatedly saying is inefficient."

Sure enough, it only took three weeks for the Mintaka City Fire Department to become the Mintaka Fire and Rescue Company, Inc. The contract must have been negotiated well before the mayor announced that the city was considering this move. She didn't get any serious opposition, and the deal went through like a flash.

Jane continued to relate the story that the social media was reporting. She noted that the announcement was made with great fanfare. It was presented in the public media as an outstanding achievement, a contract that benefited the city and brought managerial innovation to a part of government that had not been closely monitored for too long a time. The firefighters' union was outraged that it was not permitted to participate in the negotiations. It was not given access to any of the contractual stipulations besides the bottom-line amount of money involved. The union sued, but everyone expected it to lose in part because the union's contract was with the city. Now that the city was no longer responsible for fire protection, the contract was null and void. The union lawyers said they were preparing to go back to court. They said they were sure they would be able to sue to compensate the firefighters for the loss of their jobs and income. The city seemed willing to accept that, arguing that the move would save money in the end.

The public reaction seemed to be that the firefighters just had to accept their fate. That they had it pretty good and had not had to work too hard for the high incomes they were getting. They rarely had to deal with dangerous situations. People who aren't involved with firefighters have no idea what they do and how much risk their jobs involve. For one thing, their hours mean that they don't get to sleep on a regular schedule, which is already a health risk even before considering what is happening to their lungs every time they are exposed to smoke that contains a whole range of toxic substances as they put out fires.

The media did carry stories of what it meant to the families of firefighters who had been on the job for years. The fire chief predicted that the new organization would not be able to handle the kinds of things the fire department was doing these days, which now largely revolved around dealing with stress calls, not fires. Firefighters were now certified as emergency medical technicians and had a lot of experience dealing with health emergencies. Now that the new organization was hiring new, inexperienced people, he predicted that there would be lots of problems.

*****

Jane was beginning to be convinced that the new virus would not be anywhere near as virulent as the COVID-19 virus had been. The rate at which people were getting sick and dying was not increasing. Hospitals took steps to prepare to deal with the influx of patients, but their emergency rooms were not experiencing a surge of patients.

She wanted to get Dick's reaction. "I now have over two months' worth of trend data. Based on what I'm seeing, I'm ready to hazard the prediction that the SARS-12 virus will be mild. I'm not alone. The latest email from the public health association had an editorial written by leading experts. They believe that people who have even the most minimal exposure to COVID-19 are resistant to this virus. Children are not sick, just like last time. I guess we should be relieved."

"That's what the people in my lab are concluding, too," said Dick. "The issue at my end is that we've put in so much work on a vaccine that might not be necessary that the pharmaceutical company we're associated with is afraid that it will be unable to recoup its investment in our work. And you know how seriously a company that is carefully being watched by money managers and investors is taking that. I know that my lab is done with the research. The pharmaceutical company is afraid that it won't be making money on selling a vaccine for a virus of pandemic proportions. Which, let's face it, is exactly what they were putting their money on. The problem, as I understand it, is that because my lab has financial ties to the pharmaceutical company, we have to assist in figuring out what to do about sunk costs. Their people have begun to search for a new application. The easiest solution would be to transform it into a flu vaccine to be used in the autumn. But that isn't guaranteed to be a sure money-maker either. There has been some talk of reformulating it into a pill and marketing it as something to be used to prevent the common cold. Anyway, we're expected to be supportive of any new initiatives, but it's mainly the pharmaceutical company's problem."

"Won't the public figure out that the new application really doesn't work to do that, to fight the common cold?"

"Yes, but the thinking is that it would take more than one season for people to give up on it. In the meantime, just think of how many people could be convinced to buy it. Even if they just claimed that it would make the cold not last as long. That would bring in a lot of people ready to pay for a shorter cold. It wouldn't be hard to sell people on that idea even if that wasn't true. And with enough advertising, repeating the message often enough might help convince people that it was working and make it a permanent addition to people's medicine cabinets. Some people would buy it just in case, to be ready if they thought they had a cold coming on. You know, people have loads of out-of-date pills in their medicine cabinets."

Jane was shaking her head. "I know that pharmaceutical companies are very good at marketing their products. They're willing to create clever ads and spend a fortune putting them out. It can take years before someone does a study showing that some meds have little value. It's also true that people don't need much encouragement to be convinced that whatever they've decided to buy is working – ah ha – the placebo effect strikes again."

Dick had a big grin on his face. "Don't think for a moment that pharmaceutical companies aren't plotting at every moment how to make greater profits, no matter what it takes. That reminds me of what happened in 2020. Do you remember that's when twenty-six drug manufacturers were sued by the attorneys general of most states, accusing them of conspiring to reduce competition and drive up generic prices? Well, they learned from that experience. What they learned is how to conspire better. They figured out that the way they were doing it would no longer work. Friendly cocktail parties and lunches with long-lost friends – not competitors, they claimed – are now a thing of the past. What they've come up with is a new organization that credentials pharmaceutical reps. They are required to get twelve hours of training every six months to add to their very basic knowledge of biochemistry so that they can better inform their clients. The trick is that the training brings together reps from different companies for classes. The reps are hand-picked by management. The public message is that they are being considered for promotions. In reality, they are expected to report back to their companies on what other companies are working on. The information being passed on is basically a carefully packaged message by pharmaceutical companies to their competitors. The result is that companies can determine which arenas are open to anyone who wants to get involved and which are staked out by a particular company and are off-limits."

"That's a brilliant plan. It looks like they're really trying to help the buyers of their products, which includes doctors and patients, be better informed by knowledgeable persons who go out and talk to the doctors."

"Yep, sucked in again," said Dick. "But if my colleagues and I have figured it out, then other people will figure it out, and the great new credentialing arrangement may have to be revised. No one thinks for a minute that the pharmaceutical company executives will give up. They'll just keep thinking up new ploys. I'm convinced, and I'm certainly not the only one who thinks they spend more time doing that to increase the value of their stock than they spend on evaluating the work being done to develop drugs to address the diseases they claim they are interested in targeting. In fact, there are articles in respected journals on that very subject."

"I know that what you're saying is real, but it's a downer," said Jane. "Let's do something different for a change of pace. Let's go for a walk after dinner. It stays light out so late these days. The curfew won't kick in for at least another two hours. We can drive to the waterfront and walk along the lake. It's only a ten-minute drive, and there should be parking at this time of day."

"Okay, we can get some ice cream at that stand in the park."

FOUR

The evening walk and the ice cream helped Dick and Jane lift their moods. That was until they were driving home and were cut off by police cars blocking the road. They were blocking off Kenilworth Lane because the Mintaka Fire and Rescue Company was there in mass, fighting what looked like a huge warehouse fire.

Dick and Jane found a place to park nearby. They weren't usually voyeurs interested in being around to see disasters, but there was something different here that they could see as they were being shunted away from the scene. When they were walking over to get a closer look, Jane said, "am I seeing what I think I'm seeing? All those people dressed in red vests with MFRC across the back are just standing there. They're not doing anything. And look, they don't know how to unroll the hoses and hold them without the hoses waving around. Am I imagining that?"

"No," Dick said. "They are definitely looking like they don't know how to handle the equipment. See the older guy over there yelling at them. He looks frantic. He is running around yelling at different groups of guys, the ones just standing there staring at the burning building. They move when he yells at them, but I don't see them going off to do anything. They just move to a new spot."

"I see some media trucks trying to get closer, and the police trying to keep the reporters and cameramen as far away as they can. Do you think the mayor is afraid that she will be blamed for not doing enough to deal with this disaster? I don't see how she can be blamed for something that the new fire department is mishandling."

Dick's reaction was, "The reporters will have a good time with this story. It's a circus. We knew that the first thing the MFRC would do is fire the experienced firefighters and hire people eager for whatever reason to become firefighters. We knew that the company would try to get away with paying them a whole lot less and not giving them adequate training. What we couldn't have predicted is that their so-called efficiency approach to running this agency would be tested so soon."

Jane shook her head, "Yeah. I would guess that the way this story will go is that MFRC will say that they learned from this experience. And that they will have to figure out how to cover the cost of providing more training for their employees. They will float a number of different options, including cutting services, charging more for some kinds of services, or having the city kick in additional funds. I haven't read the contract the city and this company entered into, but I'll bet there is something in there about the city providing extra funds under special circumstances. And there may be something in there about who the company is expected to provide fire protection for. Maybe the company outlined the basic fire protection package with the understanding that it could charge extra based on mileage or size of the building, or I don't know what. Well, we'll certainly learn more about that contract now that reporters got such good video of what's going on during this first test of the new company's approach. There will be greater scrutiny of the details in the contract, which the media wasn't really interested in examining very closely at the time the deal was done."

Dick and Jane's predictions were front and center the next day in the media coverage of the fire and the problems that it was raising. The mayor was interviewed by all the local media outlets as well as some national outlets. The mayor's message was that the city council recognized that it was ultimately responsible for ensuring that the city was protecting its citizens from the threat of fire. She reluctantly admitted that the city would have to work out how to raise funds to accomplish that. She said that the city would try to do everything it could to forestall the need for the MFRC to institute new fees. She said she knew that the city council would definitely not go along with raising taxes.

By the end of the week, the mayor held a press conference announcing that she had formed a city council committee to consider how the city would come up with monies to support additional training for the newly hired firefighters employed by the MFRC. Who gets appointed to such committees is always interesting to watch if one is a political junky and if one doesn't have more pressing things to think about at the moment.

Over the next couple of weeks, the options the committee was considering to deal with the need to provide more funding for the newly created private-sector fire department came dribbling out in the media. Dick was following the reports on how it might be handled. He was happy to relate the story on the progress the committee was making to Jane, who said she wouldn't read about it herself but would be willing to have Dick tell her about it. He said he would be happy to give her the update on a recent media account that included some history.

One option being considered by the committee was renegotiating the existing contract with the company that got the parking meter contract. Everyone seemed to be unhappy with how that had been handled. The city used to get money from the parking meter fees charged for parking a car throughout the city. But it was time-consuming to go around to empty the meters, and it was thought to be a waste of police resources to have officers go around and ticket cars parked in spaces where the meters hadn't been fed. Collecting on the parking tickets was yet another problem because people were regularly challenging their tickets, saying the meters were malfunctioning. That meant the city had to hire staff to deal with each of the different challenges involving meters.

All in all, it was a headache. So, the city allowed private-sector companies to bid on a contract to handle the parking meters. The deal that the mayor at that time struck about twenty years ago was not exactly popular, but it wasn't nearly as objectionable as it turned out to be with each passing year. The company yanked out the parking meters and put in pay stations, allowing people to pay to park using credit cards. The machine issued a note with the hours and minutes the owner of the car paid to park. Placement of the machines caused some irritation because they were not always easy to find or far down the block. That got resolved to some extent, but not entirely, when a cell phone app became available, and people could pay that way. The real problem was the fact that the company kept raising its prices.

Dick noted that the committee was considering forcing the parking concession company to renegotiate its seventy-five-year contract, even though it still had about fifty-five years to go. He said that what the media didn't make clear was what the committee thought would allow them to renegotiate or why the company would agree to do that.

Dick went over the other options outlined in the media, which included selling off another portion of the roadway, which everyone thought had already been rejected. That attracted little support, and no matter which part of the roadway was mentioned, someone was objecting. The usual array of choices for raising funds mentioned if there wasn't a better alternative included the ever-popular cigarette tax, but you could hardly find anyplace that sold them anymore. Besides, the tax was already very high, and the proportion of people who smoked was low, so that the likelihood of a revenue stream from cigarette taxes was pretty much a lost cause. Increasing the liquor tax was always popular with some. Since the public was not ready to turn away from liquor, it was not an easy sell. Even so, liquor taxes could only raise so much, not nearly enough to cover the city's funding needs. An increase in property taxes was even more unpopular because there was general agreement that real estate taxes were not fairly assessed, with no consensus on what would constitute fairness. A city sales tax was certainly not on the table. Somebody suggested increasing the tax on empty lots. That generated some heated discussions. Would it result in the sudden sale of lots in some neighborhoods and the building of multi-family units, leading to overcrowding? Would it require the city to expend resources to find the owners, and what was the fallback if they couldn't be found? Would the city then take ownership of the lots? What good would that do? Some cities have sold the lots for a dollar in an effort to eliminate empty lots for reasons of safety and uplifting community spirits. However, the city would have to spend money to get that done, probably spending more than it could get in return.

"Well," Jane said, "we'll just have to wait and see what the committee comes up with. Whatever they decide, I expect it will involve selling off an entity that provides some form of government goods or services."

*****

Dick came home the next day and said, "It's official. My lab is done with the virus research project. The reports we're getting at my lab indicate that it's not spreading as fast as some experts feared that it would. And to the extent that people have gotten it, it seems to produce mild symptoms. Is that what your data show?"

"Yes. That's the Health Department's position too. I understand that it's not absolutely clear how many deaths can be attributed to the virus. There has been a small increase over the same period last year, but it is not a statistically significant increase. It's clearly not going to be anything like the pandemic in 2020."

"That is very good, of course. And it means that I'm back to working on finding a better treatment for arthritis. Now that's a problem that is a sure winner with an aging population. I was pleased about the progress we were making until everything shifted to vaccine research. It'll take a while to get back in gear. The three dozen genetically altered mice just arrived, and now we don't need them. We can't send them back. I told you, didn't I, that we had to get mice that had human lung cells implanted to test the vaccine because regular lab mice aren't susceptible to the coronavirus."

"Maybe these new and improved mice will react differently to the interventions you are working on to deal with arthritis. That would be an interesting, if unanticipated, outcome, wouldn't it?"

"That doesn't seem likely, but who knows. It would be hard to explain why that happened. Lungs and joint cartilage don't have much in common."

FIVE

One of the city committees that Jane's boss, Dr. Emmet, sat on was the budget committee. He called his team together via video conferencing to report that he had attended the latest meeting and wanted to convey what he learned. He said that the mayor announced that the city budget was in shortfall even after the sale of the fire department. The funds related to the sale of the fire department were still not in the city's coffers. Now that the fire department needed additional funds for training, the shortfall was more severe. Jane's boss explained that a month ago or so, the city leadership was registering worry about the expected drop in revenue that would be forthcoming due to the virus. That prediction was based on what happened in 2020. Fortunately, this year's virus was turning out to be mild, and the drop in revenue due to a rise in unemployment and closure of businesses that was projected is expected to be a lot less severe than they first thought it would be. But a number of other unanticipated events were bringing about a budget shortfall. These include the unexpected failure of one of the city's bridges, the need for repairs on the walkway next to the lake that had been washed out over the past winter and was now closed because it was too dangerous to use, and the need to upgrade two of the airport's runways. And, of course, there was the ever-present need to fund the public schools and the teachers' pension plan. If the virus had been as bad as expected, the city would have really been up the creek.

Dr. Emmet told his team that the mayor announced that she had been approached by an organization, the Education Network, created by people who had worked in Washington, D.C., in the Department of Education about a decade ago. They proposed taking over responsibility for operating the public schools in Mintaka.

They understood that they would have to accept responsibility for ensuring the viability of the pension program as well. The mayor said she thought that this was an opportunity for the city to get out from under the financial burden posed by the pension program, which had been seriously underfunded for decades. She wanted to know how much pushback taking this step would create.

Dick was sitting outside in one of their new deck chairs, relaxing, munching on some pretzels, and drinking beer, listening to Jane relate what she had heard at the meeting her boss had called that day. Jane said. "Everyone in the room was upset about turning over the schools to this organization. They knew that these people had worked for Betsy DeVos and were sure they shared her views. They were especially upset about the fact that she had supported schools that taught creationism as an alternative explanation for the origins of the universe alongside an explanation grounded in science. The people in the room whose work was steeped in scientific inquiry were not the kind of people who would welcome a private-sector approach, to begin with, but adding the Betsy DeVos element made them crazy."

Dick reacted calmly. "There are good reasons to reject a private-sector approach in this case even apart from Betsy DeVos. The record of private-sector education enterprises is not good. They vary, of course. Some with religious affiliations have high standards and provide an excellent education. Of course, they keep their scores so high by rejecting students who look like they will not perform well and tossing out the troublemakers. The secular, for-profit entities have a far more checkered record. As we all know, some of them were totally inept and went bankrupt after a short while, leaving communities scrambling to provide an education for their students. I'm not sure how the whole issue of private schools having the right to toss out students at will can be addressed.

"What will happen if the entire system is run by a for-profit organization?" He went on. "Where will they toss the students? The private schools could just toss out students and force the public school system to accept those kids. How do they say they will handle it now? I assume no one has gotten that far in the discussion."

"No," Jane said. "There were no details. No details on how much money the organization was offering to purchase the school system. No assurance that the group would have mechanisms in place to maintain the quality of education. I'm not saying these issues haven't been considered. I'm just saying I haven't heard anything about it. It'll be interesting to hear their plans for evaluating teachers."

With a big grin on his face, Dick said, "Wait until the teachers' union weighs in on this. They'll have things to say about teacher evaluation. And about teacher salaries, student-teacher ratios, bonuses for taking on additional responsibilities like coaching, arts programs, and so on. Of course, if part of the deal is to get rid of the union, the city will spend a lot of time and money in court. I assume the union will have a slew of lawyers from advocacy organizations volunteering to take on their cause. I wonder how much of the glow surrounding the work teachers do lasted after parents discovered what it was like to have their kids at home all day during the COVID-19 social isolation period. They were ready to pay teachers whatever they asked for then. But people have short memories. The organization offering to buy the school system could find a way to buy off the union by offering to increase salaries. That might work for a while until all the same issues, other than salary, come up, like class size, need for mental health counselors, adequate supplies, infrastructure improvements, and so on. It will be interesting to watch this unfold, that is, if the mayor decides to send it up the flagpole to see how it flies."

"I can't imagine," Jane said, "how these people think they'll make a profit if they agree to the kinds of things the teachers' union will demand. As we know, the typical way that such organizations make a profit is to hire workers with less experience and training and paying them a whole lot less."

Just then, her cell phone rang. Jane answered it. Her eyebrows were going up, and she was saying, "No, I didn't know that. Are you sure? Wow, that explains a lot. Good for you for digging that up. What are you going to do with that information? Tell the mayor? Yeah, you're right. It would be unfair to the mayor to let the media know about it before telling her. I can't wait to tell Dick. Thanks for sharing this delicious tidbit with me."

"Okay, what's so delicious?"

"Well. That was my friend Laurel, who is the computer geek in the department. She was at the meeting today. She did a little investigating and learned something about the people who set up the organization that approached the mayor. So, now we know how the company thinks it can afford to pay for the city's school system. It turns out that the executives in this company are also executives in a company that produces educational software, which can only be used with the special equipment it manufactures. Isn't that interesting? If every student is required to buy the software and hardware, that will bring in a fortune. Apparently, they have software that they've already created and in the process of creating more for every subject and for every grade level. There is a gold mine here with the gold just lying there waiting to be gathered."

"Oh my," said Dick. "I wish I had thought of that." Jane was looking shocked. "No, no, I'm kidding. But you have to admit that these people know how to make a buck!"

Jane shook her head. "I wonder how the mayor will react. I assume Laurel will tell her about it right away, and that the news media companies will figure it out, too. The mayor will have to worry about how the media treats the matter. Of course, you never know, the public might think that these are exactly the kind of business people who should be running the schools because they would be so efficient. The more I think about it, the more I think that is exactly how the public will react. Oh crap, why do we have so many people who can't see past their noses? Why can't they see how this will turn out? Yes, the deal will enrich the city, salvage the budget, and get out from under the pension burden, but what effect will it have on the kids? Is this software good for children's learning or just good for the company's bottom line? Is there any evidence that children benefit from using this approach? What do the teachers think? They don't seem to have been asked for their thoughts on it. How long will it take to figure out the effect of this approach, especially since there is so much resistance to standardized testing? I'm not arguing for or against standardized testing. I'm just worried about the effect of some group out there whose credentials and experience we're not sure about creating an educational curriculum and tests for our kids. Then there's the problem of costs. Surely some people will object to the need to buy this stuff. What about the families who weren't asked how they feel about it and haven't had the chance to register the fact that they can't afford the software or the hardware? How will that work?"

"I know how you feel," said Dick. "But don't get too heated up about it yet. It may not happen. Someone might point out that the parents will be paying for the software and equipment. Someone will volunteer to calculate how much it will cost parents. Hey, that might lead to an interesting fight. The parents who will suddenly object to this takeover and the rest of the people who don't have school-age children could decide that parents should be picking up the tab for their kids' education. And think the arrangement is just fine. And that it's about time that someone is making parents pay for their kids' education. All those childless families might suddenly be very much in favor of the takeover."

"Jeez, you are thinking through this a lot faster than I am. It's a lot more complicated than it looks at first glance, isn't it?"

"There's time to get some good people who support the mayor to check out what the education coalition proposing to buy the schools is up to. If the mayor and the budget committee members decide to take a serious look at the proposal, that will be the time to gear up for battle. But don't deplete your energies yet."

"Yeah, you're right. But I still think it is better to be prepared; to think about the options available to us before it's too late. But I will try to watch what happens before working up too much of a sweat for now. It's just that every time more public goods and services are handed off to the private sector, I feel that part of me is being lopped off, the part where my strongest beliefs are located. I can't help worrying that we're closer to the point where Amazon and its compatriots are in charge of our daily lives, and it's too late to go back."

"Okay, getting serious for a moment. I agree that what you just said presents a pretty terrifying picture. But if people are willing to give certain social institutions away, then we are watching how democracy operates. If one truly believes that the public should determine how society operates, then the only thing one can do is wait until the public wakes up and determines that it doesn't like the effects brought about by the decisions it has made about its social arrangements. This country has corrected the direction it is going in the past. It certainly has not corrected for all of the bad decisions the country made in the past, but I think we have seen considerable progress on some issues, especially in the recent past. I take that back. Maybe not actual progress, but at least much greater awareness. Sometimes, change requires public rebellion, protests in the streets to achieve change. Sometimes change happens with lightning speed, and no one seems to know how it happened. Attitudes about gay marriage are a good example. I don't know what you or I can do to make things turn out for the better, except for what we are doing already – contributing time and money to organizations that hire people to take a stand on the issues we feel strongly about. Furthermore, we just have to keep doing that because, as we know, all the hard work that went into achieving positive changes doesn't come with any assurance that those changes will stand."

SIX

Jane was watching the Sunday morning news shows. She turned to Dick, "I always wondered and have never asked anybody to explain why it is that the liberals (she used air quotes) are known as progressives and why conservatives (more air quotes) aren't known as *regressives*. Isn't that the dictionary definition of the opposite of progressive?"

When Dick laughed, Jane said, "I'm serious, at least somewhat serious. Why hasn't anybody raised that issue?"

"I honestly can't answer that. Why don't you contact one of the liberal media shows and pose the question to them? Or, if you prefer, contact one of the right-wing media shows. Of course, they won't bother to respond, but you might give them a bit of a scare if you say you plan to persist until you get the answer to your question. Of course, they might want to go after you. That wouldn't be good."

"I forgot to tell you about what happened to my colleague, Laurel. Remember, she's the computer geek in the office. Well, her aunt gave her a book by Rand Paul entitled The Case Against Socialism. Laurel's reaction was that she knew her aunt was a conservative, but she's a chemist. She's not stupid. She works for one of the big companies. Maybe that explains it. But it made Laurel hit the ceiling. I looked at the book. The man wrote hundreds of pages, with a ghostwriter, of course, on a topic he had no clue about. It's so off base. It's all about communism in countries struggling under the rule of dictators. He equates authoritarian communism with socialism as it operates in democratic countries. The book has gotten great reviews from similarly befuddled people. If they just checked out the first few sentences dealing with the difference between socialism and communism in Wikipedia, they would know how simplistic Rand Paul's take is."

"That's a good point. The Republicans talk about the horrors of communism. Then, say that socialism is about to be imposed on the country by liberals. They don't see that switching the topic from communism to socialism is a non-sequitur. And there are too many people who nod and say that's right."

Jane went back to watching the Sunday morning political shows. Dick was half-listening but mostly wondering whether the lawn mower would last through the season or whether he should think of buying a new one now or at the end of the summer. He was looking at his cell phone at websites selling lawn mowers.

She was giving him a running commentary. "The conservatives seemed to be set in their ways and not interested in inviting younger candidates into the fold. There is one exception, the guy running for the senatorial seat in Arkansas. Have you been keeping up with him?" She didn't wait for Dick to respond. "He is proposing privatizing Social Security. Maybe he's too young to remember what happened when that was the rallying cry of conservatives in 2007. Someone must have told him what happened. I'll bet he's hoping that his followers either won't remember or just never got the full picture in the first place. Remember how much traction conservatives were beginning to get using the standard line that business people were better at managing money, investing it, getting a better return than civil servants who didn't have business experience. Then the Great Recession of 2008 put that idea to rest. No one, not even all the businessmen who still thought they were better qualified, were courageous or, if you prefer, dumb enough to keep supporting that idea."

That got Dick's attention. "All the conservative politicians continue to say that the national debt is unsustainable. Government services must be cut back. Of course, the debt is still high as a result of the enormous tax giveaway to the rich legislated in 2017, plus the disastrous way the government handled the pandemic in 2020. This new crop of conservative politicians wants to cut taxes to provide businesses with more money to invest in their operations, which they assure us will improve the economy. You have to wonder. Every administration that has employed that tactic saw a downturn in the economy. Every administration that increased taxes saw the economy surge. You would think that they might have noticed those trends."

Jane's reaction was, "Maybe they have and are just happy that the general public can still be bamboozled into believing their bullshit line."

"Not to change the subject," Jane was eager to go on with her observations, "but my pet point of frustration is that ever since 2020, because of the pandemic, public health trends have been attracting greater attention. You would think that people would stop being surprised to hear that poor people and minorities endure more illness and end up living shorter lives. Isn't the idea that your zip code is a better predictor of your life expectancy than any other indicator a catchy enough message? I'm convinced that people simply aren't interested in hearing facts they consider depressing. They don't want to hear that suicide and homicide rates rise when conservatives are in the White House and decline when liberals are in the White House. They don't want to hear that those trends are closely linked to the drop in the country's economic fortunes in conservative administrations and an upturn in the economy in liberal administrations. I keep telling people I have the data to support that observation, and most people just don't want to hear it. Liberals just nod their heads, and conservatives say that the data can't be right, and that's that. That's apart from the nut cases who argue that fake news is being spread by spies being paid by – take your pick of any one of the billionaires who is known for his liberal views."

"I know. We've gone over all this many times before. I know it makes you really upset. Let's stop watching the Sunday morning news. All it's doing is driving you nuts. Let's try to get out and enjoy the day before the weekend is over, and we have to go back to our routines."

"Okay," Jane said. "What do you suggest?"

"How about the zoo? That is sure to take your mind off of people you dislike. The animals are always amazing."

"Great idea. I'll change, and we can snack our way through the day."

When they got to the zoo, they were met by a few people handing out leaflets. They were protesting the mistreatment of animals to provide entertainment for people."

Jane and Dick took the leaflets but didn't stop to talk with them. Jane said, "I know that these people are sincere about wanting to protect the animals from mistreatment just for the sake of someone's amusement. But the zoo is not the same as a circus. The animals are not required to perform tricks."

"Yeah, and the fact is that unless zoos work at conserving some species, those species will disappear. Zoos are now doing a lot of scientific work to ensure that they have healthy new generations being produced. They go through a lot of trouble and expense bringing animals from other zoos to mate so that there won't be any inbreeding. They do genetic testing."

"I know. The work they do is impressive. And it's supported mostly by donations by visitors and some foundation funding. They don't get government funding for that kind of thing, at least very little funding."

Dick and Jane walked around checking out the big cats, which were always interesting to watch because they seemed so relaxed, lying there, just looking around and giving out a roar once in a while. They went on to look at the chimps. That was fun, too, because the juvenile chimps were running around, and little kids were gleefully trying to chase them on their side of the glass partition. They bought a couple of water bottles before their next stop, leaning on the railing outside the pool where the seals were swimming.

Jane said, "I'm glad you suggested this. It is the perfect way to spend an afternoon. Let's sit for a while and watch people as they wander around. There are so many families here and so many kids enjoying themselves. It's hard not to smile at the kids' antics."

After they had spent a couple of hours enjoying the zoo, they decided it was time to go home. As they were walking out the gate, Dick turned and stopped to look at the sign over the entrance. "I thought there was something different about the sign, but I didn't pay attention when we were walking in because I was distracted by the people with the leaflets. Take a look. It's not the Mintaka zoo anymore. It is the Gertrude and Hans Kramer Zoo. How about that? Another entity was sold off because the city couldn't afford to maintain it anymore. I don't remember hearing about it. Do you? These things happen so regularly, they don't even make the news. Maybe it did make the news in the entertainment segment, which I ignore, so it just didn't register."

"I wonder if the new owners will keep up the scientific reproduction program. It's obviously an expensive proposition to engage in that kind of thing. I have no idea how much of the budget was going for that. I expect that it was foundation money, but the zoo itself still had to kick in funds."

"We could go to the zoo's website," Dick said. "That would tell us what the zoo's mission is these days, but I think I'll let it go. There are just too many things like this to watch and worry about."

Going home in the car, Jane said, "Dick, I don't want to belabor this thing. But I can't stop thinking about what happened with the zoo. I know what you said is right. We can't get upset and involved in every instance when public enterprises are transferred to private investors. But it is piling up. I can't help worrying about it. What's happening around us? Aren't there other people out there who are as upset as I am?"

"I know what you mean. I'm just trying to convince myself that we shouldn't dwell on these things. I can't decide if we should try to think of ways to either do something to help change things or what's the alternative, find a way to get some relief from obsessing about it?"

Dick followed up Jane's less-than-cheerful thought with, "I don't have the energy to cook on the grill. Let's think about ordering a pizza and see if there's a movie we want to see."

SEVEN

Dick called Jane at her office on Monday morning. He said, "We've been spending entirely too much time with our noses to the grindstone. We come home, have dinner, maybe watch the news on TV, read a little, and go to bed. And do it all over again, day after day. Yesterday was a nice break, but it's not enough to take our minds off all the stuff we see around us that we want to see work differently. I know we get a chance to talk to people at work, but those conversations are about work issues. There isn't much time to have a serious conversation about the kinds of things that are bothering us, serious things that require some uninterrupted time. I thought I would invite Adam and Mark over for dinner on Friday. We can get started earlier so we can be finished by the nine o'clock curfew. They're both single, so I don't think they'll be busy. I know that they're interested in the kinds of things we've been talking about. They've both mentioned things like that in passing, but we never had time to talk about them. Okay with you? I'll get some Chinese take-out on the way home?"

"Yes. That's just fine with me. You're right. We only talk to each other about serious things. It'll be good to inject some fresh ideas into our tired dialogue. I've met Mark and Adam, and from the little time I've spent talking to them, I agree they're interested in the things we're interested in."

Adam was the taller one with short, dark blond hair who looked like his face hadn't changed much since he was a senior in high school. To complete the picture, he wore dark-rimmed glasses and t-shirts with the names of bands in fashion when he was in high school. She took a liking to him the first time she saw him. Mark was shorter and darker. He wore his wavy dark brown hair longish. He biked to work. He didn't wear t-shirts regularly, but when he did, they were more likely to have messages having to do with climate change. For some reason, he gave the impression that he was ready to go to whatever protest meeting was on offer. Maybe it was his energy and enthusiasm. Dick enjoyed working with both of them.

Dick and Jane got through the week, looking forward to a change in routine that Friday night. They agreed to get together at five-thirty in the afternoon when things shut down at the lab. Mark and Adam were knocking at the door just as Dick was unloading the take-out food. They had come in Adam's car, the latest version of the electric car produced by Ford, which was getting excellent ratings.

The two guests each greeted Jane with a quick kiss on her cheek. When Dick asked if they'd like a beer or some wine, both agreed that a beer sounded good. Once everyone got settled, Dick said, "Let me tell you what prompted this invitation. I hope you don't think we're taking advantage of you. It's just that Jane and I have been talking endlessly to each other about things, and need to check to see if we're exaggerating what we're complaining about and talking ourselves into being senselessly foolish. Here's what's bothering us. Jane, do you want to explain?"

"Okay. We've been getting increasingly more discouraged watching how many of its operations the city was transferring to private investors. As Dick has already said, we keep repeating the same things in conversation with each other and need some new input. Maybe what you say will help keep us from making each other so discouraged."

Mark was quick to respond. "I know how you feel. I don't think my reaction to what's going on will make you any less discouraged. I've tried to talk to my sister about it, but she's got a family. Her kids are both in grade school, so she has plenty to distract her. I can't talk to her husband at all. He sells paper products to hospitals and health care facilities. He's been doing well. But he's developed heart disease over the past few years and has had to have stents put in. That experience has made him think he knows how to solve the problems facing the health care system. He wants the government out and the private sector to take over everything to make it more efficient. I can't discuss any of it with him without his going ballistic and my sister telling me that I'm raising his blood pressure."

Adam followed up with, "I've been talking to my father, who is a public policy professor. I've learned that I can't do that for an entire evening. I tell him I have to go home, that I'm tired and have to get up early. It's the same every time we get together. He rants and raves about what's going on. He says he has to be careful not to incite riots in his classes because his students are even more outraged than he is. He says that the people in power have all the cards in their hands, and it will take a revolution to make them give up their power. My sister can't spend an entire evening with him either."

"Well, folks," said Mark. "I read an interesting article today when I went to get coffee this morning. It's related to what we're talking about. It gave me a lot to think about. I'm happy to have this opportunity to share my thoughts with you. The article was written by a historian. He had a lot of interesting things to say about big changes in the country's history over the last century. He makes the point that the period after World War Two was marked by a sense of unity. Government agencies and the people leading them were highly respected. A lot of legislation was passed, giving the government a great deal of authority over social arrangements. He points out that society eventually rebelled because a few social critics were able to capture people's attention and appeal to some deep-seated beliefs about individual rights held by some. A growing number of people were becoming increasingly more convinced that they deserved to keep what they earned and resented having to share any part of it. Those people got a lot of encouragement from a small set of social critics, basically a small number of economists, who argued that what the government was doing was interfering with the market. They said that the market was self-correcting. The central point of their argument was that everyone would benefit if consumers could just choose according to what best suited their preferences and their needs."

The other three were looking like they were interested in what he was saying, so he continued. "That ushered in an era characterized by individualism. The author goes on to say that what's happening now is that the belief that reliance on the market is always the right philosophy has brought about an excessive degree of socioeconomic inequality. He points out that a relatively small number of people have benefited from the system that has been in place since the 1980s. They have accumulated an exceptional amount of wealth and power, which they have wielded to sponsor their ideology. They have used this power to tie individualism to patriotism and characterize any effort to constrain individualism as suspect. They have succeeded in tying criticism of and efforts to monitor excesses indulged in by the rich and powerful as socialism. The author, whose work I am citing, says that what's happening now is that dissatisfaction with the degree of individualism society has embraced is starting to swell. He says that all the protests that have been going on over the last decade indicate that people, especially those under the age of 40, are ready for the individualism ideology to be overturned. They want to embrace communitarianism, to share, to see more people benefit from what society has to offer rather than just a few."

"And," Jane said with a look of skepticism on her face, "he convinced you that this will be happening when?"

"He suggested that it took about forty years for the country to shift from relying on the government to deal with society's needs to embracing private sector solutions. And it's now well over fifty years since the last reversal. So, he says that we can expect it to happen pretty soon. He argues that the number of protests, which have been increasing over the last decade, is indicative. People are dissatisfied about a lot of things, especially the lack of jobs and stagnant wages."

"Funny you should mention what a historian has to say," was Adam's response. "I happened to read something by a historian, too. I'm pretty sure it's not the same one you're referring to. But his argument supports what your historian has to say. I was interested in this guy's approach because he wrote his dissertation on bean beetles. He was trained as an ecologist. At some point, he decided that he had learned everything there was to learn about the beetles, so he needed to study something else. He decided on humans. He uses mathematical models to identify universal ecological laws that explain the growth and decline of a species. His thesis is that society renews itself in cycles. The cycles are identifiable in the rate of political violence, which he tracked from 1870 to 2010. He found peaks of brutality every fifty years or so. He says that we are in exactly that kind of period now, and it's not clear how it will end. It could produce a civil war. Or it could mean something very different, like the beginnings of societal decline. Like what happened to the Mayans or the Romans."

Jane was looking troubled. "How come we haven't heard more about these predictions? We hear so much about conspiracy theories that explain social turmoil as something orchestrated by a powerful force behind the scenes, like the QAnon conspiracy in 2020. The followers didn't know who it was or even if it was a person or some kind of higher being. When the Q predictions didn't turn out to be true, Trump didn't orchestrate something miraculous to keep himself in office. Many followers dropped out. Others became even more extreme in their beliefs. But, I'm far readier to listen to someone who puts his name to his theory and who offers proof that I can evaluate. As far as I'm concerned, the conspiracy theories with no identifiable author might as well be the work of little green men from Mars."

Dick had a thoughtful look on his face. He said, "I need to give all of this more thought. I would like to think that the authors you cite have evidence for what they say, as scary as it is. Then we could do something about it before it gets to the apocalyptic stage."

"The historian I'm talking about makes an interesting point on that score," said Adam. "He makes the point that journalists and historians who reject mathematical modeling focus on singular events because they are interesting. But interesting events are often outliers. They ignore the arc of history." Adam was pleased to see the reaction of the others to that observation.

Dick picked up on Adam's point. "I'm afraid the media is having an important constraining impact that is keeping people focused on single events that get people upset and lead to protests. Looking at what's going on around us that way allows a small segment of the population to organize against anything that looks like it challenges their belief system. All those conspiracy theory followers are happier spreading false information, scaring people about the kinds of changes a far more substantial proportion of the population would actually like to see introduced if they weren't accompanied by what the conspiracy theorists are adding. There have always been groups like that around. It's just that it's a lot easier for right-wing extremists to communicate now. I know that has been going on for the last quarter-century, but I think those who are doing the messaging have become more sophisticated in how they go about it. We keep hearing discussions about First Amendment rights and debates about how to handle the fact that we haven't figured out how to deal with outright lies that appear on all the interactive media sites. That didn't used to be such a problem in the past, now the distant past, when there were a few highly respected media figures, and there were no electronic social media platforms like there are now, where every conspiracy theory gets repeated and elaborated upon."

Looking around, Dick could see how discouraged they all looked. He said, "in the meantime, anybody want a refill on drinks? I got some Chinese take-out. The beer will go with that. Should we have another beer or start on the food?"

Adam's reaction was, "Let's go for another round of drinks before we eat. I don't want to get distracted from what we're talking about right now."

"I agree," Jane said. "I told Dick that what's going on around us is weighing on me a lot. I can't stop thinking about it. He said that there must be many other people who feel that way. What do you think? Are there people who are as upset as I am who aren't speaking out? Not doing anything because they don't know what to do?"

Dick chimed in with: "I told Jane that is exactly what I believe. Do you think it's possible that the historian Mark is citing is right, that a growing number of people are ready to question this society's commitment to individualism?"

"That question gets a little more academic than I think most people want to deal with," was Mark's response. "But I think my other brother-in-law's observations constitute one reaction to the excesses of individualism, which not only do not help to overcome it but make things worse. He's a physician. His assessment of the public's reaction to what's going on comes out of the stress literature. He says that some people are taking the "flight" option, escaping into drugs or dropping out entirely through suicide. Other people are taking the "fight" option, turning to violence and crime. Both sets of people are doing that because they have been backed into situations from which they can't see any escape. Neither of these two categories of people is doing anything to help come up with a solution to the untenable social environments in which they find themselves."

"Yes, yes," Dick was moving to the edge of his chair, nodding and raising his voice, "and those actions are treated as the fault of flawed individuals rather than reasons that should be attributed to the flaws in the society they are forced to contend with."

"You're absolutely right. That's exactly how those trends are treated by the media," said Jane. "As you know, I work at the Department of Public Health. I wish more people would understand how suicide and homicide are shaped by the social environment in which people live rather than the psychological environment in their heads."

"Okay, let's get more to drink before we break open the take-out," Jane said. "We could have tea if anyone would like." They agreed to Jane's suggestion to switch to tea, noting that tomorrow was a workday. Then they broke open the food cartons.

"The problem," Adam said in between bites, "is that it's hard to convince people that they should think past what's best for them and think about what's best for society. That's just not the American way, certainly not the American way right now. Even when climate change activists try to point out the devastation this generation is leaving for their children and grandchildren, it doesn't have any impact. People just ignore that message and complain about how much they have to pay for gas and electricity. They are opposed to being taxed for using excessive amounts of energy. You would think they would care about the problems their kids and grandkids will face in dealing with a world in which natural disasters are the norm. The number of hurricanes and floods we've had over the past decade should convince people that all the predictions about the effects of climate change are being fulfilled, but apparently, that is not happening. The only good thing is that alternative sources of energy are now much cheaper so that there may be hope that economics in combination with self-interest will lead to a solution.”

“Hey,” Adam said as he was wiping sauce off his face, “this is delicious. Where did you get the food?”

Dick said, “I got in at that little place in the Four Corners Shopping Center. It doesn’t look like much, but we’ve liked everything we’ve ever gotten from there.”

“It’s a good thing you got it because otherwise, I would have gone home dejected. Now at least I can be happy about this discovery, a great Chinese take-out place.”

They continued to eat and to talk until there was nothing left in the take-out boxes. Jane asked if anyone wanted more tea and asked them to choose one of the fortune cookies. “Okay,” she instructed, “get ready to read your fortune to the rest of us.”

Dick said, “I’ll go first. Mine says, ‘You will receive a valuable gift this summer.’ Isn’t that nice?”

“Mine,” Adam said, “says, ‘you will enjoy developing a new friendship soon.’ I wonder if that means I’ll develop a friendship with a woman, which would be interesting. I’d like that.”

“Okay,” Mark was unwrapping his cookie, “let’s see what mine says. It says, ‘You will make an important discovery by the end of this season.’ Hey, guys, I’m the one who will find the secret to growing cartilage we’ve been looking for at the lab for the last decade, right?” He laughed and cheerfully ate the cookie.

“My turn,” said Jane. “It says, ‘you will be offered a rewarding new opportunity.’ Well, I don’t know how to interpret that. What kind of opportunity? I guess I will just have to wait and see.”

It didn’t take much longer for Mark and Adam to start cleaning up what was on the table, signaling that they were ready to leave. It was getting close to nine o’clock. They picked up the cartons and the dishes and moved them to the kitchen. Jane thanked them but said they didn’t have to do that. She said, “I’m really glad that you agreed to come over tonight. I enjoyed talking with you very much. It was great to bounce ideas off somebody new. Dick and I have talked about this kind of thing so much that we can complete each other’s sentences.”

"Yeah," Dick was shaking their hands and thanking them for coming too. "I don't think I've enjoyed talking to anyone as much as I've enjoyed talking to you guys for a long time. You said things that I will be thinking about for quite a while. It's been intellectually stimulating. I appreciate that. Tomorrow we can go back to talking shop, which can sometimes be stimulating too, but not like this."

After their guests left, Dick and Jane continued to clean up. There wasn't much to do. They agreed that they would have to invite Mark and Adam again soon. Jane echoed Dick's comment to Mark and Adam. "You're right. This evening has given me something to think about. Unfortunately, I agree with you about your skepticism about the prediction that things are about to change because people are ready to rebel against excessive individualism. I'm not at all sure what it will take for that to happen. The idea that we are in for a period of social upheaval strikes me as more realistic, but I don't necessarily trust that it will lead to a more communal and tranquil state of affairs."

"I know. There are quite a few well-organized, well-funded groups out there that are trying to convince people that we need to do something that will bring people together. But they don't seem to be making much of an impression on the people who are frustrated with the ways things are, yet totally reject any change that requires them to see past their personal interests. I'm tired. As much as I enjoyed this evening's discussion, I don't want to think about this anymore. Think there's anything worth watching on TV? I need to get distracted. Maybe I'll wake up and be less discouraged tomorrow."

EIGHT

The chances that either Dick or Jane would wake up and be less discouraged were dashed when they opened up their e-tablets to check out the news. They were sitting at the breakfast table, drinking coffee and reading the same article. A top political analyst was saying that it was not only cities and states that were dealing with the need to work out funding arrangements to fulfill long-standing commitments to the citizenry; the country as a whole had still not come out of the recession caused by the pandemic that occurred a decade ago. The country was still in a recession. The unemployment numbers were not good, but even more troubling was the fact that more people were simply dropping out and not looking for jobs. Neither Jane nor Dick considered that to be newsworthy. That was an everyday reality. What was newsworthy was that the federal government was trying to do something about it. It was again launching proposals to come up with the funds it needed to meet its commitments through what had become the single most common solution – to transfer some government entity to the private sector. They got to the same part of the article at the same time. "Wow," said Dick, "what do you think of that? Of selling off the post office to one of the package delivery companies?"

"Well," Jane said, "I guess that was inevitable. It's just that I would prefer that the contract didn't go to Amazon. I admit that Amazon does a great job of delivering everything I buy online, but I still would prefer that it face a little competition. Amazon has gobbled up too many entities as it is. I would not be surprised that it comes in with the most attractive bid and that the federal government will have a hard time rejecting it. The thing I'm most upset about is knowing that the U.S. Post Office is such a good example of an agency that Congress could have saved. It's long been the most popular federal agency. It inspires trust and loyalty. Congress could have allowed it to expand its services. It could have changed the way it was forced to deal with its pension fund. Now it's too late. Here, I've got a website that explains it. Congress passed a law in 2006 requiring the post office to pre-fund its retiree benefits for 75 years. The article puts it this way. It's like your credit card company telling you that it expects you to charge a million dollars on your card over your lifetime – please include the million dollars in your next payment."

"That's a clever way to put it."

Jane went on. "It was all those simple-minded rallying cries about the private sector being more efficient that prevented intelligent adjustments from being made when the post office could have benefited. I hope that the efficiency proponents like the way the new privatized post office works, especially when it raises its rates."

Dick had a broad smile on his face. "It will probably be a big surprise to all those conservatives who live in less urbanized areas when the new efficient post office tells them that a communal rate has to be adjusted to reflect the cost of delivery outside of city limits. And all their rural conservative constituents will have their rates hiked. I hope that gives all of them something to think about. Of course, I doubt that will affect their readiness to reject communal tax rates to cover other things. They are adamant about arguing that communal rates are socialistic, which should be ironic but isn't. Tell me, why is it that they have no objection to what amounts to a communal tax rate to maintain roads that they use, but hardly anybody else uses?"

"I remember stories about the senator, I think he was from Alaska, who had the federal government fund 'the bridge to nowhere'? He was a conservative. Amazing how bridges to nowhere can be acceptable, and funding programs providing food supplements can be objectionable to these people. I know the bridge never got built when the media uncovered the story, but that didn't change people's behavior like that particular senator or his constituents' views about who was deserving of government funds and who was not.

The politician continued to argue that people in his district needed jobs which building the bridge would have provided. Government inefficiency is perfectly fine if it's in my district is the motto all of them espouse."

"Getting back to the post office, I hope the people promoting selling off the post office will be happy paying our new corporate post office a whole lot more based on the distance the carrier has to travel. And then, there are all the advertising materials that the business sector has been sending out at a discounted rate. Of course, there will be negotiations, but I'll bet prices will go up, and they'll be asked to pay a lot more than they pay now. On the other hand, businesses may drop that kind of mailing altogether and just switch to online advertising, making Google and the other media giants richer."

Dick's smile slowly faded and was replaced with a frown. "I can't believe that the politicians won't try to do something to compensate for the fact that some of their supporters who live in less urbanized areas might have to pay more. Maybe special legislation to subsidize Amazon for expected losses in handling the mail. Wouldn't that be the epitome of irony?"

"The sale of the post office was predictable," Jane reacted after a minute of thought. "I'm disappointed that it turned out this way, but I'm not surprised. Since the post office is highly regarded, there may be protests, but people are worn out by protests. They have to decide where to put their energies. There are so many protests to choose from."

Dick nodded and said, "You're right. Given that there are so many government agencies on the city, state, and federal governments' lists ready to be auctioned off, people are having trouble keeping up. I could name a number of them, but I won't. I don't want to think about it, just in case my thinking jinxes it, and what I fear actually happens. Don't look at me that way. I have not suddenly become superstitious. I just don't want to say things out loud that will cause us to talk about them and get more upset so early in the morning."

"I'll go with that. I'll go get dressed and face another day of making an effort to hold off being depressed about this stuff. I'm not sure I can keep doing it. As I keep saying, it's wearing me down."

"Let's think about how we can deal with our frustration. I agree it's becoming increasingly harder to keep acting like things will turn out okay. They're not turning out anywhere near okay, and there isn't any reason to think that will happen anytime soon."

"Maybe we can get together with Mark and Adam again. That cheered us up last time. At least it allowed us to say things to someone else besides each other, which for some reason seemed satisfying."

"Alright. I'll ask them to come by tomorrow." He called Jane later that morning to tell her about the calls. He said, "When I called Adam and Mark to invite them for pizza and more discussion, Mark said he was happy to come because he thought our last get-together was really rewarding. Adam agreed too, but asked whether we would be interested in meeting his sister and her roommate. Adam said that his sister works for a quasi-governmental agency the city established in the wake of economic decline after the pandemic and the need for the city to find funds to support its activities. The agency's mission involves tracking the city's expenditures. It tracks changes in budget allocations from year to year and issues reports on the financial effects of changes in allocations. More recently, she began collecting data on the city's record of transferring public goods and services and its effect on the budget. Her roommate is an investigative reporter for Axium, the media news magazine that offers in-depth analyses of current social issues. I said, "Sure, we'd like to meet them. Okay with you? I told both Mark and Adam that we'd have pizza."

"Great. That sounds very promising," was Jane's reaction. "I'll order the pizzas and pick them up later this afternoon. I'm working at home today. I'll get a vegetarian one. I'll get one with cheese and another one with pepperoni, peppers, and mushrooms. And maybe some veggies for a start, so we can snack and get to know the two women before starting the pizzas. Do we have enough beer and wine? Could you pick up some more tomorrow night?"

That evening, Jane and Dick did a little cleaning up of the place in preparation for their guests the following evening. They agreed that they were feeling good about talking to more people and hoping that something would come of it. They spent the evening reading. Dick was reading a book on the Trump presidency. There were so many books written while he was in office. This one was an assessment of the aftereffects of his presidency. There were a lot of those, too, but this had gotten the most attention. Dick wasn't ready to read it when it was released four years after Trump's presidency ended. But he was interested in analyzing what changed to consider how those changes played out over time. He kept interrupting Jane to ask her if she remembered yet another crazy thing Trump had done before she told him to stop doing that because she was trying to finish her book. Jane only read mysteries at night because she read so many public health reports during the day that she didn't want to read anything serious in the evening. Dick was only on the third chapter of his book on Trump and hadn't gotten to some of the big revelations that appear later in the book, which they had lived through, but which were not fully disclosed at the time.

NINE

When they got up the following day, Dick said he was feeling more cheerful than usual. He was looking forward to seeing Adam and Mark and meeting Adam's sister and her roommate. Jane said she was also feeling good about talking with people who she was expecting to offer more information about the topics they were interested in exploring. She said sharing ideas with others had the effect of lifting a weight off her shoulders, at least temporarily. She didn't expect that they would be laying out plans for action to make the weight go away, but it was good to have more people to share her sense of frustration with.

The day went quickly for Jane. She didn't have any meetings scheduled that day, which meant that her work wasn't interrupted with video conferencing. She could devote herself to organizing her monthly report on mortality and morbidity statistics in the city and get a good chunk of it done. The report was not something that she felt good about because the difference in rates by community was not shrinking. The minority communities were continuing to register higher rates of illness and death across all the measures she was looking at. Her report included a section on special efforts to combat the stubbornly high rates in the West End community, which looked promising if the effort continued to receive funding. She knew that any effort would have to be in place for years before it would produce any positive effects. That part was hard to accept for people who were sincere but expected to see evidence of progress sooner rather than later. Jane knew that putting in more effort and more money into a dynamic public health intervention would not produce instant change. She had to keep getting the message across that it would produce significant change over time.

The intervention that she and her colleagues were following was a nonprofit called New Day in West End. It had been in place for nearly ten years. It was based in one local school. The school received funding to provide preventive health services, including free eye exams and glasses if necessary and dental care. The nonprofit got the city to turn over a couple of empty lots down the street from the school, which it turned into an urban farm. The students were involved in growing vegetables and raising chickens. The neighbors were unhappy about the rooster but were learning to tolerate him because the kids were so enthusiastic about the farm. The program operated over the summer. The students were too busy working on the farm to be bored and get into trouble. The school had volunteers teaching the children how to cook the vegetables they were growing. Because the farm produced more than they could use, the school arranged for them to sell the extra produce on Saturday mornings. The kids were amazed to discover that the school allowed them to come up with a plan for what the money they raised would be used for. That turned out to provide an important lesson in how democracy works. They could all campaign for their favorite plan, which would be voted on. All in all, there was good reason to think the kids coming out of this school would have very different aspirations than their peers in schools that did not have such active school programs.

Jane wondered if the people coming for pizza tonight had heard about this school intervention. She was ready to bet that they had not. There are too many things going on to pay attention to what's happening in one school in a poor neighborhood. If people did hear about such things, maybe they would be willing to invest in similar efforts in other schools. But of course, that would involve the city finding the funds to make that happen. In other words, it would involve money the city collected in taxes or through whatever means it was ready to employ to raise the necessary funds. Which brings us back to handing over something to the private sector for which the city could get some money.

Jane was pretty sure the proposed sale of the public schools to the DeVos spin-off group, Education Network, would not support this kind of personnel-intensive programming. She hadn't heard anything about how close that plan was coming to being a done deal. She'd have to ask someone in her office who might know more about it.

Dick's day was more mundane. He was continuing to monitor the white blood cell count of his mice to see if another gene he had targeted and manipulated was helping to alleviate inflammation. Every time he thought he was seeing something happening, it didn't seem to last. So, he just kept trying. Patience was an essential requirement for the kind of work he was doing. Fortunately, Dick was a patient man when he was in the lab, if not so much outside the lab.

Both Jane and Dick ended their work days feeling that they had put in a good day's work. They were ready for an evening of stimulating conversation.

Jane picked up the pizzas and a platter of fresh vegetables and dip for a start. Dick got home before she did and was putting out glasses and napkins. They would be sitting on the deck around the big table they got on sale at the end of last season. They had thought it might be too big, but were now glad they bought it.

Mark arrived first. He said, "Adam is picking up his sister and her roommate. They're both at Laura's office, which is located a couple of blocks from your building. They should be here shortly."

The three of them arrived a few minutes later. Adam introduced his sister, Laura, and her roommate, Nikki. Laura was nearly as tall as her brother with the same dark blond hair. Hers was long and straight, down to her shoulders, in contrast to his shorter and wavier mop. She wore little make-up and had a healthy, outdoorsy look about her. Jane thought she looked terrific.

Nikki was not as tall as Laura. Her hair was black, short, and cut at an angle so that one side fell onto her cheek. Her skin was perfect. She was wearing a t-shirt and jeans, but looked like she was modeling them. She undoubtedly got her looks and her style from the union between what they learned later was a French father and a Vietnamese mother.

Jane was smiling and telling all their guests how glad she and Dick were that they could come and spend the evening. Dick asked everyone what they wanted to drink while Jane brought out the veggies. The men asked for beer. The two women opted for white wine.

Once they all settled down, Jane asked what kind of day they all had had. Mark and Adam both said theirs had been pretty routine. Mark said, "Adam and I are monitoring our mice, checking to see the extent to which the molecule we identified, combined with the altered gene that we injected, will stimulate regrowth of cartilage cells. We know that joint cartilage deteriorates over time. It's more common and happens faster among athletes because they are more likely to sustain injuries. For everyone else, it happens with ordinary wear and tear as people age. Cartilage has a limited ability to regrow. Finding how to regrow those cells in the mice we have forced to become more athletic than they probably want to be would be a big breakthrough. We are monitoring our mice and measuring changes in cell production." Dick turned to Laura and Nikki and explained that he was doing something similar. "Right now, I'm monitoring the white blood cell count of my mice to see if another gene we've targeted and manipulated is helping to alleviate inflammation. We haven't seen as much progress as we expected, but we're holding out hope that this gene will wake up and make a difference."

Jane had heard about Mark and Adam's research from Dick in some detail. She knew that the work that all three of them were doing was not going to produce quick results and that they had to be persistent while trying to be creative in their thinking about their research.

Jane said she didn't know anything about either Laura's or Nikki's work. She asked Laura to talk about her job. "My job involves tracking data and inputting it into a matrix I designed when I first started on this project a couple of years ago. I was hired to match the city budget against expenditures. I collect information on where the money goes and chart it. Initially, my job was to watch for shortfalls and document how the money got shifted around to cover the shortfalls. This was intended to help the city do a better job of budgeting and to identify departments that were not using the funds they were allocated efficiently. It did not take long to see that the problem wasn't lack of efficiency. It was lack of adequate funding. There was very little fat in the budget, so when roads developed unexpected problems, the roads were repaired, but the money had to come from somewhere else, which reduced the funds available to that 'somewhere else.' The mayor is well aware of the challenge. However, the city council members are more resistant and less ready to accept the reality of what they are hearing."

"How much of that kind of information were the council members presented with?" Mark asked. "Did you or whoever was supposed to report on the data you're collecting indicate that moving money from one place to cover needs in another place would mean that someone always had to cut back on what they had planned to use the money for?"

"Yes. The city's chief financial officer, you know, Richard Davis, has that job. He has power points. He provides people with summaries in handouts that they can take back to their constituents. He tells them that he would be glad to talk to the constituents. But nothing he has ever said has convinced the council members that greater efficiency wasn't the answer."

"Laura, you haven't talked about the new direction your job is taking. Tell everyone how your job has evolved." Adam urged his sister.

"It has evolved. I'm now tracking the budgets of the fifty largest cities in the country. That kind of information is not always easy to find, but I can get a lot because those things do make it into the public record, even if it takes a while. The media does document some of these things, but it's one story or case study at a time, and generally, there's no connection to similar stories in other parts of the country. As to my task, there's no way to predict which cities will produce the information on time and which are slow and which will never do it. But the profile that I'm developing is interesting. You'd be amazed at the deals cities are coming up with to bring in the money they need to keep going. I should let Nikki tell you more about this part. She has been looking into some of what I'm finding."

The others turned to Nikki and nodded with encouraging looks on their faces. "Yes," Nikki said. "I have to credit Laura with making the connection or discovery. When she saw that some of the cities were transferring the same kinds of entities, things like water filtration plants, fire departments, schools, and so forth, she started looking at who was doing the buying. That's when I got interested. That's not her job. She's got enough to do to track city budgets. My job as an investigative reporter gives me the platform, and the time it will take to do what Laura doesn't have the time or the budget to do. As far as we can tell, some of the sales of public goods and services are being quietly orchestrated by a small number of private sector organizations, and some created for exactly that purpose. A closer look reveals that the new companies are being established by a very small number of rich and powerful persons and organizations. They use different names, so it is not always clear that all those companies actually operate under a single corporate umbrella. Of course, we've just gotten started tracking this, so we don't know how widespread this phenomenon is."

Mark was shaking his head. "At some level, that's not surprising. And at some level, it's shocking. No one is thinking about the consequences of this kind of thing."

"Right," Dick chimed in. "The public doesn't get to vote on whether or not these companies are the ones the public would choose to run these operations. Members of the city council don't know anything about these companies other than the glossy brochures they design and what their marketing people say about them. They certainly don't know that the companies are owned by larger entities, as you are discovering, and which they would probably not want to see gain so much control. The real owners make sure that kind of information is hard to get. I'm glad you are uncovering this kind of stuff."

"Nikki," Jane asked, "have you gotten as far as checking if these companies are publicly traded or are in the hands of private owners? I realize that the companies are not all alike but do you have a sense of what proportion of the companies will be reporting their earnings publicly or whether many of them are not required to report to anyone, just rake in the profits and put them in their private accounts?"

"I'm just getting started, but I can tell you that it's a mix. I can't tell you how many fall into one or the other category. I aim to figure out how much money is involved, at least in the cases that I have been able to track. I'm planning on adding up how much the companies I have identified have spent on buying up city goods and services over the last five years. It's complicated because some of the deals are public-private collaborations, some are long-term leases, some of it is outsourcing, and others are outright buy-outs. I'll be working on separating them and looking into what the different kinds of contracts look like. How long the deals are supposed to last, how responsibility for oversight of operations is laid out, whether the contracts give the city any say in price hikes, and so on. I know these arrangements have been going on for much longer than I realized. Getting the details straight on each of the transfers is taking a fair amount of time and effort. I'm enjoying doing this because the deals cities are entering into never cease to amaze me. My sense is that they're getting taken in a lot of cases. That they could get much better deals if they had as much high-priced talent, or as many sharks if you prefer, on their side as the private sector side has."

"What do you plan to do with the data you collect? Will your publisher – Axium, right? – publish it? It looks like it would have to be a series of articles, or are you thinking of writing a book?"

"I'm not sure. I think it would work well as a series of articles for a start. Axium doesn't have that big a circulation, so turning the articles into a book could reach many more people. One of the reasons I'm not sure about what the final product will look like is that Laura and I know that we've only scraped the surface of this thing. We're only looking at how cities are transferring public goods and services for profit. We haven't touched on how states or the federal government are doing it."

Laura picked up the story. "We've had to put our plans on hold because Nikki was in the middle of another story when we started to look at my data. She has to finish that story first. Nikki, tell everyone about the tobacco companies' new research agenda."

"The top three tobacco companies got together and formed a research institute. Its purported purpose is to identify what it is about the nicotine in tobacco that makes it addictive so that they can develop products without addictive qualities. They announced this development with great fanfare and got a positive response, even though there was some concern about collusion. But the general consensus was that it was collusion for a good purpose. Suddenly, we have a whistleblower sending the Federal Drug Administration a letter indicating that the announced agenda is not at all what is going on in this research outfit. The letter has not been made public, and there is concern about the whistleblower's safety. I got a copy because I have a friend in the FDA. What the whistleblower alleges is that, yes, the purpose of the organization is to distill the addictive ingredient in nicotine. But the ultimate purpose is to find a way to develop that ingredient so that it can be used in the production of other products. The tobacco companies realize that the smoking rate will continue to drop, so they have been diversifying. They're buying up food-producing companies, candy, and cookie companies for a start. The plan is to add the core addictive ingredient to those food products."

"Holy cow," was Jane's reaction. "Your tobacco company story is an explosive one. When do you think you will be publishing it?"

"Soon. I don't want to wait until the whistleblower story becomes public knowledge. I have to meet with the editor and legal department to make sure what we say and how we say it doesn't open us up to a lawsuit. But you can expect it to come out within days. After that, I'll have time to focus on the work that Laura is doing that I've taken an interest in."

"I can see that the data on what cities are doing with their money has the potential to be a continuing source of material," Mark said. "You've got an untapped gold mine that's not likely to run out."

"Yes," Laura said. "I'm thinking that we should try to seek money to set up some sort of nonprofit clearinghouse or maybe connect to an existing foundation that works on the preservation of our democracy. But we haven't had the time to explore all the options. We want to be careful about how we handle these data, so our efforts don't go to waste on a one-shot splash of publicity and then die out like so many other stories."

"What about the agency you work for now, Laura?" was Dick's question. "Do you think it would be interested in sponsoring what you and Nikki are talking about?"

"No. I'm basically a city-slash-nonprofit organization employee. I work for a committee set up by the city, which is supported by private funding. I'm sure the city doesn't want to get involved in something that would be highly politicized. My mandate does not extend to that, and it's really outside of the scope of what the city is ready to take on."

"Hey," said Jane, "we got so carried away with this discussion, we forgot to eat. I'll bring out the pizzas. They have to be cooked, but that won't take long. Let's get more to drink."

That broke the train of thought regarding everything they'd heard. Dick said that he needed some time to digest what he had heard and suggested that everyone come back a week later to pick up where the discussion had stopped. The others seemed okay with that idea. The conversation moved on to interesting things that they had done over the last few weeks while everyone was waiting to see if the virus would bring about all the upheaval that occurred the last time there was a pandemic.

Mark talked about learning to do stand-up paddleboarding on the lake. He had two friends who got him involved. It took him a while to learn to keep his balance. He went on to say that it was more strenuous than it looked. "It involves all your muscles at the same time. I can tell you that it's very relaxing once you get the hang of it."

Adam said he had signed up for a photography course that took the group to various urban and rural sites to do the photography. The first time they met a few weeks ago, the instructor had them walk around the downtown area and take pictures. He instructed them to look for relationships between contrasting materials: cement, glass, stone, brick, and iron rafters. They met at his studio first to talk about how the class would go. The instructor said they should send ten of their best shots to him. They would meet before the next class to discuss the photos. For the second class, he told them that he wanted them to take photos of the contrast between nature and industrial farms. The third class was to focus on the waterfront. They were to take photos of anything that interested them as long as it had water in the shot. There were six people in the course. The instructor planned to create a calendar with the best photos produced by members of the group. He would select two from each student's portfolio.

Laura said that she and Nikki went to a nearby athletic facility for exercise a few days a week. On weekends, they went biking along the lake. They had also volunteered to help with a community outreach campaign that they attended every couple of weeks. They met with people who needed help navigating city services, dealing with fundamental issues like housing, health care, schools, and so on. They said they planned to help them register to vote, so when the time comes, they won't get hassled about that.

Everyone seemed to be enjoying the pizzas. They were getting down to the last few pieces. They agreed that they had had enough to eat and drink and were beginning to think about getting home. All four of their guests thanked Jane and Dick for an evening of good talk and good eats. They said that they would be looking forward to their next session. Jane suggested switching it to next Friday so that they wouldn't have to worry about having to get to work the following morning. Everyone agreed to that suggestion.

After their guests left, Jane said, "That was very thought-provoking. I'll need to do something to come down from all the ideas that the discussion stimulated before going to bed."

"Yeah, I'll go turn on the TV and look for something that will not make me upset. Maybe a rerun of something that we've watched before. That should be good and boring, which is sure to make me sleepy. Are you good with that?"

"Sure. That sounds exactly like the kind of thing I need tonight."

TEN

The next day started as usual. Dick and Jane had a quick breakfast and dashed off to their respective places of work. It was an office day for Jane because she was handing in the monthly reports. Mark and Adam both greeted Dick when he walked by their lab, but they didn't stop to talk. He didn't get a chance to check what was going on outside of his lab until one o'clock. By then, he was hungry and ready for a break from his monitoring equipment. When he got to the cafeteria, he saw that the TV was turned on to the local news channel, and a few people were standing there watching. That was unusual because it was usually set on one of the cable news channels. He joined the group in front of the TV to watch. He saw that there was a march in front of the mayor's office. One of the protestors was being interviewed. The man said, "The water that comes out of my faucet looks funny, and I think it smells funny too. When I fill up the kitchen sink, it looks cloudy. I want to know what's in that water. I remember the scandals that took place well over a decade ago when it was discovered that Flint, Michigan's water, contained lead. We're here to demand the new water company test the water and make the results public."

A couple of other people joined the group. One of the guys standing next to Dick, whose name he didn't know, said, "Cloudy water could mean that the dissolved solids had not settled. The solids were still mixed in with the clear water that hadn't been given time to rise to the top. That would account for the funny smell, too."

Another person said, "I wonder how often the state Environmental Protection Agency is testing the water. The funding was cut when the state was struggling with the pandemic, and it never had enough money to restore those funds."

Someone else said, "We don't have the problem they have across the lake in Indiana with the steel mills releasing toxic chemicals in the water. But we do have farmers using all kinds of pesticides, plus all the animal waste that washes out into the streams that flow into the lake. That has to be monitored because it contains a lethal mix of chemicals and bacteria. We don't know if the water company is doing that."

A new person joined the group, which now included over half a dozen people. "Has anybody seen any reports on water quality in recent months?" No one said anything. The news program moved on to another issue. Some of the people in the group were done with lunch and on their way back to their labs. Two of the people went to get something to eat. Dick followed them. When the three of them were done paying for the food, they drifted to a table together. Although they recognized each other, they usually didn't get to talk to each other, other than to say hello. They reminded each other of their names and went on to talk about what they had just heard. Adam came into the cafeteria at that point and saw Dick. He waved and mouthed, "I'll join you in a minute."

When Adam sat down, they went through self-introductions again. Then they recounted what they had heard about water quality for Adam's benefit. Everyone at the table had a strong background in biology, so they knew more about water quality than most people. They agreed that they had no way of knowing whether there was any testing being carried out and whether it was being done well. Adam told the others about one of the sessions of his photography group activities that involved taking pictures at an industrial farm. No one bothered to chase him off, so he had a slew of photos that captured the contrast between the serene natural environment and the built-up, factory-farm environment. "I wasn't paying particular attention to any one part of the farm operations. I wasn't particularly interested in what the farms were doing with their waste products, but I could see the huge pond they use for that purpose. I could also see that the pond was right next to a creek. I know that the ponds are not sealed. They can easily leak into the groundwater. I was concentrating on taking pictures. I wasn't thinking about the problems the pond might be creating. In retrospect, I can see that those ponds have the potential for a real environmental disaster."

One of the other people at the table said, "We've known all along that the mix of bacteria from the waste in combination with the chemicals in the cleaning agents contains contaminants that lower the oxygen, which negatively affects fish and other aquatic organisms. I know that animal waste results in higher levels of nitrates. There is no clear evidence that nitrates are linked to birth defects and certain kinds of cancer, most notably colon cancer. But I'm not sure that's what's wrong with the water the guy we just saw on the screen is complaining about. You know it might be just the opposite of too little oxygen. It might be that the reason it looks white when he fills the sink is that there is too much oxygen in it, and there's nothing wrong with it – if it looks normal after a couple of minutes. But that doesn't mean that the water treatment company should get away with not testing and issuing reports. I don't know anything about the deal the city made when it leased the water treatment plant, but there must have been some provision for regular testing and reporting on water quality."

Everyone at the table said that they probably would have noticed if the water coming out of the faucets in their homes looked or smelled funny and would have looked into it. But they couldn't be sure that wasn't happening if the contaminant had no odor. They each admitted that they had reason to be paying attention to the fact that the water filtration company had not been reporting on water quality. Two of the men at the table said they would now call the state EPA to ask about testing. Dick said he would call the newly established water company to ask about it. With those promises in place, the talk turned to sports for a time before it was time to go back to work.

*****

Adam was meeting with his photography group again that evening. This time, they were going to a recycling operation that dismantled old cars before crushing them. He was looking forward to it. It was the kind of site that he thought could result in some dramatic photographs. They were meeting at the gate. They would be allowed to walk around accompanied by one of the employees who would make sure they weren't going anywhere that wasn't safe.

A couple of his fellow course members had already arrived, and he could see two more coming through the gates. Then a young woman he had not seen before came up to the little group and introduced herself. She said her name was Liz Sims and that she had just signed up for the course. She said someone else had dropped out. The instructor wanted to discourage her from joining in the middle of the course, but she finally convinced him when she mentioned who her father was. She said her father had been a newspaper photographer. She said that the instructor knew his work. When she told the instructor that she would go with her father sometimes on his assignments when she was in high school, that softened him up, and he agreed to let her join the class. She explained to the people she had just met that she got involved in other things when she went away to college. But now that she had a job and was spending so much time sitting in front of a computer, she thought it would be good to spend some time outside looking at the world through a camera lens.

By the time the instructor drove up, everyone in the course had assembled. He said he hoped that they had a chance to meet Liz. He then went on to issue instructions on how to approach the site. He wanted them to focus on capturing a mood. Adam thought he understood what mood meant, but had no idea how he would achieve that. Yes, the crushed cars piled on top of each other looked like a lot of destruction. It was nearly sunset. Maybe that would help set the mood for a sense of decline. He could see from the looks on the faces of the other members of the group that they weren't sure how to do that either. But that didn't stop them from taking lots of pictures. After about forty-five minutes, the instructor said it was time to leave. He said that the plan buwas to go back to his studio, look at each other's photos, and discuss them.

Liz ended up sitting next to Adam. Once they began examining the photos, the instructor identified some that he said were good in capturing the sense of destruction and desolation. He reminded them that it was often the case that you couldn't know which pictures would accomplish that until you saw what you had produced.

When it came to his turn to show his photos, Adam said he wasn't sure he had captured the mood of the place as well as he could have. But Liz was generous in praising his work. At the end, she said she was looking forward to talking with him again at the next class session. Adam reciprocated and said he would look forward to seeing her, too. The session ended with Adam feeling pretty good about his pictures and about having met someone he thought he might like to get to know better.

*****

Dick emailed the members of what he was now thinking of as the discussion group to confirm getting together again on Friday. He said they were planning to grill some brats. Jane planned to buy all the fixings on Thursday and be ready to welcome everyone on Friday.

That morning, the news media revealed that the latest agency to go on the chopping block was the regional electric utility. It had been established in the early 1920s as a publicly-owned entity. The city had provided oversight but was not directly involved in managing it. Now, the city was planning to pressure the agency to turn itself over to an investor-owned company. The move was not attracting much public interest. Dick guessed that was probably because the public did not understand what was involved in getting electricity to people's houses and places of work.

The members of the discussion group may have been more knowledgeable about the way electricity came into people's houses than the general public; still, they had only a vague sense of the possible problems the transfer posed.

Once everyone got settled with some drinks, Laura asked if they had heard about the city's plan regarding the utility. They all said they had heard that it looked like the transfer would happen, but hadn't had time to give it much thought. Laura said she had looked into it a little while ago. She explained that "some electric companies are publicly-owned and there are also some that are co-ops. But most people, about three-quarters of the country, get their electricity from a small number of large private sector companies."

She went on to say, "You probably won't remember this. One of the two largest utility companies in the country, both located in California, the Pacific Gas and Electric Company, went bankrupt after the fires that engulfed the California coast about twelve years ago. It turned out that PG and E wasn't maintaining their equipment, and the frayed lines were repeatedly touching off fires. The fires got steadily worse year after year until the state passed legislation prohibiting building in some burned-out areas to keep those areas from becoming too dense. When storms downed damaged electrical lines, the sparks caused the forest and houses in the area to catch fire. Critics argued that the company should have maintained the lines and clearing the underbrush to prevent the forest fires. The company argued that residents were responsible for clearing brush and dead trees from their property and weren't doing it. The company's arguments didn't hold up in court. The 2017 fires, which were more serious than previous fires, resulted in 87 deaths plus tremendous property losses. PG and E agreed to a settlement of $13.5 billion – that's billion with a B – to compensate wildfire victims. It's clear that the company had the funds to do a much better maintenance job, given how much money the company ended up having to pay out to victims, even as they were claiming bankruptcy. The arguments continue. Some observers continue to say that forest management is the state's responsibility. Others keep raising the question of where the money for doing that would come from if the citizens don't allow the state to raise the money to do that by taxing them."

"Yeah," Mark jumped into the discussion. "That's also bringing up the debate about climate change being the primary cause of the fires. Climate scientists keep saying that the temperature in the state has risen significantly. It was drying out more vegetation, which catches fire more easily. They are saying that the fires are having a circular effect. The fires are causing more pollution, which is causing more warming, meaning more climate change. It's an unending downward spiral. And no one seems to be ready to do something to put a stop to it."

"Yes. That gets us back to the basic issue: the private-investor electric company is more interested in profit than public safety. We know that PG and E continued to operate the same way it had been operating in the past after it declared bankruptcy. It certainly wasn't efficient before, and it wasn't efficient after it was sued for its part in causing the fires," was Nikki's summary of the situation.

Adam was nodding, "You're right. The people in California knew that was going on. You have to wonder what they were thinking. Californians were ready to agree that climate change was playing a major role in the increase in the number and intensity of forest fires in the state. But that didn't translate into support for increasing taxes to deal with its effects or to institute more government control and regulation over the private sector electric company."

"Exactly," said Laura. "Experts studying the situation said that either the state would have to raise taxes to pay for forest management or that it would have to pass legislation requiring the utility to do it, which would undoubtedly result in the company raising rates. The only other thing the state did was pass legislation to eliminate gas-fueled cars over the next couple of decades. As to who should do forest management, the public was readier to believe that the business sector would deal with it better by being efficient, more efficient than the government and that the state should institute some regulation, but not too much. They rejected the increase in state taxes option. How that would help climate control was kind of lost in the debate over taxes."

Mark was shaking his head. "Bringing up the California experience wouldn't do any good around here. People would say that our forests and our weather aren't like California's. That would be enough to end the discussion for most people. The fact that poor equipment maintenance could still cause a lot of inconvenience, like loss of heat and electricity during winter storms, wouldn't be a sufficient argument for increased regulation and against privatization. Of course, if the discussion came up in the middle of January, there might be a few more people ready to demand the government do something and might even be ready to talk about a tax increase."

"Even when bad things happen, people aren't nearly as quick to blame private sector organizations as they are to blame the government," said Dick. "What happened in Illinois around that time is a good example. I know about this because my sister lives in Chicago. The electric company there was caught bribing the Speaker of the House by offering jobs to candidates he was recommending in return for favorable legislation. The public reaction was mostly a shrug about what the electric company did, but it caused people to organize to force the politician out of office. His name was apparently in the news for months. Admittedly, he had been in that office for a long time, and many people were upset with him for other reasons. Still, the contrast in how people react to government malfeasance versus private sector malfeasance is remarkable."

With that, Dick announced that he would have to turn his attention to the grill and the brats. He got cheers for that. Mark told him that he couldn't wait to taste his cooking.

While they were waiting for the brats, Adam asked Laura and Nikki whether they had made any progress on their plan to create some kind of organization to deal with Laura's discoveries regarding who was buying all the public sector organizations. Both of them said that they had been too busy to work on that but might be able to set aside some time over the next few weeks to at least develop a proposal that they could present to potential funders.

The others tossed around some ideas about who Laura and Nikki could approach. No single nominee stood out as more likely to be interested than anyone else. They each said they would continue to give the matter more thought.

At that point, Dick brought the brats to the table, and people got the condiments they wanted and got more to drink. Once they started to eat, the conversation turned to the general topic of what else was happening in the country. There was general agreement that things had gotten worse in the wake of the pandemic, which was accompanied by continuing political unrest and economic decline. They reminded each other of the discussion about historians' predictions during the last session. Before anyone could get back to that discussion, Adam raised the question of when the country would overcome the aftereffects.

Jane was shaking her head, indicating that she thought it wouldn't happen anytime soon. "I'm very concerned about the fact that trust in social institutions is still so low."

Mark said, "That's not surprising to me. Just think of how many people lost their jobs. People couldn't return to those jobs after things started to get better because so many of the small companies they worked for were gone. The government did provide hand-outs for years after that, which helped some. It was a temporary fix, one that went on for years. The country didn't do much long-term planning for the future. The signs were there. Labor economists and lots of other experts were predicting that the country was on a trajectory that would simply prolong the pain. And that's exactly what's been happening, and we continue to see protests on the streets."

"Yes." Said Jane. "The predictions were that job growth would occur at opposite ends of the continuum, many more new jobs at the low skill, low pay end, and a small number of new jobs at the high skill, high pay end. And jobs in the middle range would just continue to disappear. The health sector would continue to be at what people called 'the driving engine of the economy.' But the health sector's continued growth was not sustainable because it was squeezing out investment in everything else. Those predictions turned out to be right on target. That and the fact that the country wasn't willing to give up the idea that the private sector would be more efficient in providing health insurance than the public sector got us to where we are now. Other countries do a much better job of handling their health care arrangements, but Americans have never accepted the idea that we should look at how other countries manage to keep their populations healthier and living longer and manage to do it at a far lower cost."

At that point, Dick said, "There are more brats." Adam and Mark said they were ready for another one.

The interruption had the effect of stopping the conversation. Adam said, "I don't know about anybody else, but I vote to put off talking about the topics we've just gotten into until next time. I'm depressed by all of it and just want to try to forget about it because it's too much to deal with. Maybe we could agree that the topic for discussion at the next session will be – decline in trust in social institutions. I would be willing to spend some time getting my thoughts on that organized. Right now, I'm afraid I would be spouting the same old tried and true comments about all the various issues we've touched on without really stopping to think about what I'm saying."

No one said anything for a minute or two. Then there was a lot of nodding. The others said they knew what both Adam and Jane were talking about. They said they would be happy concentrating on the brats without having to think about serious stuff too. So, it was agreed. They would focus on the issue that Adam mentioned the next time they met.

Talk turned to what everyone had been doing over the last week. Mark mentioned that he and some friends had decided to take their paddleboards to Chicago and paddle all along the beaches on the city's north side. He said they had a great time.

Laura and Nikki talked about working at the nonprofit. They felt that they were getting to know quite a few new people who were eager to participate in the effort to help people negotiate getting services for which they qualified.

Adam talked about the sites his photography course had taken him. He mentioned that a new person had just joined the group and that he was enjoying getting to know her. He got encouragement from the others on that score.

Jane said that she and Dick had done only one interesting thing since the last time they had all gotten together. They had gone to the zoo over the weekend. She said that they enjoyed watching both the animals and the people. Dick followed that up by asking if everyone knew that the zoo now had a new name. No one had heard that. Dick said, "Okay. I don't want to go back to focusing on the topic of selling off public goods and services. I will leave it at that."

After the guys finished eating the brats, Jane brought out a big plate of watermelon slices. They were just about gone, too. Their guests were looking like they had had enough to eat and didn't want to move. They started to talk about calling it an evening, but were moving very slowly. They all agreed that they would be prepared to discuss what was now on the agenda for next time. They said that they were pleased that Dick and Jane had started these discussions. Mark asked if they should consider finding someplace else to meet to relieve Dick and Jane of the hosting burden. But Jane was quick to say that it was no burden. Dick backed her up, saying that they really enjoyed having everyone meet at their house. Sitting around outside made it all very easy.

They agreed to meet next Friday.

ELEVEN

Jane had been in her office and at her desk for an hour or so the following day. She was feeling good about what she had managed to accomplish in that short time when the mayor's communications director, Norma Holander, knocked on her door frame, which was standing open. She was a good-looking Jamaican woman. She made a point of telling people that she was Jamaican, not African-American, because her parents instilled that identity in her from an early age.

She said, "Jane, I was here to talk to the people in the finance department, specifically Richard Davis, to see what they all thought of the mayor's plans to hand off the schools to a private investor. So, I thought I would drop by to see if you had time to grab a cup of coffee with me and share your views on that."

"Sure. You caught me at a good time. I just finished compiling the data on opioid addiction for the month. Depressing, but good to have it done. And good because there was actually a small drop in one measure, maternal deaths, for the past month in the communities that were looking pretty bad last month. Not that I'm saying it's a trend. It's just good whenever there are fewer deaths."

"Good. I'm glad to hear that, even if it's for just one month. Let's go to the coffee shop down the block. There might be fewer people from either of our offices than at the one next door, and it's quieter."

Jane told her assistant where she was going as she and Norma walked out of her office suite's front door.

Norma, who looked like she could afford to put on a few pounds, promptly ordered a latte and the specialty of the house, the extra-large almond-filled croissant. She apparently ate like that all the time and never put on a pound. Jane settled for a latte and the regular-size version of the croissant. The indulgence put both of them in a good frame of mind. Jane asked Norma how things were going at work. Norma said that the city was struggling to fulfill its responsibilities without cutting staff or services. She talked about how frustrated the mayor was about the squeeze on funds and the need to shuffle priorities constantly. She added that the mayor seemed discouraged and that she was even talking about retirement. The mayor was unhappy about leasing out goods and services belonging to the city, but couldn't come up with another alternative. That led to a discussion of the bid the city had received to buy the public school system.

Having covered how things were going at City Hall pretty thoroughly, Norma asked how things at the health department were going. Jane said that everyone in the department felt very lucky to have escaped the pressure to make cuts. She said she liked what she was doing and felt good about bringing to light the problems that specific communities in the city were facing. This did result, in a few instances, in getting more resources to those communities.

They talked about people in the city who were engaged in making life in the city more livable and those who were doing things that stood in the way. They talked about Harry Edwards, who was in charge of the parks. They agreed that he had done a great job of arranging plantings along the roads in the downtown area, and that the new plantings along the highway were a tremendous improvement. He volunteered at the Farm, which provided training for mentally disabled youth, who he would then hire to work with his people at the parks. Norma mentioned a few other people she thought had a promising future, and a few she hoped would go away.

Jane told Norma about the discussion group that she and Dick had formed and how much she enjoyed getting a fresh perspective on things from someone other than just her husband, whose views she shared but already knew very well. She said, "On that score, let me tell you about the job that Laura Wickman is doing. You know she is the one who the mayor's office recruited to track the city budget and track where money was being shifted to cover responsibilities. I don't know if you have kept up with how her job has expanded. She now follows that kind of information for fifty of the largest cities in the country. But wait, what's really interesting is what she and her roommate, an investigative reporter for Axium, have discovered. The entities being transferred from the public sector to the private sector use different names across the country, but are becoming absorbed by a small number of giant corporations. They've just started tracking this, so they don't have a really good idea of how much of it is going on, but you can see the implications.

Norma's reaction was, "Of course. Those corporations are growing into huge monopolies right before our eyes, but no one has been looking at that more closely because no one realizes how big a deal that is. Wow. When are they going to release this information?"

They don't want to do a single release. They believe that it would be a big news item for a few days and would fade like a lot of hot news items. They say that it's too big a story to let it go at that. They know that similar things are going on at the state level and even at the national level. Tracking who is doing the buying is not Laura's job. And it's too big a story for her roommate, Nikki, too. Nikki's stories typically take a few weeks to take shape. Once that happens, she moves on to another issue. She considered doing a series but felt that the story would be a continuing one, and even with a series, the story would have to have closure. Laura and Nikki considered writing a book, but again felt that it would be a one-shot deal. They've concluded that the best thing to do would be to create a non-profit organization that could continue to do that kind of work. They don't have the backing to do it. They were planning to do a proposal this week, but aren't sure where to turn to get the financial support they need."

"Humm," said Norma. "Let me think about it. I can make some phone calls and see what I come up with. I'll let you know. Then I'll want to meet with them before I do anything else."

"Norma, that would be great. I know you'll be impressed with their drive and dedication, and of course, their competence."

"I must say. This coffee break has been more interesting than I had anticipated. I thought we would just catch up. But this is an exciting new development. I can't wait to get back to the office and start making calls."

"Thanks so much, Norma, for your encouragement. I won't mention what you said to either Laura or Nikki. I wouldn't want to get their hopes up in case this turns out to be too hot a topic for anyone to touch."

"No. Don't worry about that. I know that many people want to undo the harm done by the administration in Washington, D.C., a dozen years ago. Things have been far too slow to change for the likes of many liberals and their supporters who want to see the devastation that hit the country during that period repaired. This is an ideal project for their purposes. But I agree that it would be better to wait to tell them until I line up some support."

*****

When Dick arrived at work, he found a notice posted on the lab whiteboard indicating that a meeting was scheduled for 9:30 that morning. The head of the lab would be coming to talk to the three researchers doing arthritis research about interns. He said that he had chosen their lab because the arthritis project was well designed and not at much risk of being derailed. Mark dropped by to ask if Dick knew anything more about the interns who were to be the topic of discussion at the meeting. Dick said he didn't. Mark said he had planned to do a six-week review of his data that morning to look for any indication that the cells he was cultivating were developing as he expected. But he could do that tomorrow. He said he was curious about what the meeting would be about. Dick said he was curious too.

Mark, Dick, and Adam were sitting at the conference table talking about how their projects were coming along when the head of the lab walked in. He greeted everyone and said he thought they would be pleased to hear the news he was about to impart. He said that Franklin University had approached him to ask if the lab would be willing to accept interns. The work of the interns would be monitored, and they would get college credit for their work. The lab could count on having the most able students selected for this opportunity. The lab could define the work they would be expected to do over the semester.

The three scientists did not react with great enthusiasm. Yes, it would be great to have more assistance in the lab. More could be accomplished. On the other hand, helping interns carve out a section of an ongoing research project might take more time than the results would justify. The head of the lab said he realized that they might think that. But he thought it was worth giving it a try. He hoped they would agree. This time around, there would only be three interns. It was hoped that, if things worked well this semester, this would become an ongoing arrangement.

Adam was the first to raise a question. "Would the project the intern was carrying out be something that would have to be finalized? In other words, was there an expectation that projects could be designed so that they would run for the length of a semester from beginning to end, or would the students report on what occurred during that period with the understanding that the project would continue even after the semester ended?"

The lab director said, "Ideally, the interns would be assigned tasks that could be completed over fifteen weeks, including time to write up their findings. But if short-term tasks were not possible, then the interns would be expected to outline recommendations for the next steps the research should take. We certainly wouldn't want to end projects producing promising results because the semester ended and the intern left. Projects could also conceivably end in the middle of the semester if it became clear that the research produced no significant findings. In that case, the intern would write up the findings and account for what was discovered that caused that particular part of the research to be concluded."

Mark's reaction was, "I can see that we could get a lot more done with that kind of assistance, but it would take time to coordinate and ensure continuity."

The director agreed. "Yes. There's a trade-off there. I imagine that it would work better in some instances than others. Still, I think it's worth trying. If it takes more time than it's worth, we can drop the experiment. But I think we might be able to institute some procedural guidelines that would make the process smoother and require less oversight on your part. Are you willing to give it a try for one semester?"

The three agreed that they would be willing to give it a try. Dick said, "It might be rewarding to watch an intern take on responsibility for a project in the real world rather than an academic assignment. I've always liked watching new employees learn and become more confident in their ability to translate what they learned in school to the work that takes place in an actual working lab."

The director thanked them for their willingness to give the internship idea a try. He said he would get back to them about meeting the prospective interns and the professor who initiated the idea over the next couple of days.

On the way back to their labs, the three researchers agreed to meet for lunch and talk about the internship meeting some more. Before they parted, Mark said he had participated in such a program when he was a graduate student. He didn't want to mention it at the meeting, but said he had some thoughts he wanted to share with them.

Once all three got to the cafeteria, got their food, and settled down, they were ready to talk about the internship experiment. Adam and Dick both said they wanted to hear what Mark had to say about it. Mark said that his experience was complicated by the fact that he was assigned to a researcher whose work was not going well. That made the man moody and hard to work with. Mark wasn't sure how to handle the situation. He went to the professor who had set up the internship to ask for help, but he didn't want to hear what Mark had to say. He acted as if Mark didn't know what he was talking about. Mark was hesitant about going to someone else at the lab to discuss the situation. Finally, he decided that he would be wasting his time working with the man whose research was going nowhere and that he should talk to the head of the lab. That turned out to be very messy. The lab director suspected that things were not going well for the man Mark was working with. The lab was considering letting him go.

"I didn't want to be part of a situation that would cause the guy to lose his job," Mark said. "I was stressed out. The situation got resolved when the guy decided to take a leave. He had been diagnosed with possible colon cancer and wasn't handling it well. The upshot was that I was asked to take over his research. I could see what he was doing wrong. He was using too large a dose of an interferon-related chemical on the cells he was cultivating. I reduced the dose, and the experiment started to produce positive results. By that time, the semester was over, and I just wanted to get out of there."

"What happened to the guy you were working with?" was Dick's question. "Did he get the treatment he needed for the cancer?"

"Yes. It turned out to be a benign tumor. He got the surgery for the tumor, and he was okay after a few weeks of recuperation."

Adam followed up with, "Did he come back to the lab? Do you know?"

"He did come back to the lab. But I heard from the professor in charge of internships that he was angry about how the lab handled his research when he went on leave. He said that a senior person should have been assigned to his project instead of an intern. He argued that I had caused his project to be dumped by making the changes I did. Actually, the head of the lab praised my insight and told me that I had made exactly the right interpretation. He said that there were other reasons to have doubts about this man's work, so I shouldn't feel bad that the lab let him go not long after he got back. I still feel bad about the whole episode. I know that I would have like to have worked with someone whose work was going well. As it is, this guy has tried to damage my reputation among his colleagues. Fortunately, the head of the lab said he would always be willing to give me an excellent recommendation any time I needed one."

Mark waited a minute or so and then went on. "There's more to the story. The guy I worked with, whose name you might recognize, went on to become well-known as an administrator of one of the big drug companies. He stopped doing research. He first took a job as a lobbyist for one of the big drug companies and moved up from there. I can tell you it doesn't give me much confidence in drug companies to know that this guy was able to move up in the ranks and is in a position to make decisions regarding drug development and testing."

"Well," Dick said, "that is quite a story. I'm sure the interns who come here will not have that kind of traumatic experience, given that they will be working with one of us. I guess the lesson here is to watch out to make sure that an exceptionally bright intern doesn't come in and find that the work we're doing is not up to par. It's only because you were the intern, Mark, that that happened. I'm kidding. It certainly wasn't your fault that this guy's career went astray."

"I know. But I can't help feeling that I played a part in it and that leaves me with very mixed feelings."

Dick's response was, "You know you shouldn't feel that way. Research is an arena that doesn't take poor performance lightly. You couldn't have handled it any differently than you did."

"That's exactly right, Mark. You have to keep in mind that the flaws in his research would have kept him from moving ahead even if you had had nothing to do with him." Adam said before moving on to another topic. "Let me tell you how my photography class is going. The next session is scheduled at Saint Jerome College. You know the one with that unusual chapel. We'll be taking photos of that with the sun coming through the windows, which should be pretty interesting. Afterward, I'm planning to get something to eat with someone I told you about last time. I keep thinking that my fortune cookie is coming true. It said I would meet someone, and I think I have."

Mark and Dick were both smiling and telling him that they were glad the fortune cookie prediction was correct. Dick checked his watch and said, "Okay, guys, time to get back to work, or we'll be in the position that the guy Mark worked with and have our work go to pot. Adam said, "Are you worried? You don't look worried. I'm pretty sure that isn't going to happen to mine just yet." More teasing followed as they moved away from the table and walked back to their labs.

Two days later, the lab director called and said that the three interns and their professor would be coming by that afternoon. The meeting turned out to be very cordial. The professor had done something similar at a much bigger institution, so he had a lot of experience figuring out which students would do well. He invited the researchers to contact him if they had any questions about the process, but he expected that they would all get along just fine and that the experience would be rewarding for all concerned. The interns didn't get a choice of who they would be working with. The director assigned one to each of the researchers without providing an explanation. Everyone seemed okay with that. The interns agreed to show up the following day at 9. They would learn more about the work being done in the lab then. Everyone shook hands, and the meeting ended. The director told the three researchers to come to him if they ran into any difficulties. He would contact the professor if necessary.

When Mark, Adam, and Dick were walking back to their labs, they wondered if they had ever looked so young and wide-eyed. They agreed that they must have. They also decided that the interns looked serious and agreed that things would probably go well.

TWELVE

Jane was working at home that day. She concentrated on getting files to transfer into the correct columns on her chart when the phone rang. It was Norma. "Guess what. I talked to one of the mayor's most generous donors. He manages a hedge fund. With the stock market doing so well over the last decade, he is pretty flush right now. I invited him for lunch. He expected me to talk about the mayor's priorities, but I surprised him and told him about your friends' project. He was fascinated. He said he suspected that something like what they're finding was going on, but couldn't find anyone looking at who was behind those trends. He'd been too busy focusing on the sector he has been dealing with for years to look into it himself. He is mostly interested in housing and urban development. Once I told him a little about what they were discovering, he wanted in on it. He is willing to provide the funds to set up a non-profit dedicated to tracking the ongoing shifts in control over so many public entities and to provide operating funds until it can attract more donors. He said he would personally recruit more donors because he was sure more people would be interested in this kind of information."

"That's great, Norma. How do you want to handle this? Do you want to meet with my two friends next? I'm sure that Laura and Nikki would be ready to talk about what they are working on anytime you say. By the way, were you thinking that the hedge fund manager should serve as the president of the board they will have to set up?"

"Wait, wait. We're nowhere near talking about things like a board," was Norma's response. But she was smiling in reaction to Jane's enthusiasm. "We didn't get that far. I certainly wasn't going to bring it up with him before he met them and actually signed on. As a matter of fact, the two of us should sit down with the two women and tell them about this development. That will give them a chance to get their thoughts together before we set up a meeting with my hedge fund guy. Since you will get to know who it is shortly, I should tell you that it's Josh Wilhelm. Do you know much about him and the causes he has been supporting?"

"I know the name, and I know that he supports worthwhile causes. But I can't say I know more than that."

"Okay, we can talk about what I know about him when the four of us get together. I will let you set that up. Lunch, right? We can meet at The Brassiere. It can go on my budget."

"Terrific. I can't wait to tell Laura and Nikki. I will call both of them this afternoon and set it up for next Monday. That will give them a chance to think through how they want to present their idea to you. Is that okay with you?"

"Let me check. Yes, that's fine."

Jane called Nikki, and Laura asked if they could get away for a coffee break that afternoon to discuss the possibility of getting support for their project. Both said they would absolutely make time for that.

The three of them met at the coffee shop near Jane and Laura's offices. Because Nikki spent so much time away from her office, she didn't have to tell anyone where she was going. It was a lovely afternoon. When Laura got there, Jane suggested sitting at a table outside. Nikki came by just as they were being seated.

"I can't wait to hear what you've come up with," was Laura's opening line. They ordered iced tea without really thinking about it. Jane launched in with an account of her meeting with Norma Holander, recounting what she said, that she had lined up a donor who was very interested in funding their project. Both Laura and Nikki nearly jumped out of their seats with excitement. "Wow. I didn't expect anything to happen this quickly," said Nikki. "I'm thrilled to know that there are people out there who are interested in hearing about what we are finding and, more importantly, interested in supporting our work."

"I'm not sure I know how to talk to someone like that, someone who has that kind of money," was Laura's next comment. "What kind of information will he want? How much preparation will this involve? I'm willing to do whatever it takes, and I'm just not at all sure what is involved. Will we be meeting him in person? Oh, wait, I don't even know who we're talking about. Is he willing to have you or Norma tell us his name?"

"Slow down. One question at a time," said Jane. She was acting as if she were being calm and rational, and remembering how eager she had been when Norma first told her about Josh Wilhelm's interest in what Nikki and Laura were working on. "Yes, he is willing to have you know who he is. It's Josh Wilhelm. He manages a hedge fund that has done very well over the last decade or so. He is willing to provide start-up funds to set up a non-profit organization. And he is willing to provide operational funds until the organization gets on its feet."

"Oh my god," said Laura, "I can't believe this is happening. It's like I'm dreaming. I'm afraid I'll wake up and find that I imagined this."

"No, you're not imagining it," said Jane. "You will probably get to feeling that it's real when you start doing all the work required to set this thing up. It will take a considerable amount of work."

"Yes, I was wondering about that," said Nikki. "What does that mean at this stage? What do we have to do to prepare for this meeting? Maybe a better question is, what do people do in preparation for establishing an organization that will do the kind of work we are planning? That goes to show you how new I am at this."

"I have some experience writing grant proposals," said Jane. "Which is not the same thing as what you will be writing, but there is kind of a formula when you go out to ask for money, which is basically what you will be doing. My grant proposals will give you a basic framework for the kinds of things you need to think about. I can talk you through it, but maybe it would be easier if I just send you some sample proposals that have been funded so you can get a sense of the topics that you have to address. You need an outline. Once you figure that out, then all you'll have to do is fill in the outline. Sound more doable?"

"Maybe," said Nikki. "I'm not sure. I'll be more certain once I take a look at your proposals."

"Right," said Laura. "That should help in understanding how to present the data that shows what we've found to date and what we hope to do with it."

"Jane, do you know anything about Mr. Wilhelm?" was Nikki's next question.

"No, not really. I know that he has supported some of the things outlined in the Health Department's five-year plan that focus on social determinants of health instead of the usual thing that people think will produce better health and longer life, that is, more medical care. He is mostly interested in supporting initiatives that focus on housing but education and food security too. Norma said she would tell us more about him when we meet with her."

Nikki's response was, "I'll do some investigating, so we have a better sense of who he is before we meet with her."

"Good idea," said Jane. "I think we've gone as far as we can go for now. I'll email those grant proposals to you. I'd be happy to look over your proposal once you start to develop it. You can send me a draft, and we can meet for coffee or lunch to discuss it. How's that sound?"

Laura and Nikki had big smiles on their faces and were nodding enthusiastically.

Jane went on, "Since there is no external deadline here, it would be good not to rush this. We can tell Norma that you will be working on something to show to Josh Wilhelm in a week or two. That you hope to have it ready as soon as possible, but aren't committing yourselves to a specific date. Okay? But I want to set up a lunch with Norma first. I suggested that we meet next Monday. How does that sound to you?"

They were both nodding some more with big grins on their faces. They thanked Jane for all the help she gave them, saying they couldn't imagine how they would have gotten this far without her help. They both said they couldn't wait to start working on the proposal.

Jane went back to her office and quickly got her hands on three proposals that included her name as a primary or secondary investigator, all of which had been funded. She emailed copies to both women. In her note, she added some encouraging remarks. She said she was sure they would be great at writing their proposal because they had a terrific idea to work with. And that she was looking forward to seeing the project get off the ground.

THIRTEEN

It was the second-to-last session of Adam's photography course. The class was scheduled to meet on the campus of St. Jerome's, a relatively small, respected Lutheran college in the area. Because it was summer, there wouldn't be many students. The photography class members knew that the college boasted an architectural gem of a chapel that had several wings on each side with walls that supported enormous stained-glass windows. It was a perfect time for taking pictures of the setting sun coming through the windows. When they were all assembled, the instructor said that they should pay attention to how the colors in the windows changed depending on the direction from which they were shooting. He said they would not meet tonight, but would look at tonight's photos and the photos taken during other sessions after the next and final class.

After the class broke up, Adam asked Liz if she would be interested in having something to eat. She agreed, and they went to a nearby college bar for sandwiches and drinks. They talked about their jobs. After Adam talked about what he did, Liz explained that her job was healthcare-related as well. She was a computer analyst working to develop a software program that would read dermatological slides. She explained that the objective was to have the computer program distinguish between benign lesions and those that were likely to become cancerous. The thinking behind the project came from two dermatologists who regularly took pictures of their patients' lesions. They were convinced that there was no way any single dermatologist could run across the full range of possible skin diseases. So, they decided that feeding thousands of slides of skin lesions that they collected from medical school collections into the computer was the answer. The plan was to have the computer "learn" to categorize the slides. They set up an organization that they planned to expand into other areas that they were convinced could use greater reliance on computer learning. Liz explained that once she developed the software for skin lesions, she had an offer to do the same thing for diagnostic X-rays of lungs to sort the ones that show tumors from those that do not. She said that she expected that working with X-rays would be more challenging than working with slides that were basically photographs.

Adam said he thought that her work was very interesting and asked some questions about the programming process. He asked how far along she was with her current task and how she would know when the computer had seen enough slides. She said she learned to do what she was doing mainly through a part-time job creating websites for small businesses in college. She was already a skilled programmer when she took the job. But she decided to take more courses in artificial intelligence to advance her skills. She liked what she was doing and could have gotten a much higher-paying job with a company working on artificial intelligence after college, but she felt the company was taking advantage of its employees, so she didn't want to try for a full-time job there. Adam said he would like to hear more about her work, but he also wanted to know how she liked the photography class.

Liz said it was a relief to be looking at something other than slides of diseased skin. They laughed about what a nice change it was to get away from their work settings and into the great outdoors. She said it was fun to look at the world through a lens.

Adam said he felt the same way. They agreed that they were looking forward to seeing everyone else's photos after the next class and hearing what the instructor would have to say about them. He said he wondered when the instructor would announce which pictures he selected for the calendar.

*****

When Dick sent around an email to ask the group members about getting together for a discussion at the end of the week, Laura and

Nikki begged off. They both said they were swamped right now, working on a proposal, but looked forward to sharing where things stood after meeting with Norma Holander, who had recruited a potential sponsor. They were meeting with him next week. Mark and Adam said that they thought taking a break was not a bad idea and would look forward to meeting next week.

Dick knew about Jane's meeting with Norma and the fact that Norma had gotten Josh Wilhelm interested in supporting Nikki and Laura's work. Dick was sure that they would be hard at work on a document to present to Wilhelm.

Jane and Dick were not unhappy about the break from what had become a stimulating weekly discussion. There would be plenty to discuss next time they met, starting with Nikki and Laura's proposal. In the meantime, they needed some stimulation, not necessarily the kind of intellectual stimulation that they expected from the meetings. Jane suggested that they take a one-day vacation in Chicago. It was only an hour's drive. She suggested planning on having brunch in the city and then going to the Chicago Art Institute. She said she thought there was a special show of 1960s pop art that might be fun. Dick agreed that it was a great idea. They could use a day away from familiar surroundings.

*****

Laura and Nikki were indeed hard at work on a proposal. They had a pretty good sense of the structure the proposal should take once they looked at the samples Jane sent over. They knew they had to have a mission statement about what the organization intended to accomplish. The methods they would use to achieve the objectives they set forth. The data sources they would rely on. How the information they gathered would be interpreted. How extensive their data gathering would be, in this case, how many cities would be represented, and whether they would go on to do the same thing for states and the federal government. They would have to indicate how they expected their findings to be disseminated. They would have to talk about a budget, which they had no clue how to construct.

Once they started working on the proposal, they realized that they had many questions that they weren't sure how to deal with. They were pretty sure they wanted to set up a not-for-profit organization. They knew they would have to have a board of directors, but didn't know where to start arranging for that. Someone would have to educate them about what it took to do a good job of administering a nonprofit.

Nikki suddenly said, "We need to think about getting continuing funding. We can't expect Mr. Wilhelm to have deep pockets forever. I have no experience and no interest in fundraising. I'm pretty sure you don't either. We'll have to have someone who does that for us. Maybe we can charge for the materials we produce. Or do we want to have free access to our material because, after all, aren't we doing this to educate people? Oh, Laura, have we taken on more than we can handle?"

"I know, it does sound overwhelming. I don't want to give up. We are finding stuff that people in this country need to know. Let's face it. We're researchers. We're not administrators or politicians. We need help doing this. I think it's okay to admit that. To admit that we are new at this part of what's involved in making our findings accessible to the public, and that we could use the guidance of people with experience doing this kind of thing. Let's not panic. Let's think about how we go about getting the help we need. I expect that Josh Wilhelm realizes that. Norma probably explained that we would need lots of assistance with some parts of what we're trying to create."

"You sound so calm and rational. I sound like I'm losing my mind. Okay, I'll try to calm down and do what you say. Maybe when we meet with Norma Holander, we'll have a better sense of what we need to think more about. She was interested enough to talk to Mr. Wilhelm about our project, so she should have some ideas about how to set this thing up and what we need to think about in approaching him. Didn't Jane say she already set up an appointment with Norma? I was too excited to hear everything she was saying."

Laura thought about it for a minute before she responded, "Yes, she said we're scheduled for a lunch meeting with Norma Holander on Monday. I think that talking to both Norma and Jane before we go much further will help us stop feeling like we're running around in circles."

"Right. But we do need to have a draft of our mission statement. We need to have something to say about what we expect to achieve. Remember, Jane said she would look it over."

"Okay, let's work on that," was Laura's response. "How about saying that we want to document the extent to which goods and services are being shifted from oversight by the public sector to control by the private sector? I think it's always good to use economics jargon to connect with policy wonks. It reassures them that you have read and understood their stuff. We can say that we are planning on establishing a repository of data that has been analyzed and described in language that members of the general public can comprehend. That we are focused on bringing together information on trends that reports on single occurrences of transfers from public to private control from one location to another couldn't possibly capture. Maybe we should throw in the term – meta-analysis."

"Wow. That sounds good. You've been thinking about this while I've been fretting. We have to say something to emphasize the part that I think is most startling, the part about how so many of what seem to be local private sector organizations are actually members of large, national corporations."

"Yes, I agree," said Laura. "That is a significant aspect of what we want to highlight. We can just say that. We can say that we intend to identify the private sector organizations that are taking over public sector organizations, and that we expect to outline the links the corporations may have with similar organizations. That should cover it. What do you think?"

"I think that is an excellent start. You're good at this."

"Thanks," said Laura with a big grin on her face. "I'm not sure what came over me. It must be that my pent-up frustration about what I've been working on that is pouring out. We need to say something about where we're getting the data. That's easy. I can write that up. And we need to talk about the dissemination of our findings. I know we keep bringing that up to each other. Maybe we can get some help from Norma and from Jane on that, too."

"We should have a list of things we want to cover when we meet with her so that we don't forget something. I'm thinking that we need to talk about the mechanics of setting up a nonprofit, getting a board, discussing future funding, stuff like that."

"Good idea. You make up the list. I'll work on a statement about data sources. I think that should be enough for our first meeting, don't you?"

"Yes," Nikki was nodding and looking much calmer. "I think that we're ready to talk about our enterprise without sounding like it's just a pie in the sky idea. That we've actually given it a lot of thought."

FOURTEEN

Adam was eager to get to the last session of his photography course. They would be sitting down to look at everyone's photos tonight and getting feedback. That would be interesting. They photographed the same things, but they probably ended up with very different results. Some might be special, gems in the middle of a pile of interesting but not so unusual shots.

He was also looking forward to seeing Liz. When he got to the instructor's studio, he could see a buffet of soft drinks and plenty of snacks, enough that one could make a whole meal out of. He thought that was nice of their instructor. The instructor had a screen up with pictures of the chapel windows that the students had submitted to him. You could see right away that some were close-ups that captured color and light, while others were taken from a distance and had an architectural interest. He liked both kinds.

Once everyone had assembled, gotten something to eat and drink, and settled down, the instructor congratulated them on taking great photos. He said he was getting close to selecting the twelve that would go into the calendar. He said he would choose two from each of their portfolios. Everyone looked pleased. They knew that they wouldn't be receiving any royalties from sales of the calendars. At the beginning of the course, the instructor had told them that the profits would go to art scholarships for underprivileged children in Mintaka.

The group went on to look at photos from each of the other sessions. There was a wide array of interesting shots. The students were generous in their praise of each other's photos. They didn't know who in the group took which shots, and no one admitted that the one being praised was theirs. It was all very congenial. They all talked about how much they enjoyed being part of the course. Some said they would continue to take photos on their own and asked about submitting them to publishers or other outlets. The instructor talked about art fairs, photography books, and jobs involving photography. Adam enjoyed hearing about things like that, even though he had no intention of doing anything but take pictures for his own enjoyment.

The group started breaking up, with some students staying to talk further with the instructor and others getting ready to leave. They were shaking hands with each other, agreeing that they had a great experience, wishing each other well, and saying that they looked forward to finding out which shots would go into the calendar. The instructor said he would let them know the following week.

Adam asked Liz if she would be interested in getting something to drink, and she agreed. They went to an outdoor café nearby, and each got a glass of wine. He asked her if she thought she would try to do more with her photos. She answered that she didn't have time to do that now. But she always thought the photos at art fairs were popular, and she might think about that as an activity she would pursue in retirement. Adam said, "That's thinking ahead. I've never given any thought to what I would do when I retire."

Liz said, "It's because my father was a photographer. He got to travel and take pictures of exotic places. I've always thought I would like to do that, but I'm not a risk-taker. I wanted a steady job and was not at all sure I could support myself as a photographer. But the wish to do what he did has never gone away completely."

"I admire you for working out a balance in your life. I just seem to have stumbled into what I'm doing. I like my job. I'm enjoying doing research that I consider to be important, but I can't say that I planned on this career. I was good at science and math. My guidance counselors just kind of told me what to do, and I did it. I got internships that I liked and was apparently good at. So here I am."

"Nothing wrong with that," said Liz. "It's good that your counselors spotted what you were good at and gave you good advice. I had to figure out how to combine my interest in visual art, photography, to be specific, with something practical. It wasn't too hard, but I had to do it on my own. I was good at science and math, too. Another job I had earlier in my career as a grad student was doing something like I'm doing now. I worked in a bio lab, sorting photos of bugs. You wouldn't believe how many different kinds of bugs there are. I was part of a team. Our job was to assemble photos the lab had taken over time to track how they were evolving. Tedious if you're not particularly fond of bugs."

They were both done with their wine. Adam asked if she would be interested in going out for dinner sometime. She said yes and said she would look forward to that.

*****

The interns seemed to be settling in. Adam, Mark, and Dick agreed that the best way to start was to have the interns read the documents that led to the funded research. Then go on to read notes on the work that had been done so far. They would be given a couple of days to accommodate. That seemed to be working well. Dick outlined his intern's responsibilities, which revolved around recording changes in the speed at which the mice ran on their wheels. The results would be used to evaluate improvement in mouse knee joint strength. It was now two weeks since the interns arrived, and it looked like they had settled in well.

The work in the lab was coming along routinely. The lab mice seemed to be responding to the interventions the researchers were introducing as expected. Mark was focusing on molecules that regulate the growth of proteins involved in the regeneration of cartilage. Adam was working on mechanisms designed to get blood supply to the cartilage, which doesn't produce blood cells. Dick had shifted from focusing on inflammation and the presence of white cells to spending some time creating a gel that would serve as a scaffold to contain stem cells and blood plasma to grow proteins. He had injected some of the gel into the mouse joints.

Dick was monitoring the mice to document changes that he expected to take place. He did not expect any sudden changes. Dick had been working on the gel for some time. He was starting to get hopeful that his work would make a difference. The mice were looking like they were tolerating the gel well. Dick was seeing what he expected to see. The gel looked like it was serving as a good platform for generating molecules that would be able to grow cartilage, at least, it was looking like a good platform in mouse knees. But this morning, he noticed something strange. Two of the mice suddenly looked like they had lost all the gains that he had recorded. He couldn't understand what would explain that. He went around to Mark and Adam's labs and told them what he had seen and asked them to come to look and check his findings. They did, and they agreed that two of the mice looked like they hadn't had the gel injected and were not producing new molecules. They said they would give it some more thought, and maybe they could talk about it over lunch.

Dick wondered if his intern, who was in charge of taking care of the mice, had noticed anything. When Dick asked him about what he had seen, the intern looked like he had been caught in the headlights of an oncoming car. Dick asked what was wrong. The intern said he had a nasty headache that morning and wanted to get some aspirin. Dick told him to go ahead. A little later, when Dick was standing quietly looking at the mice, thinking about possible interpretations, he saw something out of the corner of his eye moving around on the floor. When he turned around, he could see a mouse running along the bottom of the cabinets.

That explained the mystery. The intern must have let two of the mice get away and replaced them from the supply of new mice. The new mice hadn't been part of the research. Of course, there wouldn't have been any indication that any changes were going on in those two mice.

In the meantime, he had to find the intern and confirm that he had dropped the two mice and replaced them. He'd have to think about how to handle that mishap. He would also have to set out traps for the two mice. The lab had humane traps, so it wasn't difficult to capture them. However, they wouldn't be returned to the research project. This isn't the first time a couple of mice got loose. It didn't happen often. But Dick knew it had happened a few times over the years.

When the intern got back, Dick confronted him. The intern looked like he was going to faint. He was pale and sweating. He didn't look well. He admitted that he dropped the mice. He said that he wasn't used to handling mice, and they just slipped away. Dick said he thought the intern should go home for the day and get some rest. He assumed that he hadn't slept the night before because he was worried about losing his internship. He looked pretty bad. Dick said they would discuss it tomorrow.

When he joined his two colleagues for lunch, they both had concerned looks on their faces. Dick said, "Before you say anything, I can tell you that the mystery is solved. It has nothing to do with the research. It has to do with the intern mishandling the mice."

"Oh, what a relief," said Mark. "I was going through all kinds of scenarios and starting to doubt what we were doing. I'm glad to hear that it's not the research design."

"True," was Adam's reaction. "That part is good. But what about the intern? What are you planning to do?"

"I don't know. What do you both think we should do about the intern? Does it have any implications for the whole internship idea? I don't want to ruin the kid's career over a dropped mouse. We've all made mistakes. What he needs to learn is that mistakes happen, but you have to take responsibility for them. That is the honest and mature thing to do. Maybe I'll give him a stern talking to about that and leave it at that. What do you guys think?"

"With luck, that will be a lasting lesson, one he'll remember for the rest of his career. The lesson being, that if you're honest about mistakes, people are understanding," was Adam's comment.

"Yeah, I agree," was Mark's reaction. "No use making this thing into a bigger issue. No good will come from that for the lab or anyone else."

"Okay. That's settled then. I sent him home. He must be sweating bullets. He looked sick when he left. Should I call him and tell him that he still has his job, or should I let him sweat?"

Both Mark and Adam said to call him and tell him he still had his job and set a time for them to meet, but not say more until tomorrow.

*****

When Dick and Jane got home, Dick got right into the story about the mouse incident. Jane said, "I'm glad that the confusion about what was happening turned out to have a clear explanation. And, I think you made the right decision about giving the intern a stern lecture. Do you like him? Do you think he is doing good work otherwise?"

"I can't say much about him. I really haven't spent enough time talking to him outside of telling him what he was responsible for in the lab. I was planning to talk to him tomorrow about the project he's working on. I thought I would let him get accommodated to the lab before sitting down and talking with him about it."

"Well, you'll now get that chance to talk to him, but just not about what you expected to talk about. I guess you won't be giving him more challenging assignments until you see how he does after this incident."

"True. I'll talk to him about what I'd like him to work on and tell him that we'll have a review of his work in another two weeks. By that time, a third of the semester will be over. That will be a good time to see what he understands about my research project and his contribution to it."

Jane said, "My day went better than yours. I sent over some proposals to Laura and Nikki that I submitted and that had been funded. I attached a brief note on how to interpret them." She went on to tell Dick that she was looking forward to the lunch that was scheduled for Monday when Nikki and Laura would be discussing their nonprofit proposal with Norma Holander. "I know they are anxious about it because they are so new at setting up something like what they envision. They're good researchers who find themselves having to act like entrepreneurs. But I'm not worried. They're smart, and they're personable. They'll make a good impression. I'm pretty sure Norma will be happy to serve as a mentor. She'll do a good job in preparing them to meet with Josh Wilhelm. I look forward to hearing what she tells them."

Once she finished talking about her day, Jane said, "Do you want to check out the news before we settle down? I have to look at some reports that I didn't get to earlier today."

"Sure, the news is hardly ever good, but we have to know what's going on around us."

The news wasn't good from either Jane's or Dick's perspective. The mayor announced that the city had entered into a contract with Educational Advancement Enterprises, giving them control of the city's public schools. The teachers' association immediately launched a lawsuit. The service employees announced that they were setting up a meeting with their union representatives to institute a lawsuit as well. Parents were being interviewed to ask how they felt about the move, which resulted in a mixed response. Some were siding with the teachers in opposition to the move. Others were enthusiastic about the contract, saying that the teachers were more interested in job security and salary increases than in making sure the children were getting a good education.

The mayor went on air to assure listeners that the contract the city entered into ensured that high educational standards would be maintained and that the organization would do everything in its power to make sure all employees of the public school system would keep their jobs.

Dick and Jane agreed that the promises the city got from the organization were not something that the city could guarantee. The city really couldn't ensure that everyone would keep their jobs. In any case, the lawsuits that had already been launched were likely to stretch out for a long time before anything else happened. They agreed that the Educational Advancement Enterprises organization undoubtedly had much deeper pockets than the teachers' or service workers' unions. Even so, they were both sure that the unions would take the position that they had to be prepared to hold out as long as they could to win any concessions.

Jane said she wondered how much background Laura had gathered on the organization. She looked forward to hearing about that.

Dick responded with, "We haven't had the discussion group over for more than a week. Maybe Laura and Nikki will be ready to get together after they talk to Norma. We should probably wait until then to see if we can schedule another session."

"Good idea. I miss our discussion group even after such a short lapse."

FIFTEEN

Dick was thinking about what he would say to his intern when he headed for the lab the next day. He wanted to take time out to treat the event seriously without taking too much time away from his work and to make things uncomfortable for both of them.

The intern shuffled in, looking worse than he did the day before. Dick thought he'd better try to calm the guy down before lecturing him. He tried to get across the message that dropping the mice wasn't that serious an event. Not admitting to it was what Dick wanted the intern to understand was his big mistake.

The intern sat there and listened with his head down. He nodded and said he understood that he was wrong in not admitting what had happened. He was still looking panicked. Dick tried to assure him that everyone makes mistakes and that mistakes can be put aside if they take responsibility for them. Dick told the intern that he would not be dismissed and the incident would not go into his file. He said that if the intern needed help handling the mice, he should ask for assistance.

Dick reached out to shake the intern's hand, to which the intern responded, but looked like he was going to cry. Dick thought that the event was traumatic for the intern, but that he would get over it.

Dick arranged to meet for lunch with Mark and Adam to tell them how the discussion with the intern went. He told them that the kid wasn't saying much and continuing to act traumatized. Mark said his intern was acting strangely, too. Not smiling, not talking very much, and keeping to himself. Adam said he noticed the same thing in his dealings with his intern. They agreed that there was more to the story that the interns weren't admitting. The question was what to do about it.

Adam said he would talk to his intern. He would start by telling him that it was time to discuss the intern's project for the remainder of the semester in more detail. It was what Adam had been planning to do anyway. At the same time, he would see if he could find out what was going on. Dick and Mark agreed that it would be a good way of finding out if there was something that all three of the interns were dealing with, whether it had to do with the school or something else. They would wait to hear what Adam's discussion with his intern revealed.

Mark said he had already talked to his intern about the work he was expected to do. So, he didn't want to set up another talk.

Before they parted, Dick asked if they would like to schedule another dinner/discussion session that week. They both said that would be great. Dick said he hoped that Laura and Nikki would report progress on their efforts to establish the nonprofit they had talked about.

When Adam got back to his lab, he told his intern that he wanted to meet with him. The intern looked reluctant but said okay, that he knew they had to talk about what he was expected to accomplish over the semester. Adam set the meeting for three o'clock that afternoon.

Adam was pretty happy with the way his research was going, so he was in pretty good spirits when he sat down to talk to the intern. He started by asking the intern how he thought the internship was going. Was he getting familiar with the lab? Did he have any questions about how things were being handled? The intern said that he was learning a lot about how research is done in the real world. He said he was impressed with how much care went into each step in the process. He was grateful for the opportunity to work with Adam.

Adam said, "I think you fit into the lab and its activities very well. I want to make sure that you know that you can come to me to ask questions about the work we're doing so that you never have to wonder why something is being done. Then we can talk about what you can do on your own. I did an internship when I was in school and got to know the people I worked with. We still keep in touch. I thought it was an important stage in my life."

The intern looked serious but not very happy. He didn't respond to what Adam was saying the way Adam expected. Adam pressed on. He said, "I can tell that there is something on your mind. Is there something that is bothering you about the internship experience?"

The intern took a big breath and said, "Yes. Something is bothering me. I didn't know how to deal with it. I don't want to get anyone in trouble, and I know that will happen when I tell you this. But I also don't want to be responsible for letting something go that I think is very wrong. Here's what happened. The three of us interns were approached by a guy who said he was from Lifeform Labs. He said that your lab was being dishonest and stealing research protocols from the lab that this guy represents. He acted righteous and outraged. He said there was no way to correct that because you wouldn't share your results as you progressed until you got a patent. And by that time, it would be too late. Recognition for the work they put into their research would be lost forever. He said you were building your research on developing proteins necessary to grow cartilage on their findings, and not admitting it. He offered each of us one thousand dollars to copy research reports on the progress of your research."

Adam was speechless. Then he said, "holy shit."

"I know," was the intern's reaction. "I told the guy that I wasn't interested in his proposal. The other two interns said the same thing. But now that there was this incident with the two mice getting dropped, I'm not sure if Ed dropped the mice because he was anxious or if he dropped the mice because the guy from Lifeform labs got to him and convinced him to try to mess up your research."

Adam couldn't think of what else to say except, "shit."

The intern said, "I know this will all have to come out. I'm sorry if it causes Ed trouble. I don't mean to accuse him if it's just as he says that he's not used to handling mice. But the fact that there is someone out there who is ready to bribe people in your lab is just not right. I feel strongly about that."

"Thank you for telling me about this. I don't know what will happen, but you're right. Things like that shouldn't happen when it comes to research meant to benefit so many people. I'll try to keep your name out of it, although I'm not sure how I can do that. I'll have to talk to my colleagues Mark and Dick before I do anything on my own."

"I feel a real sense of relief after telling you about it all," was the intern's response. He was smiling for the first time. "I was having trouble sleeping. The whole thing was on my mind all the time. I couldn't concentrate on my courses. I just can't believe that someone would engage in that kind of dishonesty in trying to bribe us. I guess there are dishonest people in every occupation and every setting. I know that there aren't many dishonest people in this field because the scientific research community is a closed community and would identify them and make their names mud. I'm glad to be part of the kind of enterprise that treats fraud that way."

Adam was looking happy for the first time during the session, especially after hearing what his intern said about fraud. He told the intern that he was proud to know that he had someone like him working in his lab. Adam said he would be happy to provide glowing references for him for the rest of his career. He said he wasn't sure how else to reward him for his honesty. He said he was sure there would be other opportunities in the future. With that, he and the intern shook hands, and both got on to what they were doing.

Adam immediately went to both Dick and Mark's labs and told them to drop what they were doing because he needed to have a conference with them. They looked surprised and concerned but agreed to meet in the conference room on the next floor in the next few minutes.

Adam began by saying, "sit down. I've got a bombshell to drop here." He went on to tell them what his intern had said. Both Dick and Mark just sat there with their mouths open and didn't interrupt until Adam was finished.

Then they both started speaking at once. "What are you going to do?" "I haven't confronted my intern yet. Should I mention this?" "This requires serious thought."

Adam didn't take long to say more. "I obviously haven't had time to think about it, but my sense is that the issue is a lot bigger than just dealing with the intern. I think we'll have to get the administration involved. If another lab is willing to engage in bribery, then it might require legal action."

Mark and Dick were signaling agreement. "You're right," said Dick. "I should probably wait and not talk to my intern about this. He's freaked out enough for now. I'm not sure whether Harry Dennison will want to talk to him or whether he will want to have the lab's lawyer there to talk to the kid. Maybe the kid really did drop the mice because he was inept and not because he was trying to screw up the research. But, of course, he did substitute the mice. I wouldn't want to be in his position now. I'm not sure whether he thinks the problem is settled, and he escaped without things getting more complicated."

"How do you want to handle this, Adam?" was Mark's next question. "Do you want to set up an appointment with Harry alone, or do you want the three of us to be part of it? It seems that it is our work that is being targeted."

"Why don't I set it up for all three of us. That will save time if our research is being targeted, and Abacus has to do something about it."

Mark and Dick agreed that what Adam said made sense. Adam said he would go to Harry's office and talk to his administrative assistant about setting up an appointment.

Ten minutes later, Adam came back to tell Dick and Mark that he had asked the director's assistant if they could schedule an appointment for that afternoon, that it was something of an emergency. The meeting was set for 4 o'clock.

Harry Dennison greeted the three researchers, saying that he was glad to have a chance to sit down and talk to them and that they should schedule meetings more often because he was interested in how their research was going. He said he was afraid that this meeting would not be to announce that they had something good to tell him.

All three indicated that he was right about that and deferred to Adam to explain. Adam reported what his intern told him about the effort to bribe the three interns. He went on to explain about the mouse dropping incident in Dick's lab. He told Harry that they weren't ready to accuse Dick's intern of releasing the mice on purpose and replacing them with other mice without more evidence. But wanted Harry to know all the relevant facts.

Harry reacted calmly. He said he regretted that this kind of thing had occurred because it would be distracting and time-consuming. He went on to say, "I have heard that Lifeform lab was just bought out by one of the big pharmaceutical companies. I wouldn't be surprised to hear that the pharmaceutical company's first step was to press the people working in the Lifeform lab to start producing results more quickly or be at risk of losing their jobs. No more academic timetable. Now they would be on a market-based schedule. Short-term results are what the big drug companies want. I will be interested in identifying the person who made the offer to your interns. I wonder if he got encouragement to do what he did or whether he decided to do the bribing on his own to have a product that they could market."

Dick said, "How will you find out who the person is at Lifeform who contacted the interns and offered the bribes?"

Harry's answer was not exactly what the three researchers expected. He said, "The pharmaceutical companies are cutthroat. There are always things like this going on. We have a man we can turn to who is closely connected to lobbyists who work for pharmaceutical companies. He can probably get the gossip on who the new owners of Lifeform thought they could pressure into doing the bribing. I'll call him and see if he can meet me for a drink tonight. I think we can get to the bottom of this pretty quickly."

The three researchers thanked Harry for taking on the task of dealing with the mess that had developed. Harry said not to worry and was smiling when they left his office.

"Holy cow," said Mark. "That was enlightening in a way that I would rather not have been enlightened."

"Sure was," said Dick.

"I'm glad Harry is taking it so calmly," was Adam's reaction. "I was afraid he'd be really pissed off and go into a rant. But he's pretty cool, isn't he? I've never had much contact with him, but I can see that he probably has nerves of steel."

"Yeah, it's a relief to have handed it over to him." Dick was looking a lot less stressed and not particularly thinking about his intern at the moment." I'm now looking forward to seeing how this plays out. I wonder if there will be a scandal or if it'll be handled in a gentlemanly fashion as just another hurdle in doing business, something that sometimes happens but nothing to get excited about."

SIXTEEN

It was the end of the week, and the discussion group, which they were now referring to as "the group," was going to meet at Jane and Dick's house again. Dick was eager to tell Jane about the events of the day. But he would wait to do it because he would just be repeating it all in detail a little later. He assured her that life in the lab had gotten a lot more interesting today and that she would hear about it all as soon as everyone got there.

They had decided to get a couple of buckets of chicken wings for dinner. Jane also bought a tray of veggies and dip and a banana cream pie for dessert. For some reason, she had the feeling earlier that they all deserved to indulge a bit tonight. She didn't realize how right she was until Dick got home.

Jane had been looking forward to hearing how far Nikki and Laura had gotten in developing their proposal in preparation for meeting with Norma on Monday. She thought that it would be a crowded agenda tonight. She was glad it was Friday and that they wouldn't have to think about work tomorrow.

The members of the group seemed to be exhibiting extra energy tonight. Dick said, "let's get drinks first, and then I think Adam, Mark, and I need to go first to get through our story, which is certainly not a good one. Then we can go on to Laura and Nikki's story, which I expect is a far happier one, so we can end on end on a positive note this evening." Everyone agreed, although the women looked like they weren't sure what was going on.

Adam started by saying, "Let me give you a little background. We suddenly each have an intern from Franklin University working with us. This is by way of an experiment. We weren't exactly enthusiastic about having them, but were willing to give it a try. Things started okay. Then something happened in Dick's lab. Basically, his intern let two mice get away and replaced them with new mice. When Dick saw that the two mice weren't reacting to the intervention, Dick was working on the way he expected. He didn't know how to explain that. He talked it over with us. That caused all of us to begin worrying about what had gone wrong with our research until we discovered what the intern had done. We agreed that the intern should have told Dick about it. But things didn't end there. All three of the interns were acting a little strange. I talked to my intern. He admitted that someone from a competitor lab approached them and offered to pay each of them a thousand dollars to steal our research notes."

The three women all spoke at once. "That's terrible." "What a mess." "Why would the competitor lab do that? That was a stupid thing to do. Things like that never work out in the end."

"The thing is," was Dick's response, "we're still really not sure whether my intern just made a mistake because he was anxious or whether he was doing it because they got to him and encouraged him to try to mess up our research."

Jane's response was, "Well, like I said, how did they think they would get away with it? Interns don't have much training as spies. The guy trying to bribe them wasn't smart. Relying on interns was a dumb move."

"There's more to the story," said Mark. "We went to see Harry Dennison. He's the head of the lab and told him the whole story. He told us that a big pharmaceutical house had bought the competing lab. He said that he would probably be able to find out who did the bribing. That would tell us whether that person did it independently because he was getting pressure from his new employers to be more productive, or whether the pharmaceutical company was behind it. It looks too amateur to be something a big pharmaceutical company would do."

"I'm glad it's in Harry's hands now." Adam was clearly expressing relief. "We don't know what will happen next, what will happen to Dick's intern. The whole internship experiment might be abandoned. Harry didn't give us any indication that we should do anything different. So, we'll just play it by ear and day by day. Pretty intriguing, huh? Things were getting too humdrum in the lab. This will give us something to think back on for months to come."

"Yeah," Dick said. "I'm not sure we needed that kind of excitement. But I must admit that it shook us out of our routines. It forced me to go back to my research design and think about why two mice might be reacting differently. I asked Adam and Mark to try to think about possible explanations. It was a brief but healthy re-examination of the thinking that we went into this with. It caused all of us to do that."

"We'll look forward to updates on how this plays out. But," said Jane, "I'm eager to have Laura and Nikki tell us how their efforts to get support for setting up a nonprofit organization are coming along. That is something to get excited about in a good way, right?"

Both Laura and Nikki reacted to Jane's comment with big smiles on their faces. Laura said, "We'll be meeting with Norma Holander for lunch on Monday. Jane is coming too. It was Jane who told Norma about what we were finding. Norma became interested and found someone willing to explore the idea of providing us with the money to establish a nonprofit. We are working our tails off getting prepared for the meeting with Norma."

Nikki went on from there. "Jane helped us in another way, too. She gave us copies of her grant proposals that had been funded to give us some idea of what issues we need to address in asking for financial support. We're obviously new at this. It has been pretty eye-opening, thinking about things that we have never had to think about before. Like the fact that we need a board of directors, we need to be specific about what we are trying to achieve, how much money we expect to need, and a whole bunch of other stuff. When we started talking to each other about it, it didn't seem nearly as complicated. We now have a better sense of the kinds of things we need to think about. All those things make sense. It's just that we know we need a lot of help dealing with it all."

The two women got a chorus of support from the three guys in the room. They said they were sure that the two of them would manage it all very well. Dick said, "You're smart, you're highly motivated, you've got a good start on collecting the kind of data you need. You'll do just fine."

They had all been munching away and getting up now and then to get something to drink. They didn't notice that the chicken wings were almost gone. Most of the veggies were gone. Jane suggested that they all take a little more, so they could finish it all up and move on to the banana cream pie. She got some volunteers to take a few more pieces while she cut up the pie. They were all oohing and aahing about how good the pie looked. It was turning out to be a cheerful ending to the evening.

They didn't get much of a chance to talk about what they said they would talk about the last time they met, specifically, the decline in trust in social institutions. But everyone seemed satisfied to put off that topic for another time. Jane did ask if Nikki and Laura knew anything about the group that was taking over the schools. She told them what the geek in her office had found about who they were, but they didn't know if that organization was part of a larger enterprise.

"We were just getting started looking into that," was Nikki's response. "We haven't gotten very far. We have to identify all the different names of organizations across the country that have entered into such deals with cities. We'll get there. Based on our experience, we would be amazed if the group here isn't connected to a much bigger operation. But again, we don't know how big the parent organization is, at least not yet."

They talked about getting together again next week because there would be so much to catch up on, both with the goings-on in the lab and the outcome of Laura and Nikki's meeting with Norma Holander. They all agreed on next Friday.

SEVENTEEN

Monday morning, Dick wasn't sure how it would go with his intern. When Dick got there, the intern was sitting in the lab waiting. He didn't wait before starting with, "I want to say something. I've been thinking about how much I should say, but I'm just going to launch into it. I know that you heard about the offer of a bribe from a guy from Lifeform Lab. I realize that my dropping the mice and replacing them might look like I was cooperating. But I wasn't. I will admit that the thousand dollars was tempting, and the fact that I was thinking about it may have played a role in my being distracted and not being careful enough with the mice. I don't offer this as an excuse, but I want to explain what's been happening in my life."

Dick said, "Okay, I'll listen."

"It's like this. My father lost his job at the water department a while ago. He's an engineer. He hasn't been able to find another job. My mother started a little bakery and coffee shop with her friend. She's been wanting to do that for a long time. The family was all for it. My Dad agreed to take a chunk of money out of our savings to help with her start-up costs. In the meantime, my sister's asthma is getting out of control, and my parents don't have the money to get her the care she needs. I think she's pretty stressed out about the family's financial situation, which is aggravating her health problems. My Dad can't afford to pay his health insurance premiums now. I wish I could do something to help. I certainly wouldn't accept a bribe to do something dishonest. I couldn't live with that. But the fact that it would be so easy to make a thousand dollars that is just sitting there for the taking was on my mind and interfering with my work. I apologize for what I did with the mice. I was stressed out and not handling it well."

"I'm very sorry to hear how much worry is on your mind. I'm glad you told me what you've been facing at home. It helps me to understand what happened in the lab. I want to say that I want you to stay. We can start over and develop a project together, something that might help you focus rather than leaving you with time for worrying. I realize that the problems you are worried about will not go away if you don't think about them. But you could use a distraction."

"Thank you for being so kind and understanding," Ed was saying with tears welling up in his eyes. "I'm truly grateful."

"Okay, let's turn to talk about what you can do in the lab."

Dick and Ed spent the next half hour working out a plan to track mouse behavior changes, like willingness to exercise and matching that with cell growth. Dick explained that cell growth and replenishment of worn cells should result in less pain and make the mice more active. Ed responded by saying that what he liked best about working in the lab was being part of a process that could lead to making an important discovery that would benefit many people who were suffering from arthritic pain.

Dick would tell his colleagues how he was dealing with the intern's role later that day. He thought they would be pleased to hear that the kid was ready to be upfront about what was happening in his life and admit that it may have played a role.

*****

Nikki and Laura had planned to go to Jane's office so they could go with her to the restaurant rather than risk getting there and having to introduce themselves to Norma Holander. When the three of them arrived, Norma was already there. She was enthusiastic in welcoming them. They made small talk about traffic, weather, and such until they got through ordering lunch. Norma's interactional style was cheerful and easy-going. She invited them to talk about their jobs first before discussing what they wanted to do next.

Jane suggested that Nikki talk about the story she just finished working on having to do with tobacco companies. Norma's reaction was true to form for her. "Those bastards. How low can they sink in presenting what they're doing as a public good and actually knowingly planning to foist disease on the unsuspecting public."

"Okay, Laura, your turn," said Jane.

Laura explained what she was hired to do. She went on to say how the job had expanded. She outlined the insights that she had gained regarding the organizations that had emerged to accommodate the process of turning public sector organizations into private sector operations. She talked about what she and Nikki were discovering regarding the relationship between local organizations and national organizations.

Norma said she was impressed. She agreed that the public needed to be informed about the facts they were uncovering. She said that she was absolutely sure Josh Wilhelm would be ready to support their work.

She went on to say, "Let's think about what our next steps should be. Should you put something in writing for Josh to read, or would it make sense to talk to him and let him ask questions? What do you think, Jane?"

"Without having given the question much consideration, my initial reaction is that it would be good to give him a one-page statement outlining organizational aims, research methods employed to obtain information, and a short statement on findings to date. I wouldn't talk about the organization that would have to be created to do this work. That's kind of his territory. He can talk about that."

"That's good. I like that," was Norma's response. "What do you two think? Can you produce a one-page statement without putting too much time into it? You need to be clear about what you want to accomplish, but you also have to be flexible if some new ideas and ways of handling them come up. Are you okay with that?"

Both Laura and Nikki said, "Yes." "Of course, that sounds just fine." "We're just so pleased that you have taken an interest in our work and are willing to find someone who will support it."

Norma asked, "Would you be ready to meet with Josh by the end of the week?"

Again, their answers were "yes," "yes, certainly."

"Alright. I'll try to set it up for the end of the week or the beginning of next week."

*****

Adam got a group email from the photo course instructor later that day. The instructor told the students that he had selected the photos that would be going into the calendar. He asked if they would like to meet tomorrow night for a drink and look at the calendar's mock-up. He indicated the time and place where the meeting would take place. Adam was eager to see the mock-up and eager to see which of his photos the instructor had selected. He wrote back and said he would definitely be there. He hoped that Liz would be there too.

The next evening, five out of the six students in the class showed up. One person couldn't make it because he had promised his son to go to the son's sixth-grade track try-outs. They were all in a good mood, happy to have their photos become part of a calendar. When the instructor passed around the mock-up of the calendar, everyone seemed pleased. It looked pretty impressive. They agreed that the shots were all really good and were happy about the ones the instructor selected. After about an hour or so, the group started to break up. Everyone wished each other well once again and said they hoped to run into each other. They said they enjoyed working together.

Adam invited Liz to get a drink and something to eat. She agreed but looked tired and unhappy. Adam asked if something was wrong. She said, "I shouldn't be bothering you with this because we don't know each other that well. But I don't know who to turn to. It's my half-brother, Jerry. Same mother, different fathers. He's five years older than I am. He was always rebellious, getting in trouble in school, committing petty theft, and fights. He didn't get into drugs, at least as far as I know. But he has joined a radical political group and become very active in it. Have you heard about NEXT? I don't know much about the organization. All I know is that he is committed to it. He works with computers. He told me that he is creating photoshopped videos targeting politicians that the group doesn't like. Videos showing politicians in compromising situations – with a nude child, with a couple of half-nude, sluty-looking women climbing all over the men, things like that. He's proud of what he's doing because he can display his talents. I asked him if he didn't feel guilty about smearing innocent people. He said no, that he was only targeting people who don't deserve all the credit they're getting. So, it was okay to do what he was doing to stop that. He's bought into all the destructive lies that NEXT promotes. I'm just sick about it."

"You're not responsible for your half-brother's actions. It doesn't look like you can change his mind about who he is targeting and how he is doing it. He has no regrets or guilt about what he's doing. I expect that talking with him about it wouldn't change that."

"But you know some of the things this group has done. They're reprehensible. They've tried to ruin people's careers by making false accusations. Pedophilia is one of their favorite accusations. They're causing people a lot of pain. I'm afraid, from what he says, that this is just the beginning. They're aiming to target more people. I asked Jerry what the organization expected to accomplish. He said they were interested in upholding American values and punishing people who weren't doing what the NEXT people deemed to be right. He said the organization wasn't too firm about what it wanted, and he was okay with that. But that as far as he was concerned, it was standing up for American values. He couldn't explain what that means. I'm really worried that they are very pro-second amendments and seem ready and willing to use guns to make their point. I'm afraid they'll turn to violence."

Adam was shaking his head. He was trying to be supportive and sympathetic, but he knew that there wasn't much he could say that would help. He finally said, "They'll be exposed. That kind of activity doesn't last. Someone in the group will decide that enough is enough and make a killing on an exposé. If they threaten violence, the FBI will surely be watching what they're up to. The best thing you can do is stay away from it all. I know that's hard, but there isn't anything else you can do."

"You're right," was Liz's response. "I've been saying exactly the same thing to myself. But it helps to hear you say it. Thank you for listening to me. Talking about it and hearing your calm, rational reaction has been good. Thank you."

They ended up talking about the photo course, the calendar, and a little about work. Adam was not going to discuss the events that had just taken place at the lab. They agreed to do something fun together the following weekend and called it a night.

EIGHTEEN

Jane and Dick were having coffee that Saturday morning, looking at the news on their e-tablets, and not in any rush to get going. They hadn't made any plans for the weekend yet. There was nothing to be cheerful about in the news. Protests had been a regular feature over the last decade. The fact that protests were going on in California about the need for federal aid to deal with the wildfires was not new. Protests taking place in different cities for different reasons were profiled from week to week. This week, people along the Florida panhandle were hunkering down in the expectation of a hurricane. Everyone knew that hurricanes had become more frequent and more severe over the last decade. The idea that this was due to climate change was something that conservatives were still not prepared to accept. The story they were both reading said that this storm was coming very early in the season, meaning that there would probably be more storms than in the past. The story went on to say that houses had been rebuilt after previous storms with stronger foundations and further from the shore. Many more were expected to be able to withstand the winds and the rain. But the communities lost power; the roads were impassable; their water supply was contaminated. The fact that one still had a house was a blessing, but life was a struggle. Floridians didn't seem to complain about the lack of federal aid for things like education and health care. But they always complained bitterly about the lack of government aid after a hurricane hit.

Then there were the stories about police violence, which seemed to be never-ending, as were the protests that followed. Dick and Jane had talked about such incidents and the public reactions that followed repeatedly. How could those kinds of events continue to happen? The answer was complicated, but the fact that it was always a matter of a white policeman being the aggressor and a person of color being the victim was hard to ignore. It was hard to avoid the idea that there was something systematic about it. Dick and Jane knew that commissions were set up to look into most of these cases, but nothing changed. Well, that's not true. They agreed that many more white people were willing to believe that police violence was disproportionately directed at people of color. But that didn't stop what was happening.

Stories involving government decisions to transfer public goods and services to the private sector were in the business section. They were not lead stories, and people didn't seem to be upset about such things. The stories were getting more attention in recent years, but only because there were consequences for the stock market. The accounts were now regularly accompanied by estimates of the number of people losing their jobs. Another thing that was now more likely to be featured involved profiles of people who had worked hard all their lives, who had been promoted for doing a good job, and were now out of work. Each of those people talked about how hard they were trying to find another job. They were using up their savings, losing their houses, standing in food lines, and not able to afford health insurance, medical care, and drugs. The list of tragic consequences was unending.

It was easy to see why there would be protests. There were lots of good reasons for dissatisfaction. City governments had learned how to keep the protests from becoming as violent and chaotic as they had been in the past. There were always police vehicles stationed in areas where the demonstrations were staged. Everyone knew where those places were. Streets were shut off with cement blocks. Another thing that lessened the likelihood of violence was that many cities had imposed permanent curfews, including Mintaka. Cities all over the country were being shut down at eight or nine o'clock every night of the week and ten on Saturdays. It was hard to remember the days when people would party out on the streets all night.

Dick and Jane were lamenting the fact that the media was still devoting a lot of attention to violence and murder, even though the murder rate had dropped significantly from the peak reached decades ago. What kept that kind of thing going was politicians who were counting on getting support for a law-and-order agenda. Of course, some members of the public were not about to believe that the rate of violence had declined over the last decade. These were the people who were convinced that they could not trust the media to report the truth. That, plus the loss of confidence in government agencies that do data gathering, had become so widespread that presenting facts was doing little to change too many people's minds about very much.

The news media spokespeople said that they had engaged in much soul-searching. They were ready to acknowledge that so many people in the country were angry about violence because the media was focusing on stories like that. It was good to see media representatives accepting the part they had played in inciting the turmoil in the country. But it had not led to much change. The media just couldn't overcome its commitment to the long-standing journalistic slogan – *if it bleeds, it leads*. It was apparent that they were not about to change their approach as long as the public reacted with relish to reports about the *bleeds* part that plus the entertainment value of things that crazy loudmouths had to say. Let's face it. Statistics just aren't sexy. Detailed descriptions of a ruthless crime are guaranteed to overshadow statistics showing the steady decline in violence over many decades. Yes, there were repeated cases of a single individual going on a rampage. That was an entirely different problem with a far less obvious solution than the kind of thing the law and order people were talking about.

It's also true that the media had been presenting more interviews with experts across the spectrum, asking them to explain what was behind all the protests. That led to more debate about what to do about the dissatisfaction that people were registering. Some argued that anyone who was protesting was just itching to engage in violence and that the only solution was more police, police empowered to crack down on the violence. Others were arguing that, yes, the protestors were frustrated and unwilling to go quietly when police armed like storm troopers tried to disband them, but they certainly weren't starting the violence. Sure, criminals were out on the streets looting, but the looters were not the ones interested in violence for the sake of violence. They were busy engaging in smash and grab. They came along with the protestors, but they were not spending their time marching for what the protestors were calling for. They were getting right to the looting.

Jane was saying that she was happy that the mainstream news outlets were repeatedly saying that most of the violence was being carried out by members of far-right militia groups. Discussion about the influence of the religious right was now becoming more common. Media videos showed protestors, carrying crosses, armed to the teeth, claiming they were there to protect property. Members of those groups said they were patrolling the streets to preserve law and order because the police had become too restrained. Militiamen were regularly caught on camera, often with masks on, but the facial recognition software had gotten so good that just the top of the face was enough to identify someone. When the person was identified and charged with causing social disruption, that brought on more heated debate. Defenders argued that the militias were doing heroic work that regular police forces were prevented from doing by leftist politicians and courts. Those on the other side who wanted to see the militias disbanded argued that they had no right to threaten people engaged in lawful protest.

Both the police and the public had mixed feelings about cameras on every corner where protestors were likely to gather. The street cameras captured the interactions between the police and protestors. While that did result in less police violence, the "big brother" tactics were controversial. From the public's perspective, the cameras constituted an invasion of privacy. At the same time, it wasn't clear that most people were ready to argue that the cameras should be removed.

The thing that would result in the greatest change in the relationship between the police and the citizens they were charged with overseeing, according to social scientists, would be having police live in the neighborhood they were policing. After years of offering incentives to recruits, that option still wasn't an easy sell. The model was the English bobby who knows everyone in the community, meaning he knows who is and who is not a troublemaker.

Dick's reaction to what they were reading was, "It's the conspiracy advocates who are most scary. Have you heard this one? There's a group out there. I don't think it's NEXT. It's a group I've never heard of, saying that health care workers are being paid to implant microchips. And that liberal media moguls will be able to use the chips to turn people into a mindless army that will move together to take over the country and eventually the world to serve an evil "socialist" dictator who is just waiting for the right moment. The websites offer to protect followers who are encouraged to buy a medal for a mere $99 that they can wear around their necks to identify themselves as opponents of the takeover. Someone is making out big time in that scam. The website encourages followers to carry guns to be extra safe."

Dick and Jane went on repeating everything that was in the media to each other. They told each other that they had it all before and that there was nothing new to belabor. "Actually, that's not true," Dick said. He was looking like he had made a sudden, unwelcome discovery.

"You know what I just realized, that what's happening around us is not just an assorted set of distressing incidents. If you look at it through a framework that pulls it all together into one big picture, what we're experiencing is a meltdown of society. Wait, wait, I'm not going off the deep end here. Remember when Mark and Adam were talking about what historians have been saying about where we stand today? Well, there's a guy I've been following, a political theorist, not a historian, a Russian by birth who brings his cultural predilection for grand theory into his work. He says that as societies become overly complex, they become increasingly less able to bring everyone together. Social and economic inequality grows. The divide in wealth and power becomes increasingly more obvious. Political leadership is challenged. It responds by asserting its legitimacy through coercion. The country begins to spend more on policing, incarceration, on the military. To pay for that, it reduces funding for social support. That exacerbates social dissatisfaction and inspires more social protest. That process has been escalating. We watch it happening while we try to go on with our daily lives, trying to see it as just a bad period that will go away on its own. At the same time, a growing number of historians are comparing what's happening here now to what happened in Germany when the Fascists came into power. People who lived through social upheavals in more recent times in countries where dictators took over are writing books about how they continued to act as if things were normal when they clearly weren't because they were getting so accustomed to the chaos surrounding them every day."

"I'm not only depressed. Now you've got me frightened. I have to admit that what you're saying is convincing. I haven't had time to absorb everything you've said, but I can't see, right off hand, how the course of this could change in one direction or the other. People could wake up, or they could keep ignoring the signs until it was too late. What do you think will happen? I know you haven't had time to think about that. I wonder what advice the people writing about what is happening in society have to offer. I don't want to lay this on our discussion group. Let's allow what you've said to settle for a while before we bring it up."

"Okay. I think you're right. In the meantime, maybe we'll find somebody out there who has some ideas about preventing the worst from happening."

NINETEEN

Nikki and Laura had done as much as they could to prepare for the forthcoming meeting with Norma and Josh Wilhelm scheduled for Thursday. Jane wouldn't be coming to the meeting. The two women were both eager and anxious. They had done more work tracking who was turning over their school systems and the organizations that were acquiring them. So far, they had identified nearly twenty organizations in different cities with varying names connected to Educational Advancement Enterprises, Inc. The legal arrangements were complicated. The newly procured public-school systems belonged to three separate networks, which on the surface looked like regional nonprofit educational associations. But that was fiction, like dummy corporations that exist only on paper. It was only when Laura and Nikki got hold of the newly acquired individual school systems' legal charters and went through the small print that they began to understand how they were related to the EAE organization and each other.

The two women found themselves learning more about the law than they expected to figure out how the local organizations were connected to the larger parent organization. It led them to the conclusion that EAE is a holding company. It does no business on its own. Its sole purpose is to create subsidiaries, which the law refers to as daughter companies. The subsidiaries operate independently, but because EAE is the major stockholder in all the subsidiaries, it has total control over their boards and, ultimately, their operations. It receives all the profits that the subsidiaries generate.

They had a brief look at who was on the individual boards of directors. It looked like the boards were genuinely representative of their communities. They were made up of local ministers, community leaders, politicians, bankers, parents, and persons purported to be teacher representatives. Noticeably missing in all cases were lawyers and, of course, labor leaders. No one seemed to be objecting to the composition of the boards. However, Laura and Nikki suspected that leaving people who knew or might know more about corporate law and finance off the boards was intentional.

While there was no way to know what EAE's growth plans were, it certainly looked like it would continue to do what it had been doing so far, approaching towns and cities and offering to pick up the costs of running their public schools. There was good reason to expect EAE to continue to get bigger. It didn't look like it had any competitors. Of course, once someone caught on to how much money EAE was making, competitors might appear on the scene. But EAE had a big head start and might be big enough to buy out upstart competitors.

Nikki and Laura decided to focus on the public-school enterprise rather than trying to do more to track other public to private transfers in preparation for their meeting with Josh Wilhelm and Norma Holander. They couldn't say precisely how many school systems EAE had absorbed. Even so, they thought that they had enough material to present to Josh and Norma to convince them that there was a lot of this sort of thing going on and that they had the skills required to keep finding out more.

The women dressed for success for this meeting. They had shopped for clothes they thought looked like executive wear, suits, and high heels. When they got to the lunch meeting and met Josh Wilhelm, they found him to be younger than they expected, given his reputation for financial wizardry. They later decided that he looked to be about 35. He was casually dressed in a good-looking shirt with the sleeves rolled up, Dockers pants, and loafers. He wasn't wearing an Armani suit and a Rolex watch like they expected. He was attractive, self-confident, and had a ready smile on his face. The little bit of salt and pepper in the sideburns of his dark hair gave him gravitas.

Norma was her usual cheerful self. She introduced Josh to the two women. He immediately said to call him Josh. Laura and Nikki weren't ready to feel relaxed, but at least they didn't feel as nervous as they had feared they would be. After they ordered drinks, ice tea for the women, and tonic water for Josh, they spent time discussing the menu. When that was settled, Josh began the conversation by saying he was intrigued by what Norma had told him about the work that Laura and Nikki were doing. He asked how they got into what they were doing.

Laura explained what her job was, how it had expanded, and how she began to notice that many cities were engaging in the same kind of transfers, turning public sector entities into private sector properties. She said it was then that she and Nikki began looking more closely at who was involved in buying up the public sector service organizations. That's how they had gotten to where they were today.

Norma jumped in at that point. "Didn't you tell me that what you were doing most work on was looking more closely into the transfer of public school systems?"

"Yes," Nikki answered. "We have data on nineteen public school systems that have been turned into private sector operations. We're sure that there are many more. We believe that some are being absorbed by another company that we haven't identified yet. The nineteen that we've tracked have different names, mostly including the names of the cities in which they operate in their titles. They present themselves as local entities. They certainly don't provide information about their parent company very readily. It takes quite of bit of searching through the documents related to the transfer. They are all affiliated with Educational Advancement Enterprises, Inc., which is a holding company."

Both Josh and Norma were shaking their heads. "Well," said Josh. "I'm impressed. Not only did you track these school systems, but you figured out that the parent company is a holding company. Good for you." He paused to drink some tonic before going on. "What other government units have you been looking at that have been transferred?"

Laura's answer was, "We've been tracking the transfer of fire departments, water treatment facilities, and energy companies. We plan to examine how turning the post office over to a private concern is changing its practices, including the change in the prices it is charging."

Nikki turned to Laura with a questioning look. Laura seemed to understand what she was being asked. She gave a slight nod. Nikki said, "We've talked about tracking the organizations that are contracted to handle some state-level activities like overseeing public land, like parks, public roads, bridges, and other infrastructure entities. City administrative work has been leased out for decades. But no one has looked into whether the organizations doing this work are all local organizations or whether there is a single organization behind it all. Then there is federal public land that is being leased as well as sold. We're not ready to look into those things yet. Eventually, we will be looking at the transfer of federal land."

"You've got a good start," Josh was saying with a warm smile on his face, "with what you have laid out for the near future. I don't think there is any rush, so don't try to do more than you can handle initially. You'll need to devote some energy to setting up the organization that you'll be running."

Norma clapped her hands together. "Does that mean that you are signing on to support this new nonprofit organization, Josh?"

"I sure am. I think that what you are doing will be eye-opening for a lot of people. I want to be there to see how people react and what those in power decide to do about what you report. It is certain to produce some fireworks, and I want to be there to see that."

Laura and Nikki were barely able to stay in their seats. They were ready to jump up and down and cheer. Norma looked like a coach whose team had just won the playoffs. But she was not about to stop now that they were on a roll. "We need to celebrate this event, but before we do that, there are still a lot of decisions to be made. I'm not sure we need to settle all those things today, but we do need to give some thought to the kind of nonprofit organization you are planning to establish. Josh can talk to some people to see if they'd be interested in serving on the board. Right, Josh?"

"Yeah. Let me give it some thought. I assume you will also need someone to handle legal and financial matters as we set up the organization. I can probably find a couple of people to do that *pro bono.*

When the organization gets going and has a regular need for those things, you can enter into a contract with people to handle it. In the meantime, is one of you going to serve as a director?"

Nikki and Laura looked at each other. They each pointed to the other and said -- she is. Norma and Josh laughed. He said, "I can see that this will require more thought. If all else fails, toss a coin."

Norma said, "One of you can be the executive director. The other can be the research director. Who is more comfortable dealing with strangers, and who is more comfortable focusing on data?"

"We'll have to talk this through," said Laura. "I'm thinking that Nikki has been dealing with the outside world, getting her investigative reporting stories, so she has a lot more practice dealing with a range of people. I would be more than happy to serve as the research director. But as I say, we need to talk about that. I don't even know if we will be making a salary, let alone how much of a salary."

Josh was waving his hand at Laura, saying, "Yes, yes, those things are important. We'll need to work them out. I'm sure we will be able to come up with a very workable financial arrangement. I need to talk to some people I know who have set up foundations. I know it's not the same, but they'll know who would be best to consult to get us started. Why don't we plan on meeting a week from today? I think I can get some of the basics that we talked about pinned down by that time."

Norma said she should think about checking back with her office. Nikki and Laura said they should get back to work, too. Josh said he would start working on what they talked about that afternoon.

Laura and Nikki held it together until they got back to Laura's office. Then they couldn't stop hugging each other and giggling. They decided not to tell anyone about the lunch except for members of the discussion group. They were looking forward to seeing the reactions of the others in the group. They knew they had a lot more to think about now, but they just wanted to bask in the moment. They didn't want to think about all the work they knew would be involved in setting up their nonprofit just now.

TWENTY

Things seemed to be settling down at Abacus Labs. They hadn't heard from Harry Dennison about whether he had more information on the person who did the bribing, but that wasn't something that was keeping them up at night. They were pretty sure Harry would let them know once he knew the whole story.

In the meantime, the interns were working hard to prove themselves. It was only when Mark met Dick and Adam for lunch that the topic of the attempt to bribe the interns came up again. Mark had run into colleagues with whom he had gone to school, who had been working on a vaccine in another lab. They asked Mark if they had any trouble with the interns. It turns out interns from Franklin University had been placed in three different labs. According to Mark's friend, the interns in the other two labs had been approached by someone offering a one-thousand-dollar bribe for lab notes on vaccine development. Mark said that the Abacus lab's interns told them about it, but they had turned down the offer of the bribe. Mark's friend then went on to explain that his lab partners followed up on who was doing the bribing. His friend said he thought that the NEXT people were behind the bribery.

Mark asked if his friend knew why NEXT was doing what it was doing. The friend explained that, as far as he could tell, it was to discredit science; that the NEXT people thought that they could recruit more members by building on the prevailing distrust of vaccines. They thought they could do that by portraying the scientists doing the research as driven by greed for money and fame. Saying that scientists were being paid off by a group of billionaires from Switzerland, paying them to produce a substance that would make the people who got the vaccine susceptible to government messaging and eventually mind control. Mark told Adam and Dick that his reaction was: "What out and out bullshit!"

Dick said, "damn, those NEXT people are really crazy."

Adam's reaction was, "That's the most preposterous thing I've ever heard. I didn't tell you guys that the woman I met in the photography class, who I've been seeing since then, told me her half-brother is a NEXT member. She kind of unloaded on me because she's so stressed out about it. She said he's irrational, and she doesn't know whether she should try to do something, like tell someone about him."

"I'm not sure what anyone can do about a person like that," was Dick's response. "She could contact the FBI, but only if she could tell them about something he was planning to do, not because he has crazy beliefs."

"I don't think she wants to have anything to do with him. But she worries that he will do something bad and that she will feel guilty about not doing more to stop him."

Mark was looking grim. "That's a tough spot to be in. Tell her he's not her responsibility. I'll bet the FBI already has him on their radar."

The three of them were quiet for a moment. Then Dick said, "I kind of expected to get together for another discussion session tomorrow, but we didn't confirm it. I'm interested in how Laura and Nikki's project is going."

The other two said that they would be happy to come.

Dick called Jane and asked her to contact Nikki and Laura about tomorrow night. Jane said she was eager to hear how their lunch with Josh Wilhelm went. She hadn't wanted to contact them before lunch because she didn't want to put more pressure on them.

When she called Nikki and Laura, they both said they thought that there was a tentative plan to get together and were counting on it. They were looking forward to telling the others how their lunch went.

Jane and Dick agreed that it was warm enough to sit outside on the deck. Jane said she would make chili and get something for dessert. She wouldn't be going into the office tomorrow, so she'd have plenty of time to run to the store and get the chili fixings. Dick said he would check on the drinks supply. They were both cheered up by the prospect of meeting with the group.

Once that was settled, Dick told Jane what Mark had found out about the interns being bribed. He said he thought that would come up during the discussion tomorrow, so he didn't want to dwell on it tonight. Jane said that she hoped that what Nikki and Laura had to say would bring enough cheer to overcome all the worrisome stuff that was going on around them.

That is precisely how things went when everyone got there. Laura and Nikki were all smiles, making it very clear that they had good news to share. So that was the main topic on the agenda. As the two women recounted how the lunch went, the others kept raising their glasses and toasting them. They asked a lot of questions, some of which the two women could answer and others that they said they would have to work on.

There was talk about who should be on the board. Laura said, "We were hoping that you would agree to serve on the board, Jane."

Jane looked surprised by the suggestion. She said, "Well, I'm honored to be asked, but I'm not sure that I'm the kind of person you need. You need people with big bucks and connections to people with big bucks. I don't qualify for that."

Nikki's response was, "We also need people on the board with scientific credentials who know something about doing research. You certainly qualify for that slot."

"Well, if you are looking for someone like that, I would be happy to serve. I look forward to hearing who else you've got in mind, what other slots you've identified."

"We've given that some thought," said Laura. "Josh Wilhelm said he would check with some of his friends to see who would be a good fit. So that takes care of the rich and well-connected slots. We thought we could also benefit from having someone from a consumer watchdog group and maybe even a representative from the public service employees' union."

"I'm impressed," said Dick. "Not only do you sound like you've given this a lot of thought, but you also sound pretty sophisticated in your understanding of the role the board needs to play. How close are you to actually setting this up?"

"That depends on Josh Wilhelm to a great extent," said Nikki. "He is the one who is arranging the funding. We won't be moving forward until that's in place. But I don't think it will be too long before we can get going. Of course, we haven't got the lawyers involved yet. Josh said he'd probably be able to find people who would be willing to do that *pro bono*. We need lawyers to help us write the charter and get that approved by the state. Assuming all goes well at every step, I think we will be ready to create a website in four or five weeks. I'm not sure whether we should quit our jobs just yet."

Another round of cheers went up as the others assured them that they were on their way to making a difference in the public's understanding of what was happening as cities turn public-sector goods and services into private-sector enterprises.

Everyone was happily eating and drinking while listening to Laura and Nikki. Mark said he regretted introducing a sour note in the evening's discussion but wanted to hear the women's reactions to what he found out about the bribery scheme. He went on to explain that interns in other labs were bribed by members of NEXT, and something about what his colleagues said they thought was motivating the NEXT people. Jane had heard some of this already, but Nikki and Laura expressed shock. They all lamented the fact that it was tough to reason with people who held such bizarre ideas. More than that, they expressed frustration about social media's inability to deal with the messaging by people promoting the conspiracy nonsense.

"You would think that the social media organizations, who have all that technical talent, could not only figure out how to sort out facts from fiction but find a way to deal with it. I know they've been making progress on that front. It's just getting it to happen contemporaneously, as someone is spouting false information is still a challenge," said Mark. "Yeah." Adam picked it from there. "The government needs to protect the First Amendment, but does that mean that crazies can be allowed to develop sophisticated messaging platforms that deal in lies but succeed in making themselves look like respectable sources?"

"The example that critics constantly use," Jane interjected, "is that you don't allow someone to shout fire in a crowded hall or stadium because of the chaos that would cause and possible loss of life. If the First Amendment doesn't allow for that, I don't understand why it allows for people to cause as much harm shouting what they are shouting about individuals and organizations they disagree with."

Dick was shaking his head, "I think that argument has been made without much dispute, but no one seems to know how to set boundaries about what can be said and what can't be said on social media. Even outright lies can be published about public figures without legal ramifications. The social media giants have tried to insert corrections at the bottom of quotes from people telling lies, but it hasn't made much difference. The most troubling thing is that all those communication specialists agree that if a lie is repeated often enough, people will begin to believe that it's true."

"This is getting depressing," said Mark. "And we were enjoying hearing happy news for a change. I'm counting on the information that you two (looking at Laura and Nikki) come up with to make a difference in people's understanding about what we are seeing happening as a result of the abhorrence of taxation that somehow got ingrained in the American mind. I read someplace that Paul Ryan, you know, he was speaker of the House of Representatives during the first decade of the twenty-first century. He's from this state, saying that Ayn Rand's book *Atlas Shrugged* was what he was basing his political philosophy on. I don't think many other conservatives were ready to make that kind of admission. Maybe they haven't read the book. But what's going on now sure looks like the formula that Ayn Rand laid out."

Adam had a wry smile on his face, "If you believe the picture of government she presented as being on target, then I can see signing on to her formula. However, you have to be pretty delusional to think that there is some kind of sorting mechanism that directs confused, incompetent people into government jobs and clear-thinking, smart people into private-sector jobs. Each sector has its share of smart people, and each has its share of dimwits. Then there are the ones ready to engage in fraud. Based on the news, more of them are in the private sector, which makes sense because they are more likely to measure success in dollar terms than other accomplishments."

TWENTY-ONE

Mark was still thinking about last night's conversation as he was driving to Galena to see his sister, Nancy, and her husband, Ned, for lunch and an afternoon visit. His other sister was married to a doctor, who Mark thought was too intense but interesting to talk to. The sister in Galena was married to a businessman, the owner of a company that supplies hospitals with paper products, including gowns and masks. The COVID-19 virus gave his company a tremendous boost in profits for a couple of years. That made it possible for him to expand. He was now supplying more hospitals, plus an increasing number of nursing homes as well.

Mark got along with his brother-in-law as long as they didn't get into conversations that touched on politics. Ned was politically conservative, distrustful of evidence-based science, and ready to reject any ideas that were in conflict with his views. Listening to Ned's ideas about what was wrong with the country was hard. But Mark wanted to see his sister, so he was willing to put up with having to listen to what he considered to be Ned's uninformed opinions. One of the things that they had long disagreed about was the need for universal health insurance coverage. Now there were more things to disagree about. Ned obviously thought masks were a great idea since he was selling them, but he objected to masking being mandated. He thought it infringed on individual rights.

Nancy taught eighth-grade English. Mark often thought that it was a good thing she didn't teach something like social science, or she would be disagreeing with her husband all the time. Ned and his wife's sister's husband, the doctor, really got into it on the issue of health insurance, among other things. Sparks flew during those discussions. The family knew that they couldn't be near each other during holiday family dinners.

It was cloudy when Mark started out, but it turned sunny as it got closer to noon. By the time he arrived, it was dry and plenty warm enough to sit in the screened-in porch to have lunch. Nancy suggested that they go right to the table where he could have coffee to start or wait to have it a little later. Mark said he would love to have coffee after the drive. However, Mark said he first wanted to see his nephew and his niece, who were ten and eight, respectively. They were in the yard tossing a ball and letting the dog get worn out, chasing between the two of them, trying to catch it. They were laughing and looking like they were enjoying themselves. They suddenly noticed Mark and came running in to greet their favorite uncle.

Mark had to admit that the scene made them look like a model suburban family. He hoped that they could stay away from controversial topics and that he could just enjoy seeing the kids and his sister. But, of course, it wasn't going to turn out that way.

After a short while, Nancy said lunch was ready, and all she needed was help to bring out the dishes. She called the kids and asked them to set the table. Ned asked what everyone wanted to drink. Once everyone was settled down, Nancy talked about the short vacation they were planning before school started. They were going to rent a cottage on one of the nearby lakes and spend the time boating, fishing, walking the trails, and visiting quaint little towns. It sounded idyllic. The kids said they were looking forward to the vacation, but they were also eager to get back to school to see their friends. Ned talked about how much his business was expanding now that he was selling supplies to nursing homes. Nancy asked how Mark's research was coming along. He explained how it had been interrupted by work on a vaccine, which was then abandoned. Mark decided not to talk about the intern fiasco his lab just went through.

The kids gobbled up lunch in no time and asked if they could go back to play with the dog. Nancy said yes, but first, could they take some of the dishes they were finished with to the kitchen. With that out of the way, the three of them could get into an adult conversation.

Ned started by pressing Mark to explain how his organization handled working on something that would not produce a financial return now that it looked like there would be no need for a vaccine. Mark explained that the federal government provided funds for the research. The thinking was that it was necessary to be prepared in case the virus began to spread. A vaccine would avoid the disaster that occurred in 2020 when the infection rate skyrocketed. Hospitals were overrun, people died, businesses closed down, and people lost their jobs. "You know how bad that was, since so much has changed since then. So many businesses closed, and people lost their jobs. We still haven't fully recovered. The people who are in a position to provide federal funding wanted to avoid a similar disaster this time around."

Mark explained that once the public health experts became convinced that this year's version of the virus was disappearing on its own, the lab's findings were passed on to the pharmaceutical company that the lab had ties to. The drug company was now investigating alternative potential applications of their findings.

That got Ned on his old hobby hors,e griping about the government spending tax-payer dollars on things that he was sure taxpayers wouldn't agree to if they were given a chance to register their opinion. He said he was afraid that government interference posed an increased threat to our capitalistic system. He then said, "I've never asked you this, Mark, but I suspect that you'd like to have the government put more restrictions on capitalistic enterprises and impose a system closer to socialism. How do you feel about that?"

"Ned, let me be clear. I'm a capitalist. It's the best system for handling the distribution of goods and services that people can choose to purchase. Competition has been an important force responsible for introducing new and better products. It has cleared the market of products that, for whatever reason, the public does not want to purchase. But it is not a perfect system. It requires regulation. I assume that you agree that the government needs to step in when organizations grow so big that they turn into monopolies and effectively eliminate competition. Do you agree about the role of government and monopolies?"

"Yes, of course, I agree that the government has an important role to play in breaking up monopolies and ensuring marketplace competition."

"Good. Now, Ned, how do you feel about oligopolies? You know, like the three American automobile companies before foreign manufacturers started selling cars in the US? Or how about the market dominance of the three major soap companies, the two big soft drink companies, four airlines, the three major health insurance companies, and the three major generic drug companies? Then there is Amazon and the social media giants. They are all playing by capitalist rules. In each of those cases, the leading corporations have been so efficient that they could take over their competitors. Having either absorbed or put their competitors out of business, they eliminated a lot of administrative waste by consolidating, which, at least in theory, is good. Reducing administrative costs also means they got rid of a lot of small companies and their employees. Lower costs in doing business should result in lower prices. That hasn't happened. When there are only two or three businesses that sell the same thing, those companies don't really need to compete in price or quality anymore. If one introduces a change in its product, not necessarily a real improvement, but one that they can sell the public on, the others follow. Prices are remarkably similar and move up at the same steady pace. Far more money goes into advertising than research aimed at innovation. Here's my question: Isn't it just fiction to keep treating the increase in the number of oligopolies and monopolies as the outcome of greater efficiency?"

"Mark, you're exaggerating. There's plenty of competition in the sectors you mention. They're constantly innovating. They're keeping prices low. What do you want to see, the government setting prices?"

"Of course not. I'm telling you I accept the fact that there is no substitute for capitalism when it comes to goods and services that people want. Even though I disagree with you that the companies are keeping their prices low. They are raising them as much as they can to satisfy their stockholders. My concern about the role of capitalism has to do with goods and services that are not a matter of preference but a matter of need. I don't think that capitalism works well at all when it comes to basic goods and services that are life essentials. The country has a mixed economy reliant on both a private sector and a public sector. The only question is the balance between the two. The public sector is responsible for ensuring that we have clean air, clean water, safe highways, safe drugs, and safe air travel come to mind. We could be doing better in those realms, but where I think this country is failing badly is in ensuring access to health care and ensuring that all children get a good education. Those are core public-sector functions. Selling health and education in the marketplace to the highest bidder creates serious problems."

Mark's sister had been quiet until now. That was not unusual. She rarely disagreed with Ned in public. Mark wasn't sure whether she was readier to differ in private. But now that the topic of education had come up, she was prepared to register her opinion. She said, "The fact that children are required, by law, to go to school does not guarantee that they are learning what they are supposed to be learning. The schools in this country are very different from one another. Schools in wealthy neighborhoods are well supplied with the latest technology, pay teachers higher salaries, and have more extracurricular programs. And the buildings are well-maintained. That's in contrast to schools in poor neighborhoods, especially minority neighborhoods, where the schools are poorly maintained, are not welcoming, and don't have enough high-tech equipment for each child. There is no way to say that our educational systems are doing a good job. International comparisons make clear that our kids aren't doing nearly as well in math as kids in a lot of other countries."

Ned was shaking his head and frowning, "Nancy, you and I have been over this territory many times. You know that I think that it's the parents' fault if they're not interested in making sure their kids are getting a good education."

"True," Mark jumped in, "parents bear primary responsibility. But what about the parents who find themselves in difficult circumstances beyond their control? We have an intern in the lab who is struggling. It turns out his father is an engineer who just lost his job. The father's been trying to find another job with no success. His wife just started a bakery/café, which used up much of the family's savings.

But it's just getting going and not making much of a profit yet. The intern's sister has asthma. The family doesn't have the money to pay for her care. She has to stay home from school because her asthma is not under control. So that brings up our health care arrangements as well as our educational system. Think these people deserve help, or should we just let them struggle until they can work it out? Maybe sell their cars, their house to make ends meet?"

"Things like that happen. The father will find a job, and things will get better. That's not the typical story. There are many more people who are just not trying to get a job. The government is supporting them with welfare payments, and they're not interested in working. It's people like that who are responsible for the economy going downhill. If they took the jobs that are out there, they wouldn't have to get welfare, and I wouldn't have to be supporting them with my tax dollars."

"First, I'm not at all sure that the intern's father will get another job, a job at his skill level, given what we are seeing happening in how work is being organized with fewer people required to do the work. More middle-class people are struggling and not finding jobs at their skill level. But as to the question of welfare, I didn't expect to get into this with you today, but as long as we're on this topic, what do you mean by welfare? What counts are welfare?"

"You're just trying to make this difficult. You know what I mean."

"No. Actually, I don't know what you mean. That's why I'm asking. Do you consider social security welfare? How about Medicare?"

"No. People paid into those programs. I'm talking about things like aid to women with dependent children."

"Ned," Mark started to laugh, "The Aid to Families with Dependent Children program ended in 1997. You haven't kept up."

Ned was not happy to have Mark laughing at him. "Whatever the program is called now. It doesn't make any difference. It still gives money to women who don't bother to get married and make sure their children have fathers who support them."

"It's called Temporary Assistance to Needy Families—two things you need to know. First, most people stay on it for less than a year. And two, it's run by states, but virtually no state pays over fifty percent of what it costs to live, even if one were working at a poverty-level wage. I happen to know that because I have a friend, someone I went to high school with, a woman whose husband walked out on her and took all their savings. She's an English teacher as a matter of fact. Nancy, do you remember Leslie? Well, she and I have kept in touch because she lives near me and we run into each other. She told me what she had to go through. She has two kids. She had no alternative but to apply for TANF and food stamps, and Medicaid. She stayed on those programs for about six months until she got a teaching job in the fall. There are a lot of cases like that.

He went on, "I don't know how you feel about this, but a lot of the TANF money ends up going to private companies to do training, including offering classes that middle-class people can take. In the end, less than 10 percent of eligible people get cash assistance. Are you still convinced that there are welfare queens out there?"

"What about food stamps?" was Ned's response. "I read that people are selling them for cash so they can buy drugs."

"Where do you get your information from, Ned? You need to dig a little deeper if you want to argue about this kind of thing. To qualify for food stamps, a person must work thirty hours a week. There's no way around that fact. If wages were higher, people wouldn't need food stamps. If the government increased the minimum wage, you wouldn't have to shell out nearly as much money in tax dollars to provide food stamps. Employers would be paying people enough so they wouldn't have to rely on food stamps and food banks. By the way, the program has been providing about $1.50 per meal or $4 per person per day for the last twenty years. You think the government is throwing too much money at these people? Wait, there's more. It's a simple economics lesson. For every one billion in food stamps, the country has gotten one and a half billion in return in economic activity through the thirteen and a half thousand jobs it creates. Food stamps are not cash. The recipient goes out to the grocery store and buys food with those stamps. That benefits the economy. If the government spent that much money on education, it would produce an even greater return in terms of jobs and economic activity."

Ned was now looking like he'd like to lash out at Mark for being so oppositional to everything Ned believed. Nancy could tell that it wouldn't be long before Ned would be yelling and calling Mark names. She said that they had been sitting long enough and suggested that Mark take the kids and the dog for a walk to the park. Mark readily agreed. Ned didn't say anything. He just sat there, looking like he was fuming.

Mark's walk with the kids helped distract him from thinking about how rigid, backward, and uninformed he thought Ned was. The kids took him to a local park where they got a chance to hit the swings. The dog was happy to watch. Mark knew that his visit was over. There was no way that conversation would turn to general topics that they could agree on.

The kids were happy, chattering away as they walked back. They were disappointed to hear that Mark was ready to leave. Nancy stepped out of the house when she saw him and agreed that it was time for the visit to end. She said she wasn't sure how to explain why Ned reacted to Mark that way today. That he didn't get anywhere near as upset when he talked to her about the things he believed. He was willing to listen to her when she challenged him. But with Mark, he always acted ready to go into battle. "Oh well. He'll get over it by the time we see each other again. I know he'll look up everything you said to check it out. Maybe he'll change his views. Even a little would make a difference."

"He may, but he probably won't. Anyway, it was good to see you and the kids. Call when you have a chance."

TWENTY-TWO

When Dick, Adam, and Mark got to the lab on Monday morning, they each found an email from Harry Dennison asking them to come up to the conference room to hear what he had found out about the attempt to bribe the interns. All three were happy to talk to Harry, but they were pretty sure that they had gotten the basic story from Mark's friend. They weren't expecting to hear anything too surprising.

When they entered the conference room, Harry said I've had coffee and rolls brought up because I think you'll need some energy food to deal with this. The three of them looked at each other in surprise. Mark said, "I ran into someone from another lab who told me that there was an attempt to bribe his interns, too. They concluded that NEXT was behind it. That it was an attempt to discredit scientific research into vaccines."

"Yes, that's true. I called some friends in Washington who have been looking into NEXT activities. What's interesting about what they told me has to do with who is funding NEXT. It appears that the group is getting contributions from the National Rifle Association. If that seems strange, it's because it's not actually NRA money. It's being funneled through the NRA, which is getting a relatively small contribution from the actual source of the money. Presumably, as a fee for doing the funneling. The source of the money is actually a shady Russian organization that doesn't make anything or sell anything. It's a dummy corporation that has a lot of money. The government is looking into the source of the money."

"Holy cow," said Adam. "That's probably not the only thing that the shady organization is funding. The funders must be responsible for arranging for the photoshopped pictures that have appeared on the internet, smearing people who are promoting socially beneficial legislation."

"Yes, according to my sources, the Russian organization is part of the Russian secret service. Although the Russians are sophisticated enough to figure out how to mess up American minds on their own, there is someone close to the administration in 2018 and 19 who has been spending a lot of time in Moscow having meetings with members of the Russian government. He is being closely watched by our side. The feds haven't tried to stop him. I expect they're building up a file on his activities so they can charge him when they're ready."

"This is no small matter," was Dick's reaction. "How did we get in the middle of it? NEXT is becoming more bold and more outrageous in its claims. That's making it more of a player among the fans of conspiracy theories. These people learned a lot from the tactics used by the alt-right a dozen years ago. Repeat, repeat, repeat. It works like advertising. If people hear it enough times, they don't have to remember where they heard it or who said it. They accept it as fact because it is repeated so often, and everyone seems to have heard the same thing. Isn't there somebody out there trying to do something about this kind of indoctrination?"

Mark was shaking his head and looking glum. "That's the trouble with access to the technological wonders of social media. Technology has gotten ahead of society's ability to set norms and establish rules for its use. It's brought out all the charlatans who took to it immediately. It's how some politicians have gotten so well-known. They say outrageous things, and the news media picks it up because it makes for good copy. The public has reduced its tolerance for polite debate, which it considers boring. Just think of how extreme and violent films have become over the last few decades, and people can't wait to see them. People want action. Kids' video games have come under scrutiny by some committee in Congress for allowing violence to become routine. Kids grow up with a distorted sense of how disagreements should be settled."

"You're right," was Harry's response. "NEXT is playing a huge role in fostering social disruption on a number of other fronts, according to my sources. They're working on convincing the public that climate change is a hoax. They're funding white supremacist organizations. They're paying thugs to break up peaceful demonstrations against racism and police violence. They've done such a good job of spreading fear among white working-class men that the thugs are viewed as heroes by some of those people."

"If the folks in government agencies who monitor this kind of thing know what's going on, why aren't they doing more to stop it?" was Adam's question.

Harry's answer was, "What would you have them do other than what they are doing? The police do arrest the thugs if they damage property or hurt anyone. That produces anger on the side of the white working-class types who want the protestors arrested, not their heroes who are out there protecting people's property. Explaining that some shady organization is paying the thugs to do what they're doing is dismissed as fake news. The fake news label is now a fixture. It has delegitimized efforts to present facts. Facts are no longer facts. They're just a version of reality that people feel they can choose to accept or not. Time and time again, it turns out that the people arrested for engaging in violence aren't involved in the protests. Meanwhile, the right-wing media keep saying that all the protestors are interested in is taking advantage of an opportunity to engage in looting. So, the police should gas them, beat them, and arrest them all. I'm not at all sure how we're going to get past this."

Dick's reaction was not a comforting one. He said, "and it's only going to get worse. As more middle-class folks with college educations lose their jobs and as companies do everything they can to lower labor costs, they'll be struggling like the white, working-class folks without college degrees and people of color have been doing all along."

Harry's response was more potent and more forthright than they expected. He said, "True. Socioeconomic inequality is getting more extreme. The system is set up to support socialism to back up the stock market and capitalism for everyone else who is left to compete for the scraps. A small proportion of people are getting richer by the day, but most of the middle class is experiencing a decline in its standard of living. The safety net is not designed to help middle-class people who cannot find another job. And the unemployment rate has been continuing to climb little by little as middle-class and working-class people lose their jobs and can't find new ones. They blame themselves. They're ashamed. That leads to depression. The result is escape into drug addiction or suicide. The minority suicide rate, which was always much lower than that of whites, has been increasing over the last couple of decades. Poor minorities have always been less likely to turn to suicide. The black female rate of suicide has traditionally been just a small fraction of the white rate, especially the white male rate, which was always highest across racial and gender groups. That's the reward members of minority groups get for moving into the middle class: a higher suicide rate. They have always had good reason to believe that they were being discriminated against. That doesn't produce shame. That produces anger, especially among the males. Anger leads to violence, which too often results in homicide. The homicide rate is lower than it was decades ago, but it's now rising again. To the extent that socioeconomic equality is a major factor, then there is a solution. But getting that idea across to people is not easy. The very notion of doing something to overcome inequality is perceived as a threat by the very people who would benefit most."

"Well, guys, have more coffee and sweet rolls to keep up your energy," Harry's invitation to have more coffee was incongruent with the sober look on his face and what he said next. "We're not going to solve the problems we've been discussing here. Thank goodness nobody is objecting to us working on arthritis treatment. Even the science deniers don't mind us doing that."

Dick, Adam, and Mark each thanked Harry for bringing them up to date on the bribery episode. They thanked him for the opportunity to talk and hear his views about what was going on in the world around them.

They walked back to their labs, saying that it was good to know that Harry had connections in Washington that his contacts were on top of the NEXT story. They were also pleased to have had the opportunity to hear what Harry thought about more significant issues facing society at present. They agreed that what he said painted a dismal picture, but it was good to know that they shared an understanding about it all with someone like Harry.

Dick went back to his lab, reflecting on what he and Jane had talked about. What Harry was saying sure did sound like society was on the edge of collapsing. He kept his thoughts to himself but was beset by dismal thoughts and found it hard to concentrate on work tasks.

TWENTY-THREE

When Dick got home that evening and told Jane about the meeting he and his colleagues had with Harry Dennison, Jane sat there with her mouth open, listening. She didn't say anything for some time. Then she said, "I shouldn't be surprised about what NEXT is doing. But I am. Things like this didn't happen in the past, did they? Or is it that we just didn't hear about it?"

"I've had a little more time to think about that. I think things like that did happen, but they weren't as likely to attract the attention of as many people. Groups like that were doing their thing in isolated pockets of society. The fact that the internet allows so much hate speech and false information to spread so widely is what's changed. People who feel that they are not being listened to can now feel part of something bigger. They can have targets identified that they would not have targeted on their own. They can have someone to blame for what they feel is unfair and who is getting support for that."

"It reminds me of our conversation last night."

"By the way," Dick now had a grin on his face, "this should cheer both of us up. Have you heard about the fifteen-year-old Indigenous Canadian teenager, Nokomis? Her name means "daughter of the moon." She has become a media celebrity in Canada. She has turned the tables. She is calling people of European ancestry undesirable immigrants. She argues that they were unclean – they brought diseases that indigenous people had not been exposed to before. They signed treaties that they then proceeded to violate, making it clear that they are cheats and swindlers. They went on to destroy sacred lands and symbols. They killed animals with abandon. To this day, they continue to kill animals for entertainment. They separated children from their families to indoctrinate them, imposing a foreign set of religious ideas and values on them. She has been speaking on campuses in the U.S. Her saying that European whites are dishonest and dishonorable is making many people both in Canada and the U.S. uncomfortable. She is not seeking reparation, which she says would take too long to figure out. But she does have a clear objective. She wants all the treaties signed by "the dishonest, invading immigrants" to be upheld. That's sure rubbing all those stuffy Anglophones in Canada who embrace English traditions the wrong way. It's making the white American establishment types edgy because they are having trouble coming up with a response. The whites in both countries have been acting like they are solely responsible for holding civilization together for so long. They don't know how to handle being labeled as an invading horde of disreputable immigrants. It's cheering to watch that kind of thing."

"I know that she is gaining a following in this country," was Jane's reaction. "I know that she has organized protests in areas that she has identified as places where treaties have been violated all over this country. They're mostly in the West and states with a lot of open country. That, added to the continuing protests over racism in urban areas, is driving all those conservative old white men nuts. The ones who didn't think they needed to achieve much more than being born white are the ones who are most upset. I know there are a lot of hard-working white people who have lost their jobs, who feel that they have worked hard, watching their efforts turn to dust. Unfortunately, they've been convinced by those who are benefiting from what's happening to blame the protestors for what's going wrong. If they joined the protestors in getting the government to take stock, to deal with the demands of the indigenous people and minorities, everyone, including whites who are losing their jobs, would benefit. I know that's not about to happen after all the years that conservatives spent stoking distrust in the government."

"You're being serious," said Dick. "I'm taking a break from being serious and just enjoying Nokomis making all those old, white farts sputter with fury because there are people in this country more interested in what she has to say than what they have to say."

"As an added note, I just ran across something that I have to admit that I haven't had reason to think about before. I'm reading a mystery, not something I'm claiming to be scholarly, but the main character, a western sheriff, states that Indians don't want to be called Native Americans. They want to be recognized as members of nations of their own, not as Americans. They consider their tribes to be nations. Did you realize that?"

"Yes, I knew that. But, like you, it's not something I have had much reason to think about. Although I think it is something that deserves much more attention than it is receiving."

*****

The following day, Jane opened her email to find an article circulated by the head of her agency, just published online by the American Journal of Public Health. It was a study comparing the quality of care in for-profit versus nonprofit nursing homes. Although the study findings didn't reveal anything new, the difference in morbidity and mortality rates was much higher in for-profit nursing homes than had been true in the past. Because the number of elderly needing assistance with daily living tasks was steadily increasing, the matter had taken on greater significance over the last couple of decades. The article reported that nursing homes run by nonprofits were much better run. Inspections indicated that, according to all the measures used to evaluate nursing homes, the residents of nonprofit homes were doing better – they had fewer falls, fewer bedsores, and were less medicated. The patient/staff ratio was much higher in nonprofit homes. Some for-profit nursing homes had no nurses on the premises during the evening and nighttime hours. Finally, the residents registered far greater satisfaction with the care they were receiving in nonprofit homes. The study was based on the Centers for Medicare and Medicaid evaluations.

Jane was sure that the public health community and families of nursing home residents would demand stricter government oversight when the media picked up the findings. But she was also afraid nothing would come of that. The report would attract a lot of attention for a while, and then interest would fade as the families' energies wore down. The private sector nursing home industry has regularly claimed that any adverse reports that appeared in the news media constitute fake news. The fake news charge has certainly become a handy retort to be trotted out on all kinds of occasions over the last dozen years. It has been bandied about so often that the public seems to have stopped listening and just believes what their gut tells them to think. Unfortunately, their guts are too often addicted to alt-right media sources that trade in conspiracy theories.

A big part of the problem was that the number of people employed by CMS charged with inspecting nursing homes had dropped drastically during the time the conservatives were in control of the Senate. Fewer inspectors meant inspections weren't being carried out once a year as required by law. The number of inspections was also inconsistent from one state to another, again probably because of a shortage of inspectors. The number of inspectors might not increase because the private sector nursing home industry has ramped up its lobbying efforts to argue that inspections interfere with the work going on in the nursing homes and that they constitute government interference in the operations of private businesses.

Politicians in cities across the country seem to have bought into the private-sector nursing home lobbying. They haven't been ready to argue for more oversight over the operations of the for-profit nursing homes. One of the big reasons politicians have been sympathetic to the private nursing home industry has to do with its readiness to buy up downtown office buildings that have lost their clients and turn them into assisted living facilities and nursing homes. Politicians celebrated it, saying that the downtown streets would get new life. The staff at the facilities would be interested in eating out, maybe doing a little shopping. The hope was that some of the residents would be doing that too. It was true. You could see more people on downtown streets than had been the case in the recent past. The nursing home companies were being credited with helping the economy.

While it was clear why politicians were willing to turn a blind eye to the adverse reports coming out on for-profit homes from the Centers for Medicare Services, it was also hard to ignore the fact that the for-profits were getting more citations issued against them, more fines, and more payment denials due to failure to meet federal standards. They have continued to operate the way they do because the media wasn't spending a lot of time focusing on the adverse reports. There are so many other problems occupying the media's attention that nursing home issues have not been at the top of the list of issues to focus on.

Jane wondered if her agency would be putting out a statement in reaction to the findings. The mayor wouldn't be thrilled about it because she had been counting on the nursing homes saving downtown. The mayor was depending on the stability they were expected to provide to entice developers back to the city. Jane had heard the mayor talking about her vision of turning downtown into an environment where people could live within walking distance of restaurants, stores, and small parks without the need for cars. Like European cities. Everyone was anxious about turning around the effects of the exodus out of the city around the time the pandemic hit. Not only were people working from home, so that companies were cutting back on office space, but many people moved to the suburbs to get some space so they wouldn't feel locked up in their apartments.

Jane didn't have to wait long for her agency's reaction to the report on the need for increased inspection of nursing homes. She got a draft of a letter that the head of the city's Department of Public Health would be sending out to the media. He wanted her and a couple of other staff members to review and comment on the draft. Jane thought it was a measured statement that drew attention to the need for more funding to ensure that housing of the nation's elderly population was receiving the attention it deserved. To ensure that health and safety measures were being upheld. She returned the draft, saying that it was precisely what was needed and required no changes.

TWENTY-FOUR

Everything seemed to be coming along as expected in Dick's lab. The mice were happily growing cartilage, maybe not very fast, but still showing signs of growth. Dick and his colleagues were becoming more confident that their efforts to make it grow stronger would succeed. Knowing that they couldn't make it grow faster, they told each other that patience was a virtue, even if it made for long periods of waiting to see results.

The three of them met for lunch. They had planned to discuss how they would evaluate the interns when something on the TV seemed to catch people's attention. The reporter was pointing to a chart indicating the steps used in water treatment. He said that the complaints of residents who said their water was cloudy and smelled funny got the attention of the state EPA. Dick said, "I remember sitting here a few weeks ago watching some guy being interviewed who was saying that." His colleagues said they, too, remembered watching that segment.

Mark said he called the state EPA when they heard the interview with the man complaining about the water coming out of his tap. He then went on the internet to find out that there were about 15,000 water treatment plants across the country. He wasn't all that surprised because every town needed to deal with making sure the residents got clean water. Some bought their water from a larger city. Others relied on wells, in which case the source of that water had to be tested.

The reporter announced that the state EPA just released something called a Consumer Confidence Report, which the EPA said was a regular report on water treatment across the state. They asked each other if they had heard that such a thing existed and speculated on what "regular" meant. They agreed that they had not heard about it before. It turned out to be a water quality report that goes through an assessment of the stages of water treatment, beginning with where it is collected, and goes on to review the steps involved in quality testing. The report found that the coagulation and flocculation stage had not been handled correctly by the Mintaka plant. This is the stage at which sedimentation occurs. The process allows the separation of dirt and other particles. The sediment is called floc. The clear water that is left then passes through filters like sand or gravel. The next step is disinfection with chlorine or a related substance. After that, the water is ready for distribution. Each filtration plant is responsible for finding a way to dispose of the floc it collects. That part of the process did not seem to receive much attention. And it was pretty clear that no one was monitoring that part of the process. No one was complaining about it either. Maybe that would be the next problem the EPA would be facing, or maybe not.

The reporter went on to say that the agency would be doing a more thorough study to identify any additional contaminants. And that a report would be coming out shortly. The three men speculated on what that might mean. They wondered if it meant that the EPA inspectors had found something else in the water to worry about.

Adam said he would be interested in knowing how many of the plants had been turned over to the private sector. "Maybe Laura and Nikki can tell us. I would be amazed to discover that someone has taken the time to compare the water quality provided by private-sector-owned plants versus the public-sector-owned plants. It's highly unlikely that the Consumer Confidence Report would do that. I look forward to talking to Laura and Nikki about this. We should get together to catch up on how they are doing, setting up their organization."

Dick said, "I'll get it organized for this Friday."

*****

Josh Wilhelm got in touch with Nikki and Laura via email to tell them that he had good news. He suggested that they meet for lunch the following day. Laura called Nikki to make sure they could both make it. Nikki told her that even if she had something scheduled, she would cancel it, but she didn't have anything on. They told each other how excited they were to have this happen. Laura said she would get back to Josh and say that they were happy to meet for lunch.

Josh invited them to his office on one of the top floors of a downtown building that had been able to keep most of its occupants. He said he would have lunch brought in so they could talk without being interrupted. They met in a conference room overlooking the lake. Josh looked relaxed. They could see that he had some piles of paper sitting on a side table. He welcomed them and said, "Let's have lunch first before looking at the materials I've prepared. I ordered lobster salad sandwiches. I hope you are both lobster fans. I could get something else brought in if you'd rather not have that."

"Who doesn't like lobster?" was Laura's response. Nikki said she loved lobster. With that settled, Josh assured them that the water they were served was bottled water and was not coming from the compromised water filtration plant that had been in the news.

Laura said, "On that note, we've been tracking how many water treatment facilities have been turned over to the private sector. We will get quality reports from the EPA by zip code, but identifying ownership is a bigger job. As far as we can tell, a substantial number of plants have changed hands in recent years. We'll keep at it."

Nikki added, "The EPA site says something about everyone getting an annual water quality report as of July 1 of every year. We'd never heard of such a report. If you want information about water quality, you're on your own. You have to search for it. I doubt that a lot of people know they can do that. The people in Flint, Michigan, certainly didn't know that they were drinking lead-poisoned water. I know that happened a long time ago, and most people have forgotten about it, but there are lasting effects. The children whose brains were affected will never regain what they lost. That problem continues where property owners have not replaced lead pipes. But that is beyond the scope of what we are dealing with."

They finished the sandwiches and got coffee. Josh brought the papers to the center of the table. He said, "First, let me tell you that

I set up a checking account that will provide you with the funds you need to get an office, equipment, supplies, etc. I have some contacts that will give you a good price on all that. There are so many offices that have closed down that you can get high-quality, slightly used furniture and equipment for very little. Owners of office space are eager to get renters, so you'll have a lot of choice."

He went on to say, "I've given a lot of thought to who you should ask to be on the board of directors. I know that you've already got Jane Sherman, the epidemiologist at the Department of Public Health, on board. That's good. Here are some other suggestions. I haven't said anything to anyone, so don't feel any pressure. I thought having someone associated with the public employees' union might be good. They are the people who know about the agencies being affected by the public sector to private sector transfer. And they are the people losing their jobs."

"Right," said Laura. "We thought that getting a public sector union person would be a good idea."

"Okay, good. You need some folks who would be willing to come up with some money. I think one of the officers who heads up the network of community banks in the area would be good. Unlike the great big banks that favor big companies, this network of community banks is more likely to lend to small businesses in the area. They are more interested in making sure the community is flourishing than the big banks."

"We hadn't thought of that. That's an excellent idea." Laura went on to say, "We thought it would be a good idea to have someone with media connections on the board for a couple of reasons. That kind of person would help present our findings to a wider audience, which would get us more attention and perhaps additional funding. Do you think that would be a good idea, or should we try to accomplish that another way?"

"I think that is a great idea. I hadn't given that any thought. Let me think about who might be good in that role. But maybe we can wait on that until there is more on the ground for that person to work with."

"That makes sense," was Laura's reaction.

Nikki was kind of hesitant and having a little trouble getting the words out. "We need someone to chair the board. We were hoping that you might agree to do that. Maybe just for a while until we get the organization off the ground. I know that's a lot to ask given how much help you've given us already and how much time you've taken out of your schedule to do it, but we would be really grateful."

Josh said, "I'm flattered to be asked. Of course, I'd be happy to serve as chair of the board. When you get established, you may find someone perfectly suited to the role who has a passion for the job. That would be great. In the meantime, I'll do everything I can to help you get started."

Laura and Nikki were talking at once. "That's wonderful." "We're so relieved." "We've enjoyed getting to know you and feel very confident that you are the best person for the job." "This means we can go forward with what we're doing and not worry about things that you know so much more about than we do."

"Well, good. That's settled. For now, I've got some incorporation documents here for you to look at. A friend of mine who's a retired judge drew these up. He was fascinated by your project and would like to be involved in some way. He was willing to draw up the documents without charging you. They're not complicated. But you need to know what you're signing. I understood that you, Nikki, would be the director of the organization and that Laura would be the research director. Is that right?"

"Yes," Laura said. "I think we're comfortable with those titles. I'm not sure that they'll make all that much difference in the way we work together. I do think Nikki is better at dealing with all kinds of people than I am, but we're both good researchers."

"That's what I thought. There is one other thing, have you given any thought to what you want the organization to be called?"

Nikki and Laura began to laugh. Nikki said, "No, that's amazing. I hadn't given that any thought at all. Have you, Laura?"

"No. That's embarrassing. We should have come up with something at the beginning. At the moment, I have no idea what it should be called. That's homework for us. We need to think about it and agree on something."

"I'm sure you'll come up with something," said Josh. "Why don't you spend some time looking for office space. I'll get you in contact with my friend who can set you up with furniture. Once you have an office and a name for your organization, we can contact the people you want to serve on the board. I don't see anything else we need to decide on right now. Oh yes, here is the information on the checking account I set up. You can start using it at any time."

Laura said, "I don't know how to thank you. You've made it possible for us to do something that we only dreamed about. Now it's a reality."

"Yes," said Nikki. "You've allowed us to start a whole new exciting life. I hope that we don't disappoint you."

"Don't worry about it. You are being entrepreneurial, which involves risk. But you are doing it for a very different reason than many people eager to become entrepreneurs. You're doing it for the good of others, not for personal gain. I respect your ambition and am very willing to go along with you on any risk that involves. Let me know when you find some space and want to get together again."

TWENTY-FIVE

That evening, Nikki and Laura agreed that it was time to let their employers know what they were up to. They would have to give two weeks' notice and get their work passed on to the person who would replace them. They could take the next day off to look for office space. That shouldn't take too long. As Josh said, office building owners had office space going begging. They agreed they should look downtown, not necessarily in the fancy building that Josh had his office in. But something that had been well maintained. Maybe one of the buildings that the city had offices.

When Laura told the mayor's assistant that she was leaving, the mayor's assistant looked somber. She said she was disappointed and that Laura was letting down everyone who supported her. When Laura told her why she was quitting, the assistant threw her arms around Laura and said she had a fabulous reason for leaving. The assistant said she would arrange a party in her honor next week. She was sure everyone would wish her well and be eager to help her succeed. She said she would work with the mayor to determine what would happen to her position. The assistant took a minute to give that some thought. Then she said that, given what Laura would be doing, maybe there would be no need to fill her position.

When Nikki announced that she was leaving and why she was leaving, her colleagues wished her well, but she could sense something else there. She concluded that they were envious. They could see that she would be doing what she wanted to do, focusing on issues that she cared about, not chasing stories assigned to her by other people. Nikki had loved her job uncovering wrongdoing, but she was glad that she could concentrate on an issue that would be more than a short-lived story before she had to focus on something new. That was exciting in its own way, but not as rewarding as hanging in and going into much greater depth. A few of her colleagues suggested going out for a drink to celebrate. She said she would be happy to do that.

Nikki and Laura took time out to look for office space the next day. While they were doing that, they talked about the widely-touted assessment offered by a well-known economics professor for the disconnect between what had been the steady rise in stock market value in contrast to the steady rise in unemployment. His assessment was that the recession brought on by the coronavirus was primarily responsible. He pointed to the skyrocketing rate at which mergers had been occurring and the consolidation of corporate power that resulted. It was what Laura and Nikki were seeing. His analysis provided a more complete explanation for what they had been seeing and hearing. He said that antitrust enforcement was almost non-existent. The reasons were obvious. For one, the Justice Department had not been fully rebuilt after the devastation Barr, the attorney general in office when the coronavirus broke out, inflicted on the department. Congress had not increased the Federal Trade Commission's budget to provide it with the personnel to deal with antitrust. The professor said a big loophole in the law allowed so many mergers and take-overs to take place over the last decade. Antitrust enforcement could not be invoked if the businesses that were being taken over would have failed anyway. In other words, the big companies would not be increasing market share because the small companies wouldn't have been there to do business anyway. That occurred, of course, because Congress provided bailout funds, which major companies quickly took advantage of. Congress didn't do nearly enough for the small companies that had struggled for as long as they could before they eventually had to shut down.

The economics professor explained the stock market's success with a tongue-in-cheek summation – who doesn't love to invest in a profitable monopoly? Laura and Nikki agreed that there was no arguing with his assessment. The rich, that is, those with money in the stock market, got richer. Those who lost their jobs or worked for meager wages and getting no benefits were on a downward spiral in every way possible. They were becoming poorer and sicker. The conversation didn't put either of them in a good mood as they started looking for space to begin their new venture. It did confirm that they would have a lot of choices because so many small organizations had closed down.

Once they looked at the first office, they were focused on what kind of office space they wanted. The realtor showing them the rentals had three spaces for them to look at in three different buildings, all close to each other. They liked all three spaces. There wasn't much difference. They each had some advantages and disadvantages, such as having a coffee shop in the building, consideration of who else was on the floor and whether they would be noisy neighbors, the kind of security the building offered, and, of course, the rent, which was almost identical across the three. They decided on the space in a building a block from city hall. It was a high floor with a lot of light and a reasonably good view for a downtown building, even if it didn't look out at the lake. It was where quite a few public defenders had their offices. The bottom floor had a cell phone provider operation and a roomy Starbucks, which seemed to be doing well. The building was old but reasonably well-maintained. They signed the contract. It all seemed to go so fast.

They decided to stop for coffee before going back to their own offices to sort out what they would be taking with them. They talked more about the economics professor's assessment and the role the federal government played in allowing the country to go down the path it was going.

Laura's next comment was, "Maybe we can discuss all this with our group. Have you heard anything from the others?"

"No, but I'll bet they're eager to hear how things went with Josh. We should tell them that we'd like to get together. I'll call Jane and see if they think we should meet."

Laura's call resulted in a plan to meet the coming Friday. Nikki said, "Maybe we can ask for their help in coming up with a name for our new venture."

"Great idea!"

Nikki and Laura spent the week getting the furniture and sup-plies for the new space. They couldn't set up a new phone and register the new business until they had a name. That would be next week's task.

*****

When Friday came, the group was eager to hear how Laura and Nikki's plans were progressing. Jane had decided that it was time for pizza again. Once they got seated and had the pizza in front of them, they asked the two women to give them a blow-by-blow account of how things were going, which they did.

Once all the questions about quitting their jobs, finding a new space, and getting it set up were covered, Nikki said, "By the way, we need a name for our organization. We haven't had time to think about that. Got any suggestions?"

No one said anything at first. Then they all had sugges-tions, including some that were off the wall. Among them were – Investigations Inc., New Directions Corp., Mergers and More, Inc., Aid to the Dependent Rich Sector, Consolidations, and Realizations, Growing the Private Sector, From Public to Private, Inc. The sugges-tions continued. They were getting giddy. Then Adam came up with The Public Record.

"Hey," said Laura. "I kind of like The Public Record. What do you think, Nikki? What does everyone else think?"

There was general agreement that it was the best of all the sug-gestions on offer. Mark said it was nonthreatening. Jane said it was simple and urbane. Dick said it sounds like one of the cable network news shows, but that was just fine.

"Okay," Nikki said. "We've got a name, The Public Record. That will allow us to move forward. Get a phone, a website, stuff like that. It's a relief."

"Yeah, the more I think about it, the more I like it," said Laura. Then she went on, "While we've been doing all the work involved in setting up a new office, we've been talking to each other about an article by a famous economist that we wanted your take on. He explained why the economic indicators are so confusing; why the stock market is doing so well while the unemployment rate and business closings continue to plague the country. He made several points related to the growth of monopolies and the stock market's positive reaction to that."

Laura recounted the primary points of the argument. She said that they already knew the private sector buyers of public sector operations were generally connected to much larger organizations. They were interested in the extent to which the trend was resulting in more monopolies. And they were interested in hearing the group's take on the state of the economy, the disconnect between the primary indicators like stock market expansion and the rising unemployment rate, and why that wasn't getting more attention.

"Wow," said Mark. "You don't fool around when you pose a question. That is one big question. I don't think there is a quick, easy answer. Off the top of my head, I would say that the people who are benefiting from the stock market are doing their best to influence politicians to convince the country that all is going well and that a healthy stock market means that economic recovery is taking place. And that jobs will be coming back very soon."

"I agree," said Dick. "You can hear that message in what some senators are saying about privatizing public land. The effort to stop that, once the new administration took over after 2020, has run into legal hurdles and continued opposition from conservatives in Congress. The conservatives keep saying that selling the land to developers will result in loads of high-paying jobs in mining, logging, and energy development. They argue that environmental groups want to tear down the economy. Investigative reporters, you know about this, right, Nikki, have uncovered documents that reveal ultra-conservative groups disparaging the monuments located on public lands that are sacred to indigenous people. The message is that private companies will provide jobs. And prohibiting corporations from using the land denies people jobs is convincing to people who are desperate for jobs. They don't realize that the corporations will be using high-tech equipment, employing highly trained engineers to operate it. The relatively small number of jobs available to people without that kind of training would be hazardous and not all that well paid because so many people would be willing to work for low wages just to get a job. It's a no-win situation, but people are desperate. You can sell any lie about the economy if you promise that there will be jobs in it."

"It's like the health care sector," said Jane. "The sector continues to grow. But it's highly segmented. The number of doctors hasn't been increasing. There is still a serious shortage of nurses. The growth in jobs is at the low-skilled, low-pay level. There is a tremendous need for nursing aides in hospitals, home health aides, and nursing home staff. Jobs that are exhausting because they involve constant attention and even some heavy lifting. They involve dealing with patients acting out and expressing their anger about their situations, which nobody can do anything about. And, there is no job ladder up from those jobs."

"Talk about increasing the minimum wage for those low-level jobs has resulted in action in a few cities. The effort to increase the minimum wage at the federal level keeps getting hit with a lot of resistance from politicians in southern states," was Adam's observation. "The story is always the same. It gets repeated over and over. But the basic lesson is certainly not getting across to the electorate, which only hears that their taxes will go up. There is no question that the cities that have introduced a higher minimum wage have seen their cities flourish. Companies move there because the cities are vibrant and attractive to the highly skilled workers ready to move there. Yes, housing has become expensive in those cities because there is so much demand, and the cities recognize that. They have been trying to work on it, admittedly not very successfully. In the meantime, the cities that have not raised their minimum wage have people standing in line at food kitchens because their wages aren't enough to feed a family. That kind of picture does not encourage companies to move to those cities. The property values are a lot more reasonable, but there's no demand either."

Nikki said, "This is exhausting. We've had a great but tiring week. I'm ready to call it a night. I think the conversation is stimulating, and I want to get back to it. But my eyes are crossing, and I'm not processing what you're saying well enough to retain what is being said from one moment to the next."

"I'm ready to go home and go to bed, too," said Laura.

The others agreed that the conversation required more attention and energy. They decided to pick up where they left off the next time they got together. Everyone wished Laura and Nikki continued luck with their venture. There was some talk about getting together next Friday, but everyone agreed to put off making arrangements until next week.

TWENTY-SIX

Now that they had a name for their organization, Laura and Nikki called Josh to tell him so that when he talked to people, he could refer to something that sounded like it was real. Josh said he liked the name. He reminded them that they needed to check to be sure it was not trademarked. Then they would need to register the domain name with the state. He said it wouldn't hurt to call the Small Business Administration to be sure they didn't need to apply for any licenses and permits. He didn't think that would be necessary, but it was good to check.

The two women thanked him for the advice. They told each other that they knew that there would be a lot to do to set up the organization, but they sure didn't realize all the different things they would have to think about. They agreed that they were lucky to have Josh to turn to.

The first thing they did was check to see if anyone was using the Public Record name. They discovered that a couple of small newspapers used it in their titles after the city's name. But no one had trademarked the name. That was a relief. They were already getting used to the name.

The next thing they would have to think about is the meetings with the people they wanted to ask to serve on the board. Josh would, of course, be there to lend *gravitas* to the affair. They were well aware of being two young women with little experience in running an organization. They didn't want to be discounted as idealists who couldn't be counted on to make a success of it.

Now that they had the organization's name registered, they could get a phone line and have professional cards printed. There was no time to think about a design or symbol. For now, the cards could be straightforward. Later, they could get someone to do graphics and set up a website. "Oh god," Laura said, "will we ever be able to get to do the work we set out to do and stop having to do all this preparation?"

"We're getting there. Don't get discouraged. We've accomplished a lot in a short time."

"You're right. I bounce back and forth between feeling elated and feeling overwhelmed. I'm having an overwhelmed moment. Besides, I'm itching to get back what we were working on."

"I know exactly how you feel. We have to help each other get through this part so we can get to what we set out to do in the first place. Let's get the things done that Josh suggested. Then we can call him and ask about setting up a lunch with the people he suggests for the board."

While they were talking, Laura got a call from Jane. Jane asked if there was anything she could do to help them at this stage. Laura put Jane on the speakerphone and recounted what Josh had said. Jane said she thought they had everything under control. She was looking forward to the first board meeting once the two members they were trying to recruit signed on.

*****

Adam and Liz were planning to get together for dinner that evening. They were meeting at a new Thai restaurant that hadn't caught on yet. It was quiet so that they could talk. Liz looked stressed out. When Adam asked if she was still concerned about her half-brother, she said yes. "I follow what NEXT is doing, and that stresses me out. I know my half-brother is in the middle of it. I expect that he will go too far and get in trouble with the law. That's okay with me. I just worry that he will do something destructive and hurt people. The line that NEXT is pursuing now is that a far-left cult is controlling people's cell phones. That the phones have been programmed to insert mind-altering messages that will cause them to rise up and storm the offices of major corporations, to destroy capitalism."

They ordered drinks but said they would wait to order food.

Adam said, "I imagine that a lot of people in this country might be ready to hear that message, given that they've lost their jobs because of the actions of some group of evil conspirators. But I don't think there are too many people out there who can claim that they are hearing mind-altering messages on their cell phones. Messages are being propounded on social media that are anything but hidden, messages about Satanic cults that engage in pedophilia. It's like the Middle Ages. I expect that they're ready to have witch trials. It's hard to be shocked by anything that appears in the media. There is no indication that those on the left have much interest in storming corporations. They may march to send a message about product safety or something, but not storm the place. That is in contrast to some on the right who have stormed places that they were convinced were the places where the Satanic cults were engaging in sexual child abuse. Remember the guy who came blazing into a pizza parlor ready to shoot people because he was convinced that it was operating as a cover for Hillary Clinton's pedophilia ring? I know that happened a long time ago, but it was pretty bizarre that he believed that kind of right-wing nonsense and acted on it. It wasn't due to a mind-altering message via his phone. It was out there in the open on extremists' media sites."

"Satanic cult nonsense and hidden cell phone messages are only two of the conspiracy theories NEXT is promoting. They're also telling people that something is being put in drinking water, known to make people more complacent. It's to stop them from challenging those who are doing the cell phone messaging to turn them into a mindless army. There's more. They're also arguing that vaccines are making people sicker. There's even a racist edge to that message. They say that the vaccines are being given to white people at a greater rate than to minorities because there is a plot in the public health community to make whites sicker."

Adam was shaking his head, "I hadn't heard about those things. They're beauties. Hard to believe that anyone is buying into that stuff. Those folks never seem to tire of coming up with conspiracy theories, and their followers never seem to doubt that the theories are true. It makes you wonder what it is about conspiracy theories that have this power."

"And of course, they're continuing to promote their photos, the ones showing people engaged in pedophilia. There's a contingent that never gets tired of that. You have to wonder why they're so fixated on pedophilia. It makes one wonder what it was in their background that makes pedophilia so captivating to them."

"That is a haunting question. But, Liz, you are not responsible for anything your half-brother does. If the people monitoring the internet can't do anything about the messaging, there is certainly nothing you can do. While a segment of the population looks at this kind of thing and thinks that the people behind it are kooky and make jokes about what they are promoting, the people who need to hear that aren't listening. People on both sides only listen if the ideas they are committed to are being discussed. There is no debate. Their side is right, and there is no reason to listen to anyone who disagrees."

"I wish someone would emerge who people across the board could trust. Do you think that could ever happen again? Someone like Walter Cronkite. I know that is ages ago. But people across the country trusted him to provide them with accurate information. There's no one like that now."

"Well," Adam took a minute to think, "as so many political commentators and historians say, the country has gone through a lot of political turmoil since it came into existence, and eventually, things got straightened out. I'll admit it looks pretty bad right now, but this level of turmoil can't last. At least, I don't think it can last. Let's get something to eat and turn to something more cheerful. I'll tell you what the two women in my discussion group are doing. You'll be impressed."

Once they got their food and Liz heard about The Public Record. She said she was very impressed. She asked a lot of questions about what the two women had found. That turned the conversation to the state of the economy, which wasn't a particularly happy topic, but it was a lot better than talking about conspiracy theories. The evening ended well. They agreed to do something over the weekend that would be distracting. They would both try to think of something.

TWENTY-SEVEN

Dick and Jane had decided to go on a riverboat tour offered by the Chicago Architecture Center Foundation in Chicago on Saturday. Jane said she had done the tour years ago and wanted to see how things had changed. She knew there had been a lot of development along the river since she had done the tour. But there were also a lot of office building closures over the last decade. She knew Chicago had a plan in place to deal with the changes, but didn't know if it was working. The city had developed its riverfront. She hoped that the cafes and shops had managed to survive.

Over coffee that morning, Dick told his colleagues about the riverboat trip he and Jane were planning. Adam asked if he and his friend, Liz, could come along. He wanted members of the discussion group to meet her. Dick said, "Sure. That would be fine. He was sure it would be okay with Jane."

Dick and his colleagues spent some time talking about how their work was going. They wondered if Harry Dennison had gotten the story on who was responsible for bribing their interns and what happened to that person. They decided to wait another couple of days before calling to ask him.

As it turned out, Harry left a message for the three of them that he had tracked down who was responsible for the bribery and wanted them to come up for coffee later that morning so he could tell them about it.

They met in the conference room. Harry looked pretty cheerful. He had ordered sweet rolls again. After getting their coffee and rolls, the guys settled down to listen. Harry said that someone approached one of the pharmaceutical company researchers. The person who did that, his name is Jerry Sims, said he wanted the researcher to contact the interns and offer them $1000 to pass on the research data they were working on. The pharmaceutical company researcher said he wasn't interested until Jerry Sims showed him a picture capturing him and a young woman embracing, standing in front of his car. The woman was not the man's wife. She was a lab assistant in the pharmaceutical company. The researcher tried to get out of it, but this Jerry person convinced him that he knew his wife's name, children's names, and address. Jerry said he would happily ruin the man's career if he didn't cooperate.

Dennison explained that Sims was an operative for NEXT. "He seems to be high up in the hierarchy. We turned him in to the police. He was arrested on a felony charge, which carries a one-year state prison sentence. His lawyer might ask the charge to be dropped to a misdemeanor, resulting in a one-year local jail sentence. However, we have evidence of a lot more wrongdoing on his part, which the prosecutor might decide justifies more charges. I doubt that he'll be willing to reduce the charge to a misdemeanor. We'll be watching to see how it goes."

"That's great. I'm glad he'll get his just rewards," said Dick.

Adam followed up with, "what happened to the researcher this Sims guy threatened? Did Sims carry through with his threat to contact the guy's wife?"

Dennison said, "As far as I know, the man told his wife about the affair. They had been having problems. They agreed to see a marriage counselor. As far as his job is concerned, he is involved in a vital project, so the pharmaceutical company didn't want to fire him. But they said he would be asked to take some time off once the project he was working on was completed, which they estimated would take another three months. The man accepted the directive to take time off without pay. He was grateful that he was not being fired. The company agreed to have him return to work in another of its research facilities on the outskirts of town. They came to a mutual agreement to drop the matter of his participation in the bribery effort because it actually didn't go anywhere."

Dennison continued to look cheerful. He said, "It's unusual to find scientists engaged in criminal activities. They're just not good at it. There have been a few colossal cases, but that's rare. I'm glad this episode is over, and everyone can forget about it."

The three researchers thanked Harry Dennison for keeping them in the loop. They all said it was good to have the episode resolved.

When they were in the elevator, Adam said, "I have to tell you something. This Jerry Sims is the half-brother of the woman I've been seeing over the last few weeks. She has told me that she is fine with him being arrested. She thought that it was sure to happen sooner or later. She was worried that he would do something to harm somebody before he was arrested. I'm sure she'll be relieved."

Mark's reaction was, "It's a small world, isn't it? What were the chances of your friend's half-brother being our culprit?"

"You better call her and tell her what happened," was Dick's advice. "She'll be interested in hearing that he's going to be off the streets and out of commission for a while. Of course, he'll be back, but now he'll have a record, so he'll be watched more closely."

Adam was looking uncomfortable, "Dick, are you still okay with us coming along on your riverboat trip? It's okay if you're uncomfortable with having Liz there."

"No. She's not responsible for her half-brother's actions. Besides, from what you said, she's sure not defending his actions either."

"Okay. I'll call her about the trip. I think I'll ask her to get together to tell her about her brother. I don't want to do it over the phone."

*****

When Dick got home and told Jane about the meeting with Dennison, and that the culprit turned out to be Adam's new girl-friend's half-brother. Then he told her that Adam had asked, before they had the meeting with Dennison, if she wouldn't mind having him and Liz join them for the riverboat trip. He said, "I told him, okay, and I was sure you wouldn't mind, but that was before I knew about her brother's arrest. We could come up with some excuse and cancel it if you want."

"No. It's fine. She can't be blamed for what her half-brother does. I'm glad that Adam found someone he is interested in spending time with. I look forward to meeting her."

*****

Adam called Liz and told her about the riverboat trip. She said she thought that was a great idea. Then he said, "Let's get together tonight for a drink or dinner. I've got some news I want to share with you."

Liz said, "Fine. A simple dinner sounds good to me. I'm kind of tired of what I'm doing, so I need something to look forward to. The promise of taking that boat trip will keep me going until the weekend."

They met at a bar near her office. Liz didn't look anywhere near as troubled as she did the last time they met. Adam was sorry that he would have to bring her the bad news. On the other hand, she might see it as a relief.

She asked what the news was that he wanted to share with her.

Adam said, "I'm the bearer of news that is up to you to interpret. I'm not sure whether you will see it as good or bad news. It's about your half-brother. He was arrested on a bribery charge. I don't think I told you about this. But the interns working at our lab were approached by someone who wanted the notes on our research. Your half-brother played a major role in that." He went on to tell her the whole story.

Her reaction was somewhat of a surprise, but not really. She said, "I'll drink to that. He'll be off my radar for a while. Of course, I'm sorry for the trouble this caused at your lab. But it means that Jerry has been caught. I'm glad about that. He needs to go to court and hear the prosecutor lay out the charges against him and hear the prosecutor outline the harm he is doing. I don't think that will be enough to change his mind. Maybe the stint at the prison will make an impression on him."

"I expect that prison has had that effect on some people. Let's hope that the experience will make your half-brother see the light. Maybe if he gets connected to a good counselor, he will be forced to reassess his actions and alter his beliefs. Of course, if he gets mistreated, he might turn into a more sophisticated and hardened criminal."

"I don't think that will happen. Maybe that's wishful thinking, but he wasn't interested in making a lot of money in what he was doing. He was doing it because he could show off his talent. Maybe the prison will find a way for him to use his talent more constructively."

Adam could see the change in Liz. She acted happier and more relaxed. They went on to have a lovely evening, talking about their college years, the books they enjoyed reading, the movies they liked. The more they got to know each other, the more they seemed to like each other. They agreed that they were looking forward to the riverboat trip.

TWENTY-EIGHT

Laura and Nikki were spending most of their time moving and organizing their belongings in their new space. But they managed to get a few hours in over the week, doing the work they were interested in getting back to. They agreed to look at the latest effort to trade government assets for cash, which had hit the public media, involving the sale of public land. They discovered that there was an online auction site that was offering up government land. The property was not clearly identified. The website referred interested persons to another site, which was apparently headed by an ultra-conservative think tank. They didn't spend much time tracking down who was behind the site just then. The basic argument for selling the land was that developers would provide so many jobs that the economy would be booming for years.

The two women knew they couldn't spend more time trying to figure out who was really behind this effort. It sounded shady, but determining whether there was anything illegal about it would take a whole lot of time and effort. They would get back to it once they were fully settled in.

They still had to call Josh and meet the two people he was suggesting as board members and, of course, get them to agree to serve before they could work on a website. They decided to focus on the board before doing anything else. Josh said he would set up two separate lunches with the people he had in mind. He would send over their resumes for Laura and Nikki to look at. He said he was pretty confident that both people would be happy to serve on the board. He knew them slightly and had excellent reports on both of them from the people he talked to.

The women agreed. He called back a little while later and said the lunches were set up for the day after tomorrow and the day after that. He was sending the resumes now.

Nikki and Laura looked at each other with smiles on their faces. Nikki said, "My head is spinning. But I haven't been so psyched in a long time. I need to get focused instead of indulging in fantasies about how much difference we're going to make."

"I know what you mean. I keep thinking of how we'll get people to recognize what is happening and rethink their stance on government and taxes. I know that is unrealistic. But if we get a few editorial opinion writers to notice, I'll be happy."

"Good way to look at it," was Nikki's response. "I think you're right. Getting people who write op-eds to pay attention would have a big impact on the discussion about the government's role in society and the taxes it needs to do that. I guess we shouldn't get our hopes up that high because we'll be that much more disappointed if nothing much happens. But that won't keep me from working to achieve what might be idealistic and highly unrealistic goals."

"Go for it, girl! I'll be there right along with you." They high-fived each other and got back to sorting out the files they brought with them, both feeling better about doing the tedious task of sifting through piles of paper and files.

They talked about meeting with Josh and the community banker the following day. Josh had just sent over the two resumes. They looked at the resume of the bank representative first. They liked what they saw. He was involved in setting up an organization that dealt with housing issues in one of the minority neighborhoods. The organization was designed to help with everything from arranging for mortgages to finding honest and competent contractors. That effort grew, turning into a training program for community leaders. He volunteered to help his kids' school raise money for an arts and music program. Once that was established, the mayor asked him to serve on a committee to select the new school superintendent. His resume included a long list of activities that the two women thought gave him a lot of insight into dealing with a range of organizations across the board, from government to nonprofits to corporate."

When they met for lunch, they liked him immediately. For a banker, he was very informal in the way he dressed and the way he presented himself. He was in his forties, starting to get bald, beginning to develop a gut. He came in, looked around, and gave them all a big smile. He introduced himself as Mike Blew and said to call him Mike. He said he knew a little about The Public Record already and what it stood for from talking to Josh, but wanted the women to talk more about their project. When he heard what they hoped to accomplish in more detail, he said he knew many people who would be interested in their findings.

They told him that they were glad to hear him say that because they knew it was important information, but weren't at all sure how many people would pay attention. Mike reassured them that people were standing in line trying to learn more about what was going on. He would look forward to helping in any way he could.

Josh certainly looked pleased about the way lunch was going. He told Mike about Jane being on the board and outlined her credentials. Mike said it was good that there was someone with a scientific research background on the board. Josh also mentioned that he would be interested in seeing someone from the public service workers union on board because so many of them lost their jobs when private sector organizations took over. Mike said he thought that was an excellent idea.

They parted with plans to hold the first board meeting in a week or so.

The next day, Nikki and Laura were pretty upbeat about meeting the person from the union. If he were anywhere as easy to get along with as the banker, they were going to have a great board. His resume indicated that he was in charge of the union's political program at the national level. He had a lot of experience making sure that the members had a political voice and would be able to hold politicians accountable. Earlier in his career, he had represented home health workers in New York and adjunct college faculty in Illinois. He was responsible for writing policy position papers that were featured on the union's website. He was a University of Wisconsin graduate in political science. He had been an organizer since college, when he did an internship with the AFL-CIO.

Josh was already seated when the two women came in. They were recounting how well yesterday's lunch went when Josh waved to the man walking in. The man wasn't smiling. He looked formidable. He was fiftyish, had short dark hair with a lot of grey in it, and an aristocratic face. He introduced himself as Albert Rollins. He looked like someone who no one would consider addressing as Al. He wanted coffee before anything else. When they got their drinks, he said, "I know a little about what you are working on, but I want to hear about it from you."

Laura launched into an explanation of what got them started working on the transfer of public goods and services to the private sector. She talked about the public schools and why that would bring profit to the new owners. She mentioned the other entities that they were tracking. Nikki could see that Laura was starting to talk too fast. She was nervous.

Suddenly, Albert looked at both of them and said, "damn! I hope you pin the ears back on all those bastards who are milking everyone dry. They're getting rich and fooling the folks who are opposed to taxes. People out there will just be paying these rich bastards a lot of their hard-earned money instead. Sign me up for whatever you need to do to get the kind of information you're gathering out there." He was chuckling and looking absolutely delighted. His whole demeanor changed. He didn't look forbidding at all. Nikki and Laura were both sighing with relief.

Josh said, "I knew you'd feel that way, man. You didn't disappoint me."

"I have to admit that you had us scared for a moment," was Nikki's comment.

"Yeah," he said. "I'm good at that. I've had a lot of practice dealing with pompous administrators who are used to dealing with people who are afraid of getting fired. They're not used to anyone standing up to them. I thought I would give you a sample of the performance I like to give in dealing with those kinds of people."

Josh said he'd seen the performance before and knew what to expect. Laura said she wasn't prepared and was glad to know that it wasn't how he would be acting in interactions with them. "It was pretty intimidating."

Albert said he was pleased that he had that effect, but wanted to reassure them that he'd save the act for when he thought the folks they might be dealing with were acting like they were used to getting their way.

They went on to discuss some of the findings the women had come up with. Albert kept up the positive comments. As the lunch was coming to an end, Josh said he would email everyone with a date for their first board meeting.

"Oh my gosh," Laura looked like she suddenly remembered something important. "We don't have enough space in our office for a meeting. What should we do about that?"

"I think the building has a lot of empty space, including meeting room space," was Josh's response. "I'll bet you could arrange to use one of those meeting rooms. If management requires you to pay for use of the room, that's okay. But I bet they won't. They'll want to keep you happy, and it won't cost them anything. They are counting on you growing and needing a bigger space. If they treat you well, you'll rent a bigger space in the building. Keep that thought in mind when you ask to use a meeting room."

Laura and Nikki thanked Josh for the advice. They thanked Albert for agreeing to serve on the board and said they were looking forward to learning how to deal with all the pompous, self-important types they were likely to encounter from him. He said he'd be happy to provide training.

After the meeting ended, Nikki said, "Let's call Jane and ask her to meet with us to debrief. I could use a debriefing, and Jane is always level-headed. I'm looking forward to hearing her reactions to how our lunches went. Besides, she needs to know who the other people are on the board that she'll be serving with."

They met Jane for an afternoon coffee break. They told her about the two men they had just met who would be serving on the board. They recounted how the lunches went. She was amused by the performance Albert staged. She said she thought the organization was off to an excellent start. She was glad that most of the work of setting it up was now complete and that they could get back to doing the research they planned to do. Jane said she was looking forward to the first board meeting to meet the others and see what ideas they had for how the organization would operate.

TWENTY-NINE

Laura and Nikki had now entirely severed their ties to their previous employers, had their departure drinks with colleagues, and were pretty much settled into their new space. They even got the use of a conference room at the end of the hall for their first board meeting settled. The management said they could reserve it anytime they needed it, but would be charged a small clean-up fee. They looked at the room and decided it was pretty impressive and well worth the clean-up fee.

They were geared up for getting back to focusing on what they set out to work on, agreeing to concentrate on the public-school system transfers. They managed to identify a total of twenty-seven cities across the country that had turned their school systems over to the private sector, initially smaller cities in the eastern part of the country, then "rust belt" cities. The names of the new organizations were different in each case, usually starting with the city's name, followed by an impressive-sounding label like Educational Enterprises, Inc., The Learning Corporation, Advanced Education Systems, Inc. Transfers west of the Mississippi didn't begin until later. They hadn't tried to track those yet. From what they could see, the newly established privately held school systems had board members who were respected locals, but curiously, there seemed to be no lawyers or accountants. The person heading the operation was generally not a local. These were business enterprises run by businessmen with some local representatives who were carefully vetted and found to be sympathetic to the cause of turning over government entities to the private sector, but no one who was likely to raise questions about legal or financial issues.

It took a lot more digging to find the connection among all these disparate enterprises. It looked like the enterprises all got funding to make the transfer from public to private from a single bank just outside of Washington, D.C. That was strange since these entities were scattered across many states. Then Laura found that one of the backers of the transactions in every case was HND, Inc. Searching out what HND was about took a lot more effort. They found that it was a holding company. The HND company must have grown out of the initials of the first names of the three founders, Hendrik DeVry, Noor Bergen, and Derrick Voss. When Nikki and Laura went on to find out who these people were, they found the three were from Holland, Michigan, and had worked for Betsy DeVos when she was Secretary of Education. They would have to check if they were related to her. It was not clear whether some of the money to set up this company came from her and her family's fortune built on the success of the Amway enterprise.

What had become clear is that a single organization was behind the transfer of so many public schools from public to private ownership. It was responsible for introducing software that all the school systems would be required to use, and computers that they would have to buy to use the software. The software and hardware had been installed in some cities some years ago. HND had been reaping the rewards of that arrangement, allowing it to buy out school systems in more cities.

Nikki and Laura couldn't find any evaluations of the performance of the school systems owned by HND. There were interviews with a range of stakeholders reported in local newspapers. Teachers' reactions were consistently negative. For a start, experienced teachers were let go and replaced with recent grads. The new hires were required to have computer training rather than disciplinary training. There was apparently less need for disciplinary competence since that was taken care of by the software.

The new private-sector owners also fired the maintenance staff and outsourced maintenance to local private janitorial services. The janitorial services companies all employed people for a partial workday. They paid no benefits and paid the workers minimum wage for the hours they worked. The new school system owners also reduced the number of clerical and administrative staff. The reactions reported in the media were mixed. Some people thought this was an indication of the business savvy on the part of the new owners. Others said that reducing the number of employees from teachers to maintenance staff meant that there would mean more unemployed people. It wasn't just a matter of a single school. The school system in a city employed a lot of people. They argued that the local economy would suffer because those people would be spending less in the local stores, and some would have trouble paying their mortgages or rent. The effect would be small at first, but it would snowball. Those who lost their jobs wouldn't be able to sell their houses and move someplace else to get a job because no one would want to be moving to an area where the unemployment rate was increasing. The cities would lose tax revenue requiring the cities to either raise real estate taxes which was a non-starter, or find something else to sell off or lease.

Some parents, not clear how many, persisted in saying that they liked the fact that a business was in charge. They said they were confident that the organization would be efficient in handling their affairs as well as the education of their children.

The teachers who had been let go argued that the business wasn't giving individualized attention to the kids, that they had no way of knowing which kids needed more help because they weren't doing any grading. The company took the stance that children learned at different rates, so it was detrimental to their self-esteem to give anyone a low grade. The software was designed to allow the children to learn at their own pace.

As far as Nikki and Laura could tell, kids were promoted to the next grade without any indication of whether they had learned what they were expected to learn in each grade. When asked how they liked their classes, the children varied in what they said. Some said they liked learning on their own and that they were learning a lot. Some said the lessons were boring. Their answers were hard to interpret. Was it boring because it was too simple or too complicated? More kids came down on boring because it was too simple, and there was nothing to do after they got through with the lesson. Quite a few said they didn't like the math instruction. They said that it wasn't clear enough. If there was one thing all the kids agreed on, it was that they couldn't ask a question if they didn't understand something. The company's reaction was to instruct the teachers to tell the children to go over the lesson again and again until they gained complete understanding.

Because HND, Inc. was a privately held holding company, it didn't have to issue an earnings report. So, it was not possible to calculate how much money the owners were making. What was clear is that the company was expanding, buying out an increasing number of public-school systems with all the effects that it was having on the communities in which it was operating.

Laura and Nikki had gathered enough information about HND, Inc. to present to the board members at the forthcoming meeting, with the understanding that there was a lot more out there. They needed to think about how they would show the work they had accomplished so far. They were tossing ideas around. Would it make sense to present brief reports on other public to private transfers rather than doing a more complete report on the school system transfers? Could they come up with a formula so that information on several sectors could be presented in an organized format, regardless of what they thought of as the public sector categories they were looking at? They decided to do a brief, informal sketch of their findings rather than spending time trying to organize their findings into a systematic report to be used to present data in the future. After all, that was why they had a board to help them sort out how best to present the results of the work they were committed to carrying out. Maybe they should talk to their discussion group about it, too.

Nikki said she would call Jane and see if they could get together and get some feedback from their friends. Jane said, "Sure. I'm certain everyone in the group is eager to hear how things are going for you. Let's do it on Friday. I will get it organized."

Just as Jane predicted, as soon as they walked in, the other members of the group said they were eager to hear about the progress Nikki and Laura were making in setting up their organization and hear whether that had taken up all their time or whether they were able to continue working on their research too. Since the Chinese take-out was so successful the last time, Dick got it again. Everyone was in a cheerful mood. They all said something along the lines of – there's nothing to cheer about out there, so we're counting on hearing good news from you.

Nikki told their friends about the two men who Josh had suggested as board members. She talked about how the meetings went. Jane had heard about that already, so she was sitting back and smiling, waiting for Nikki to describe the meeting with Albert. The guys all said they were impressed with how much the two women had accomplished in such a short time. Nikki went on to say that they couldn't have done it without a lot of help from people like Jane, for a start, then Norma, and especially Josh. She said they were glad to be mostly past the initial stages of setting up the organization and back to doing the research they set out to do.

Laura picked it up from there. She talked about what they had discovered about the transfer of public schools to private ownership.

Their friends had a lot of questions. Once Laura had related as much of the story as they had assembled, she said that she and Nikki were not sure how to present the information and asked whether anyone had suggestions. She told them that they had thought about a single format or outline for presenting findings about transfers going on in other sectors. But they weren't entirely comfortable with that. They were tossing around headings for the information like history, development, scope, or size, earnings if they could get them, impact on stakeholders, including employees, clients, and community.

Jane said she thought the outline of topics was excellent. But she could see that the stories would be long. Maybe they needed an abstract or summary at the beginning of the whole story. She added that she wasn't sure what should go in the abstract.

"This is not directed to what Jane was saying, but it's a thought I want to share," was Mark's contribution. "In thinking about history, it might be good to have a section on how we got here in general, not in any one specific case. On why it is that so many people are convinced that the business sector can do a much better job of handling public sector affairs of why *efficiency* keeps coming up as a critical concept. I know presenting that kind of analysis is not central to what you're doing, but it would be good to have a statement about the significance of that kind of thinking. It could be a stand-alone piece on your website. I'm sure that there are organizations out there that are responsible for promoting the idea that government is inefficient and that taxation should be severely curtailed. I can think of a few names of people behind those organizations. I don't know if you're interested in writing that kind of thing, but I'm sure you could find support for it in the writings of highly respected scholars. I think it would be an informative background piece."

Dick said, "I just ran across something that would contribute to that kind of account. It's about the Koch brothers. Remember, they were among the five richest men in the country during the first decades of this century. It's a piece on what they tried to accomplish. Charles Koch gave speeches for decades condemning what he called *confiscatory taxation*. He was on a campaign to dismantle regulatory institutions. He made considerable headway using a variety of approaches. He used his fortune to pay for an army of lobbyists, sponsored a handful of think tanks, and established what was supposed to look like a grass-roots organization called Americans for Prosperity. The Koch brothers didn't waste their money getting involved in political elections. They targeted their efforts by going right to the seat of power on such matters – the courts. The courts have always played an important role in defining the government's regulatory power over corporations. Their ultimate aim was to install judges favorable to their objectives. Charles Koch paid for judges to attend seminars in ski resorts and beach resorts where he presented seminars. He said his objective was to educate the judges so that they wouldn't be taken in by what he called *junk science*. He devoted a lot of attention to refuting evidence that pollution was responsible for climate change. Since the Kochs had the money to do it, they spent millions in a campaign to convince the public that government is the problem and that corporations would run things in a more efficient and orderly manner if they were not hampered by government regulations."

Adam was nodding, "The Koch brothers have had plenty of company in promoting that message. Every town has a Chamber of Commerce and Better Business Bureau that echoes that message. Then there are all the Milton Friedman acolytes who get trotted out to argue that consumer choice is crucial to this country's existence. It's only when you get to specific cases that people are willing to see corporations as self-interested and greedy – like the case of the pharmaceutical industry. It's the least trusted industry in the country and has been in that position for many years. Some other industries that you might think could be blamed for all kinds of damage aren't treated that way, the coal industry, for example. Everyone knew it was responsible for a major share of what was polluting the environment and causing early death among the workers. Still, people didn't rail against it, probably because it was dying on its own. The fact that miners lost their jobs and were struggling to find new jobs was another reason people weren't interested in arguing for the industry to shut down faster. There's not nearly as much talk about the damage coal is doing these days. Coal lost out in the market on its own because it became more expensive than green energy."

Nikki turned to Laura and said, "Laura, what do you think? I'm beginning to think that we should be saying something about how we, as a society, got here, about what explains the deep-seated negative attitude about taxation in this country. The success that conservatives have had in tying taxation to socialism. They've managed to equate it with communism, and Americans aren't stopping to think through what that means. I'm not sure we should take on the challenge of educating everyone about that, but I do think we should do something about distinguishing between what the private sector is good at and what the public sector is good at and how taxes fit into that picture."

That statement got a lot of approval from the others. Laura said she hadn't thought about doing something like that, but said she could see how it would be an excellent opening to diffuse attacks from conservatives who might argue that they were just trying to tear down the economic system in the country that had been so successful and just needed some minor adjustments. They needed to clarify that, based on their findings, what was needed was a more extensive examination of the belief system on which the anti-tax sentiments were based and flaws in that thinking.

The others all said that they would be happy to read and comment on a draft of the statement when it was ready. Laura and Nikki thanked everyone for their support. Nikki said it increased her sense of confidence, knowing that they could turn to their friends for ideas and help in putting the ideas that came up as they were doing their research into a well-reasoned and concrete narrative. Everyone seemed to think that the evening was very productive and went home with good feelings about Nikki and Laura's new venture.

THIRTY

The first board meeting of The Public Record took place the following week. Laura and Nikki assured each other that they would be able to talk about what they were finding with some confidence. They were pretty sure everyone in the room would be in their corner and happy to support their efforts. The meeting was scheduled for ten in the morning. They ordered coffee and rolls. The conference room provided an impressive setting. They were looking forward to hearing what the board members would have to say.

Josh Wilhelm opened the meeting, made introductions, and welcomed everyone. He followed that with a short opening statement on how the organization came into existence and its objectives. He said he thought each of the board members had given the project some thought and was ready to work on not only advancing its goals but also furthering those goals. But first, he wanted to hear from Laura and Nikki about their work.

Nikki said she would present their findings on the transfer of public schools to the private sector, which was the most recent research they had been doing. And that Laura would follow up with some questions that they hoped the board could help them answer. They had been mulling over questions regarding how to present their findings to the public.

As Nikki talked, the board members interrupted with questions to clarify and expand on some of the research findings she was presenting. They made a number of comments about how amazing it was that no one seemed to realize that a single organization was absorbing schools across the country. And what impact their findings would have when the people realized that a small group of individuals was making a great deal of money without having to report it to anyone or do much analysis of the effect of the transfers, most notably on educational outcomes.

When she finished, the board members expressed enthusiasm about how much work they had done on school system transfers. Then Laura took over. She went through the questions they had come up with regarding how to present their findings. She said they were thinking of starting with a statement addressing the public attitude toward taxation and the belief that corporations do a better job of handling things like public education because they are efficient and the government is not. She asked for their input on that and advice on presenting information on transfers in other sectors.

That resulted in a broad discussion with no conclusive answer. The group moved on to the next topic regarding what should go on the website and what it should look like. They continued to talk about how the information could be disseminated. They took up issues such as whether the organization should have enrollees. Should they ask for contributions or charge for subscriptions to regular reports? No one seemed to take a firm position on any of the issues. They all said these were big decisions, and they needed time to give them more thought.

Nikki came back to the question of whether they should have a statement about what was responsible for the public's attitude about taxation. The board members all agreed that they should develop such a statement. But that was all that they could agree on. Josh suggested they try having an email roundtable of comments on the issues they discussed after everyone had some time to give it more thought. Not that everyone was expected to have comments, but if they did, they could share them and have a continuing discussion before they met again. Everyone agreed to do that. They all said something to the effect that it would be a good way to stimulate ideas and give people time to digest the ideas, which didn't necessarily happen during a time-limited face-to-face meeting. With that, Josh thanked everyone for participating in a productive first meeting of the board and said he was looking forward to working with everyone.

Laura and Nikki each said how grateful they were that the board members were willing to participate in this venture. Laura said she was looking forward to the e-mail roundtable. She said it would stimulate them to work harder on something they knew the board members were interested in supporting. Nikki said talking to the board members provided her with a boost in energy to do what they were doing. Everyone shook hands and left with good feelings about what had happened.

Jane stayed behind and walked them back to their office. She told them that she thought the meeting went very well, that the board members were a good fit, and she was sure that they would work well together in the future. Nikki and Laura said they might need to take a lunch break before getting back to work to unwind from what was a more intense experience than they realized while it was happening. They both admitted that underneath it all, they had been pretty anxious. Jane said they deserved to celebrate getting their first board meeting over with and having it go so well. The three decided on having lunch at a little French bistro a few blocks away.

When Nikki and Laura got back from lunch, they debated what they should turn to next. They settled on working on the privatization of water departments. They knew about the concerns reported in the media regarding the quality of the city's water supply in the wake of the sale of the water filtration operation to a private entity. They knew that the private-sector company now in charge had gotten rid of engineers and other senior staff members and hired people with far less experience and training. That wasn't what hit the media. The thing that did make the news was that the water wasn't being tested for safety, and the results of testing, to the extent that it was taking place, the results were not being reported to the public. Not that the citizens had been paying attention to the reports until that one person told the media that his water smelled funny and looked funny. Then the press swarmed in. The company responded by saying it had been releasing reports regularly. The fact that no one knew where to look for the reports was something the media was happily focusing on. The company continued to reaffirm its position that the water was perfectly safe.

Now that Laura and Nikki were looking into who was supplying the country with drinking water, the picture was becoming more complicated than they had expected. For a start, privatization of water treatment facilities had been tried a few decades ago. United Water, a branch of the gigantic French water company, Suez, had entered into contracts with several American cities. What happened next should not have been surprising. The promise of cutting costs through greater efficiency did not hold up. United Water did cut costs, but customer satisfaction was offset by infrastructure break-downs, which required water boiling alerts. Not only that, but the promise of efficiency was refuted when the company failed to link new residents to services and collect the money it was owed. One city after another canceled contracts with United Water, including Atlanta, Camden, New Brunswick, and Gary. Stockholders also bailed out because the profits they were assured would be forthcoming did not materialize. The venture crumpled.

Cities in the southwest for whom water supply is a more significant concern have not opted for privatization. Some took a very different approach than one would not have predicted, given the region's well-established allegiance to political conservatism. Some cities, such as Las Vegas, for example, turned to the government to set water usage rates that penalized excessive use. "Who would have thought?" was the reaction of those documenting the scenario. Hotels were required to use recycled water as much as possible – in fountains, for watering lawns, and for laundry. Parking lots were penalized for allowing runoff. They were encouraged, mind you – not required – to construct lots with permeable materials enabling water to be absorbed. Of course, if they didn't do that, they were fined for failure to recycle. Front lawns were outlawed. The city achieved a rate of about ninety percent of indoor water use being recycled water. It became apparent that turning from privatization to the combination of taxation and regulation resulted in an enormous reduction in fresh water usage, lower prices, and a tremendous increase in customer satisfaction.

Las Vegas' experience did not stop conservative politicians from arguing that allowing the market to set the price of water would do a better job of addressing the need to ration water. That people would respond to pricing and find ways to use less water as the price of water increased. The same arguments just continued. The response of the liberals was that pricing doesn't work that way. Just look at the golf courses that get watered every night, while homeowners find that they can take showers only every other day and can't flush their toilets regularly. The liberals were happy to further push their side of the argument by noting that private water companies and public water companies didn't have any competition. People couldn't choose to buy less expensive water from another company. There was no reason for private companies to lower prices, especially when stockholders pressed for higher returns. Public water systems were more responsive because constituents pushed local politicians to pay attention. Admittedly, politicians were ready to take up the issue only after the local media spotlighted rising dissatisfaction with water-related issues.

Liberal news outlets published editorials written by environmentalists who argued that scientists and engineers should be allowed to deal with what were basically technical problems. They said that turning over the pricing of water to a cadre of financiers was sure to result in the same simplistic answer that conservatives use whenever the question of how to distribute scarce goods and services comes up for discussion – the market.

But history keeps showing that long-standing simplistic ideas just don't go away in the face of piles of evidence debunking those ideas, most notably when public services are at issue. That is what explained how Water Works Inc. was buying up one water treatment plant after another. The public just wouldn't abandon the idea that a private company would do a better job than the government. Nor was the general public taking the time to become informed about everything that happened in the past when some cities did privatize their water departments.

When the water treatment plants were turned over to the new set of investors, they were renamed with impressive titles, just like the school systems, with the city's name in the title. There was no reference to Water Works Inc., the parent company. But Laura and Nikki's research showed that the company was the sole owner of all the city operations being transferred. Because there is no recognition of a single private-sector buyer, each city deals with the company in charge of the water filtration plant in its city, and the problems that come up there, with little recognition that the same issues are coming up in other places.

The newest problem facing the water filtration companies revealed by the Environmental Working Group, a well-respected advocacy organization, is that a source of water contamination affecting drinking water in forty-nine states was not carefully monitored. The problem was not exactly new. The Environmental Protection Agency has known about the set of contaminants they were targeting for over four decades. The contaminants, polyfluoroalkyl substances, PFAS, are known to cause cancer and learning problems. This is a class of 5,000 substances. Concern about the substances came to public attention most recently due to a lawsuit by residents in a town outside of Philadelphia. The suit revealed that the EPA has relied on voluntary guidelines to regulate the level of PFAS and that it had never issued a citation when the contamination levels exceeded guidelines.

Laura and Nikki were amazed to find that the EPA guidelines specify a 70 parts per trillion level for two of the compounds found to be most dangerous. But the scientists who launched a lawsuit that grew out of their research said that one part per trillion would be a more appropriate limit. The scientists provided a graphic visual image of what that amount would look like – a grain of sand in an Olympic-sized swimming pool.

The DuPont chemical company was the culprit identified in the lawsuit. What else came out as a result of the lawsuit was certainly a surprise. It revealed that the federal government was a major polluter. That was established when someone reported that the Naval Air Station in Texas was using a newly developed firefighting foam in training exercises. The foam contained a host of pollutants and was simply being dumped on Navy property, ending up in groundwater. That lawsuit forced fire departments across the country to look more closely at the chemicals they were using to fight fires to see whether there was reason to suspect a relationship to causes of death among firefighters. The reaction of firefighters was just beginning to gain traction.

Congress was informed of the risks connected to the firefighting chemicals produced by DuPont but refused to impose stricter rules and regulations. It continued to advocate voluntary self-monitoring.

In the meantime, Laura and Nikki discovered that a whistleblower had released internal documents indicating that the top three chemical companies, fearing the onslaught of lawsuits charging them with water contamination, agreed to form a holding company, which is what brought Water Works Inc. into existence. Not surprisingly, that's where the funds to lease water treatment plants all over the country were coming from. The chemical companies knew they had a problem with chemical pollutants, including PFAS contamination. They agreed to work together to create alternatives to the toxic chemicals. At the same time, each of the companies was employing armies of lobbyists to convince Congress that the chemicals they were manufacturing were vital and should not be restricted. And, they were employing armies of lawyers ready to argue that any effort to restrict what they were manufacturing was an unlawful restraint of trade.

The two women did not expect to run into this treasure trove of information on what happens when this particular public sector entity is sold off to the private sector. Nikki said, "How are we going to put this all together into a coherent story? There is so much technical information. I know that our sources are reliable, and I'm not afraid that we would be found guilty of making up this stuff, but I'm not sure that the chemical companies would not try to make that claim and cause us a lot of trouble."

"I've been thinking the same thing. I don't think we should go it alone on this. Maybe it would be a good idea to do a draft of what we are finding and send it off to the board members. I'm sure they all have more experience in dealing with potential lawsuits than we do. Besides, I think they'll find our report very interesting. We certainly haven't tracked all the cities that could be on the Water Works company list. I just had a thought, and maybe we can get Albert to have a chat with the company executives." That brought a smile to both their faces.

"Let's work on a draft and send it to the board. It might be interesting to get our discussion group to hear about it." Nikki stopped for a minute and, looking somewhat concerned, said, "To change the subject. You know I've been thinking it's unfair to let Jane and Dick do all the hosting. Maybe we should start a potluck kind of get-together. I don't expect any of us to volunteer to bake casseroles, but we could do the shopping and bring stuff."

"You're right. I've been feeling guilty about that, even though Dick and Jane never seemed to mind. But we should suggest another get-together and go the potluck route."

"I'll do that," was Laura's response.

THIRTY-ONE

When Laura called Jane to suggest getting together and doing it as a potluck, Jane protested at first. But then she relented, saying, "Maybe that's a good idea. It will result in some variety. I must admit Dick and I were getting into a rut in thinking about what we should serve. All right, do you want to arrange it?"

"Yes, Nikki and I will take care of it. Next time, the guys can work on it."

"Fine. Have you come up with something that you want to talk to us about?"

"Yes," said Laura. "We have. It's about water treatment plants. The story keeps mushrooming, and we're afraid we are about to step on some very important toes. We'll lay it all out. We're planning to get the board involved, too, so you'll be hearing it twice."

"Sounds intriguing. I look forward to hearing what you've found out."

That afternoon, Nikki and Laura wrote a short summary of their findings on water treatment plant transfers. They stressed the point that some very big players were behind the shift of water treatment plants from public to private ownership to the Water Works, Inc. holding company. Once they had a draft, they sent it to the board members and asked for comments. They indicated that they were concerned about their chances of having Water Works instituting a lawsuit as a harassment tactic.

While they waited for the board members to respond, they started to work on the privatization of fire departments. It was something that the city had already privatized. And it was already evident that privatization did not help to overcome the city's fiscal problems. As everyone would remember, that's when the city ended up transferring the school system to get the money to fund further training for the new recruits the private-sector company had hired to do the firefighting.

One of the most surprising pieces of information Laura uncovered was that the Boeing corporation was the largest private fire protection company in the country. Its firefighters worked at Boeing plants in several states, primarily Washington and Arizona. Boeing was not interested in expanding its firefighting services to cover the municipalities in which it was located. But its operations were often cited as an example of how well a private company performed in handling firefighting when cities got interested in moving toward privatizing their fire departments.

Laura and Nikki found a growing trend toward the privatization of fire departments, generally in smaller cities. The arrangements invariably took the form of the city outsourcing fire protection services. As might be expected, there was considerable controversy about this trend. People were expressing strong feelings about it in the face of the rising trend. Some communities in rural areas in the West took the most libertarian route. They opted for signing up for a subscription and paid for fire protection on an individual basis. The residents in towns in those areas were not interested in that option because their houses were too close together. No one wanted to be next to a neighbor who opted out of paying for fire protection.

The name of one organization kept coming up, Fire Protection Inc. The company's website offered a list of reasons to opt for its services. It claimed years of experience, which allowed it to design firefighters' jobs differently than they had been designed in the past. The job provided regular hours and high pay, but the benefits were not as generous as those offered by public fire departments. The company introduced some services that brought in income, which the firefighters were expected to take on when they weren't engaged in firefighting, such as safety inspections and recommendations. Sale of and installation of fire alarms. Fire safety training classes for corporations and schools for a fee.

Cities were also readier to outsource ambulance services that fire departments had been providing for years. That saved cities quite a bit of money. But the ambulance story wasn't settled. Most cities weren't opting to use a single company and instead were giving licenses to any company that met some basic criteria. The result was that the companies had different prices. There was no way to know which company would come to the emergency and how much it would charge. The cities had a central number for ambulance services and sent the closest ambulance. City government representatives were getting complaints from angry citizens about how much the ambulance companies were charging. No one was deluded enough to argue that market competition was the answer. Customers could not be expected to shop for the best price during an emergency. According to all those who had needed an ambulance in the recent past, cities weren't working quickly enough to solve the problem. This was a problem that did not look like it would be addressed anytime soon.

The cities that signed on with Fire Protection Inc. reported being satisfied that the arrangement allowed them to save costs. However, how much they saved was not being studied. Amazingly, the last comprehensive study calculating how much privatization of fire departments affected city budgets was conducted by the state of California in the 1990s. It was a careful calculation revealing that some savings were achieved. But, of course, things have changed since then; population density has increased, for a start. And, the effects of climate change had resulted in a vast increase in the number and severity of forest fires. Nevertheless, Nikki said she thought the report provided a good start for the issues to look at in evaluating the impact of privatization of fire departments. Of course, it was not something that she had any intention of taking on.

The arguments against the privatization of fire departments were similar to those against privatization in general, but the market for such services stood out as a significant obstacle. Cities interested in issuing a request for bids typically received a single bid or no bid at all. There were simply not many private firefighting companies out there, and there were certainly none standing in the wings ready to compete. If there were no competitors, then the company that won the contract would have little fear of losing the contract. Another concern was that if the private company found it was not making enough profit, it could cancel the contract, disrupting services. That could be serious, and there were cases where that happened.

Laura told Nikki that she felt that they were opening a huge box of scraps of paper with lots of notes that they would have to sift through to get a clear picture of the extent to which fire departments' privatization was occurring. She was pleased that they had loads of new material that they would be able to look at and organize over time. But she said she thought it looked like a huge challenge. They decided to set the privatization of fire departments aside for the time being.

There were other issues that they wanted to look at. Not that they were going to work on them all at once, but they were eager to pin down the list of issues they would be looking at so that when they ran across relevant material, they would be able to "file" it for future reference. Some of the public-to-private transfers were more complicated than others. Laura said she thought they should probably put off looking at police departments' privatization because that was a very messy case. Ever since the protest marches became a regular part of life in so many cities protesting the treatment of people of color by the police, calls for defunding the police were being registered all over the country. It took time for cities to figure out how to handle that. The responses were different from place to place.

Nikki's reaction was, "I agree. But privatization of the police is a very interesting case, and I'm looking forward to getting back to it. The literature on that is often connected to the privatization of the military. Now that's a highly controversial issue that has gotten attention in Washington but not in the hinterland. Did you know that the person who is most closely involved in private military operations is Eric Prince, Betsy DeVos's brother? He heads up the Blackwater organization. He has made out like a bandit. I was amazed when I found that there were more Blackwater forces in Iraq than American army forces. And they were being paid up to $1,200 a day. By contrast, army sergeants were $85 per day, and the general, David Petraeus, was paid $493 a day. Can you believe that? The whole thing hit the press when Blackwater operatives were accused of killing civilians, including children, in Afghanistan. The fact that they were convicted but got a presidential pardon attracted a wave of public outrage. But interest lasted for a couple of news cycles and then died down. I'm not sure how much time and effort we should devote to the privatization of the military. I'm ready to leave that until much later. In the meantime, how about going back to the sale of public land?"

"Yes, that sounds a lot less hair-raising. I know that some of the presidential orders allowing for the transfer of public land have been rescinded after the Trump administration was out of office. Still, the government may not be able to void all the contracts. There's also an extensive record of the arguments, both pro and con, on the selling of government land. Let's see what we can find. We can spend the morning on it, see what we come up with, then decide whether to continue."

"Good plan."

A few hours later, they were ready to compare notes. Nikki started. "I hadn't thought about this before, but public land can mean a lot of different things – natural forest, natural wildlife refuge, national recreation area, natural wilderness preservation area, national resource land. And, of course, public land can mean federal, state, and local. I think we should focus on federal land first, don't you?"

"I agree. I was concentrating on what the federal government owns. It owns about 640 million acres of land. That's more than a quarter of all the land in the country, mostly located in twelve western states. What I found surprising was that there is no single law that gives any of the four agencies in charge the authority to acquire or dispose of the land. The Bureau of Land Management has broad authority, and the National Park Service has no authority. The Fish and Wildlife Service and the U.S. Forest Service are somewhere in between. There's something else that's strange: the Bureau of Land Management, the Fish and Wildlife Service, the National Park Service, all fall under the Department of the Interior, but the U.S. Forest Service falls under the Department of Agriculture."

With a frown on her face, Laura jumped in, "Yeah, the lack of a law governing the disposition of the land explains how it was possible for the president to simply have signed a proclamation in 2018 eliminating protection of two million acres of public land – the Bears Ears National Monument and the Grand Staircase-Escalante National Monument. He single-handedly made that land available for mining and drilling for oil without requiring the companies involved to pay a penny for the privilege. The indigenous population and environmentalists were outraged because it put those lands at risk of destroying important Native American archeological sites. Environmentalists were furious because it put prized hunting and fishing areas at risk of contamination."

Nikki's response was, "We'll have to spend a lot more time on the extent to which the oil and gas companies are benefiting from the use of public land. Not only are they using the land to drill without paying for the privilege, but they are also engaged in a variety of fraudulent activities. I was reminded that the Department of Interior's staff was so depleted a decade ago that it was doing little to no oversight to ensure that the companies were complying with pollution standards. And there was no way to know whether the companies were reporting the volume of extraction accurately, meaning that the government was very likely not receiving the royalty payments that it was due.

"The most recent scam that I ran across was online lease sales, and it has been going on for years. I discovered a whole slew of problems related to that. For one, the sales are not announced to the public. Conservation groups sued to get that changed. On top of that, the bids are anonymous. The oil companies argued that they needed to protect their competitive interests. To assist in that cause, the oil and gas industry created a trade organization with a branch that employs "lease brokers" who do the bidding on behalf of the companies. That protects the identity of the companies doing the bidding. The only opposition to all of this comes from environmentalist groups, who obviously don't have the resources available to them that the oil companies do. The oil companies just keep coming up with new ways to thwart the system whenever the environmental groups institute a campaign or go to court to stop the grabbing of public land."

Nikki and Laura were taking turns reporting the results of their research efforts to each other and getting more animated as they talked about each new set of findings. It was Laura's turn. "I wasn't surprised to find that the oil companies have been trying to survive the downturn in the use of gas and oil in the wake of the pandemic by entering into a series of mergers and acquisitions. In 2020, the price of oil per barrel dropped so radically because no one was flying, and fewer people were driving to work. There were 9,000 gas and oil companies at the beginning of the year. Only the biggest companies were engaged in all three of the business streams: upstream – exploration and production; midstream – transport and storage; and downstream – operating oil refineries, petrochemical plants, retail outlets, and such. The smaller companies were involved in only one of these streams.

Interestingly, it was the big companies that experienced most of the drop in income. Small companies did not suffer as much financially because they had started producing more diverse products long ago. I had no idea that oil was involved in producing so many products – not just gas and jet fuel. Oil is used in lubricants, waxes, agricultural chemicals, pesticides, asphalt, synthetic rubber, plastics, pharmaceuticals, and water treatment chemicals. The list just goes on."

"But big oil is hedging its bets on the future of oil and gas in buying up public land." Nikki jumped back in and was on a roll. "They've been using some of the land for wind and solar farms. That has attracted the attention of conservation groups, who are not surprisingly wary about it. They're reporting that the big oil companies don't appear to be doing any drilling on the land that they are acquiring. They are buying up land leases and stockpiling them. Because they can do it anonymously through subsidiaries, there is no way to know who holds the leases. They're moving to use the land to invest in green energy, which is great in one sense, but the fact that green energy will now be in the hands of oligopolists is certainly not a good thing."

"Hey, Nikki, I ran across something that I thought we could work into the story of how our country got to where it is today, where public attitudes about a bunch of stuff come from. Listen to this. Jimmy Carter put solar panels on the roof of the white house to indicate his administration's concern about greenhouse gas emissions. Isn't that amazing? I had no idea that the role of oil and gas in air pollution was recognized to be a threat back in the late 1970s. Then Reagan got into office. He promptly took them down and eliminated a lot of the regulations Carter had instituted. You know that all those historians that Adam, Mark, and Dick talked about during our dinners treat the Reagan era as a turning point in social attitudes about things like government regulations, taxes, and the efficiency of the business sector."

"That is interesting about the solar panels. I'll bet hardly anybody remembers that. But, you're right. That's what I'm seeing too. It's when a lot of things involving the economy changed. And now the writing is on the wall. The big oil companies, in fact, all big companies, have been doing what happens in most industries at some point. The successful companies have been buying up smaller and mid-sized companies. They will stop when there are only three or so left to avoid having the anti-trust regulators come down on them. The Justice Department has been making a concerted effort to overcome the disaster that it suffered while Bill Barr was in charge. Once he departed in 2020, the department hired more people to investigate and prosecute antitrust violators. But so much damage had been done that it's now years later, and the department is still not up to speed and as effective as it was before Barr decimated the department."

"In the meantime," Nikki added, "the big oil companies pressed Congress into imposing limits on foreign oil and gas. That worked for a while. Now the same companies are becoming more actively involved in international politics than they were in years past. It's as if there is a single book of instructions out there that all big companies follow. They all take the same steps: get rid of competition through mergers and acquisitions, cut costs by reducing the number of employees, build up lobbying efforts to prevent any attempts to regulate the industry, and finally turn to globalization to avoid paying taxes. And it is obviously working! We'll have to remember to include that sequence when we work on the country got to where it is today."

Laura and Nikki agreed that privatization of public land was a much bigger issue than they had anticipated. But they decided that they had done enough on the topic, for now, recognizing that there was so much more that they could do. First, they would have to try to identify who was buying public land. They would have to look into the financial reports of the companies involved. Maybe that would reveal transfers of funds used to purchase and lease land going to third parties. The women would have to make the findings they were coming up with into a coherent story that everyone would understand without devoting an enormous of time figuring out all the steps the companies took to get to where they are. They were eager to do that, but there was only so much they could do given the rapidly expanding list of topics they were developing.

They reminded each other that they hadn't considered what states and cities were doing with public land. They knew that there were controversies all over the place about the use of public land in cities across the country. Those should be fun to look into because local issues always attracted a lot of interest and were generally well documented by local media. States were less transparent. They also had been engaging in public-to-private transfers all along. It would take some effort to track them all.

"Remember the stories about the Chicago lakefront?" Nikki asked. "The city was ready to sell off land to open a Star Wars museum in the park on the lakefront. That didn't fly after the media got hold of the story. Opponents argued that the city had no right to give away rights to the land. And that it was unfair to deprive people in that part of town of park and beach access that they were clearly enjoying. After that, there was a long battle about whether the Obama library would be built in the park. The argument opponents offered to build the library on parkland next to the lake was that there was plenty of land away from the lake that could be used without taking away public park space."

With that, the women agreed that they had done enough on public land, for now, whether it was federal, city, or state. They were looking forward to sharing what they had learned so far with their friends on Friday.

THIRTY-TWO

By the end of the week, all the board members had responded to the draft on water department transfers that Nikki and Laura had sent out. They got some suggestions for information that should be included and where the text could be expanded. However, all the members of the board said that the story was solid and well-supported. One suggestion was to summarize the collusion among chemical companies as an introduction to the whole story. Josh's message was longer. He said he'd been thinking about the drive to privatize government functions and how that turned out in cases that had an impact on housing, the area with which he was familiar. He thought that they might be interested in the Fannie Mae and Freddie Mac stories. He said it was a complicated story best related in person. Would they like to meet for lunch?

Nikki called him to say yes, they would be interested, and where they should meet. Josh said he'd be happy to come to a coffee shop near their office. When they got settled with some coffee and sandwiches, he said, "Get ready for a complicated history lesson. This is the history of the rise, fall, rescue, and who knows what's next of The Federal National Mortgage Association, otherwise known as Fannie Mae. The organization was chartered in 1938 in the wake of the Great Depression. Home loans before then were short-term and had balloon payments, which many people couldn't come up with. It was common for people to lose their houses when banks foreclosed on their loans, but that was far more common during the depression. Fannie Mae's purpose was to buy mortgage loans from banks, bundle them into securities, and sell the securities. Because Fannie Mae was so big, it was in a position to get low-interest loans. It was able to buy the loans from banks and make money by turning the loans into securities, which they could sell to investors for a profit. It had no competitors in what became known as the secondary mortgage market. Are you following me so far? It gets more complicated. I'll give you a list of references that you can tackle on your own if you're interested."

Nikki and Laura tried not to look totally confused as they assured Josh that they were interested in hearing more about these agencies and would be glad to read the material that he said he would provide.

So, he went on. "Freddie Mae had strict guidelines for the kinds of loans it would back, based on the Federal Housing Administration and Veterans Administration lending rules. But then comes the big turning point. The politicians in charge of the government at the time decided to privatize Freddie Mae in 1968 because the private sector would be more efficient, right? In 1970, the same politicians created a new agency, Freddie Mac, the Federal Home Loan Mortgage Corporation. It was set up as a for-profit organization that would compete with Freddie Mae. At the same time, the government dropped regulations restricting risky lending practices. The newly minted private-sector agencies began selling their bundled securities on the New York Stock Exchange. I expect that you can predict how that turned out. Banks, which were no longer bound by any restrictions on the loans they could offer, were eager to enter the secondary mortgage market. The banks began lending to anyone interested in getting a mortgage without checking to see if the applicants were likely to be in a position to pay for the mortgage. This became known as the subprime market. As a result of the banks' lending practices, foreclosures began to increase, housing prices began to drop, and the banks engaging in this practice began to fail. That brings us to the Great Recession of 2008. Fannie Mae was delisted from the stock exchange because its stock fell below the minimum of one dollar as required by the stock exchange. At the time, Fannie Mae and Freddie Mac had owned or guaranteed about half of the country's $12 trillion *yes with a T* mortgage market. The risk was that the two organizations would collapse because their stock had become so devalued. If that happened, mortgages would be much more difficult to obtain.

Besides, the bonds that Fannie Mae and Freddie Mac had sold had been bought by money market funds, retirement funds, international investors like the Chinese government, and so on. There would be a massive national and possibly international financial crisis if the housing market continued to spiral down and if more banks failed. There was no alternative. The federal government put the two agencies into "conservatorship." The U.S. Treasury advanced the funds to save the two agencies. In other words, they were *de-privatized*. The government did the same thing for the automobile companies, but that only lasted for a short time. Nothing changed until the Trump administration began promoting efforts to re-privatize the agencies. In the end, that effort went nowhere. Fannie Mae and Freddie Mac continue to operate with government oversight. What do you make of this saga?"

"Well, that is quite a tale of disaster," was Laura's reaction. "There are obviously some important lessons to be learned here. I'm sure that, as you say, most people don't really have a good grasp on what happened. They know there was a recession in 2008 and think that the most important part of the story is that the government stepped in to save the banks and the auto industry. That is certainly the way I understood it. The big complaint was that the government didn't step in to help ordinary people who lost money or lost their jobs during the recession. What happened with regard to Fannie Mae and Freddie Mac is something most of us, me included, heard very little about."

"I second everything Laura just said. It is all much more confused and maybe even obfuscated than what I thought had led to the Great Recession," was Nikki's contribution.

"Okay, you two. I will let you decide what to do with this information. I expect that you will have to give some thought to whether you want to include it in what you're doing, because there is no way to make the story shorter and easier to understand. Let me know if there is anything I can do to help you get deeper into all the stuff you're getting into. Just keep telling yourselves that you are doing something significant that will force people to confront ideas that they aren't examining very carefully."

Both women thanked Josh for putting them onto a story that, as Laura said, was something that they should definitely include in what they were doing. "The story has a long enough history coming full circle to show the effects of privatization writ large."

The two women left the lunch meeting, agreeing that they would have a lot to talk about when they met with their friends that evening. They had not had time to give any thought to their promise to bring food for the group. After tossing around ideas about the foods they liked, they agreed on lasagna. They would order it from one of the small family restaurants south of the downtown area.

******

The lasagna was a success. It came with garlic bread, which everyone dug into right away. Mark, Adam, and Dick said they were all buried in familiar routines and had nothing to report, so they were eager to hear how things at The Public Record were going.

Laura looked at Nikki and said, "Do you want to tell them?" Nikki nodded.

The others looked unsure why the women reacted the way they did, but they looked ready to listen. Nikki explained that they had lunch with Josh and that he had introduced them to the workings of Fannie Mae and Freddie Mac. She went on to relate what they heard from Josh, with periodic invitations to Laura to ask if she was telling it right. When she got through with the story, their listeners just sat there. When they did say something, what they said was something to affect – they learned a lot; they didn't have a clear idea of how the two agencies operated before this; and, they certainly had no idea about the shift from government sponsorship to privatization back to government the two agencies had undergone.

Jane interrupted the flow to urge them all to have more to drink, which they did while they continued to comment on what Nikki and Laura were saying. By the time they started on the lasagna, they were pretty much talked out about the two agencies.

Dick was the first to move the discussion beyond talking about the two agencies to some of the lessons based on what he had just heard that gave substance to the big picture. He mentioned consideration of the impact of privatization in the name of efficiency, the benefits of competition, and the role of government in coming in to stabilize the economy. Everyone agreed that there was a lot to untangle here. Then, Dick startled everyone by announcing that as far as he was concerned, efficiency was actually beside the point. What good was it when one looked at how the private sector operated when it began to offer subprime mortgages? "Let's face it. Greed is a more apt concept here than efficiency."

"You're exactly right. Efficiency is a useless concept in so many cases. It plays no role in dealing with social issues like mental health, addiction, and sex abuse. I know those are the themes I always come back to," said Jane.

"Efficiency is great until it turns into a monster like Amazon, buying up companies along the way as it becomes so efficient it doesn't have competitors," was Mark's contribution. It was getting harder to add something to the conversation. Everyone was eager to say something. Adam said, "Right, and remember what we were saying about monopolies and oligopolies? That's what happens when efficiency has no limits. People don't have a choice when Walmart moves into town. They can't really do anything to stop Walmart from taking over. Choice is something that conservatives keep stressing, but that's a fantasy. Walmart decides whether it will take over the town and its economy or not. Amazon decides which kinds of companies it will buy out and which merchants it will promote. The market is good at creating conditions for the most aggressive companies to gain control over the distribution of goods and services. Is that what privatization proponents are after in lauding efficiency?"

Laura and Nikki had been watching the back and forth in what they had started when Nikki got back into the conversation. She said, "The lesson I take from the Freddie Mae and Freddie Mac story is that taxes saved the country from going into a tailspin. If the government didn't have the money, gained largely through taxation, to save the banks and other businesses like the car companies, what would have happened? It wasn't only the economy that was about to fail. It was our whole way of life that was in deep trouble. In other words, the chaos that would have followed if the government didn't step in would have demolished democracy along with society as we know it."

That stopped the conversation. "Jeez, Nikki, let's not tiptoe around this – tell it like it is. Holy shit. You're right. That is exactly what would have happened," was Adam's reaction.

"Do you guys know what we're saying here?" Mark wanted to get his two cents in. "We really are forecasting doom if things keep going the way they are going. If people don't recognize that the slogans they're ready to promote, like individual rights, choice, efficiency, lower taxes, small government, reducing regulation, and on and on, have real consequences when taken to the extreme. And the extreme is what we are seeing unfold."

"I know we are all sounding like crazed alarmists," Jane said, trying to inject some calm into the discussion. "I know what you're saying is true, but maybe it won't be as bad as it looks to us right now. The generation following the millennials is better educated and less committed to individualism. They are already having a positive political influence. The country always bounces back, doesn't it? I'm trying to look at the glass being half full rather than half empty."

"Right. We should not leave tonight without at least holding out hope that people will wake up and things will fall into place when that happens. That the historians who say that change comes in waves are right and that we are witnessing the top of a shockingly big wave that will ebb away over time." Adam was offering Jane his support. But everyone was looking tired and discouraged despite Jane and Adam's efforts. They were ready to go home and go to sleep to avoid thinking about all of this. Maybe what they were talking about would all look different tomorrow.

"Before you all leave," Laura said, "we had so much to tell you about what we were finding regarding the work we've done in other areas before what Josh told us about Freddie Mae and Freddie Mac came up. We wanted to get your reaction to all those things. Can we plan on getting together again, soon, to do that? Please, we'll try to be less gloomy in reporting what we are finding."

The others agreed. They said they wanted to be supportive of Laura and Nikki. Nikki responded with, "Can we plan on next Friday? It'll be the guys' turn to bring food." She was smiling about what that might look like, "I'm looking forward to that." With that thought in mind, people said goodnight.

THIRTY-THREE

Laura and Nikki were feeling pretty good about how much information they were able to gather. They could see how upsetting what they were reporting was to their friends, friends who were highly educated and well-informed. Their friends were shocked by what they had heard. While they agreed that they weren't happy about the distress they caused their friends, they told each other that the reaction they got to what they were reporting to their friends looked like it could have a powerful effect on the broader social conversation if enough people reacted that way. Maybe people would begin paying attention to what was happening around them. Nikki and Laura reminded each other that expecting that kind of change was excessively optimistic. But getting some people to take notice would be better than watching society slide into a situation in which everything was run by a handful of anonymous entities whose main objective was a stock market success and humongous rewards going to the handful of people who managed to work their way into executive suites. The two of them were psyched-up, in fact, so psyched-up that they were at their desks on Saturday and would probably put in some time on Sunday too. They agreed that they might need to go on a lengthy bike ride to get rid of the muscle aches from sitting in front of their computers so much. They spent the rest of the week putting their findings into better order. By Friday, they were ready to present a more organized portfolio of findings to their friends.

Adam and Mark spent some time on Friday morning thinking about what they would bring for dinner that evening. They decided on Mexican food. They ordered dinner for six from *This Side of the Border*. The order started with guacamole and chips, tacos as the main entrée, plus side dishes, and churros for dessert if anyone still had some room. It was a feast. The others greeted them with cheers when they set the food on the table. The mood was more cheerful than it had been by the time their session ended the last time they saw each other.

Jane, Dick, Adam, and Mark all said they were ready to hear more about Nikki and Laura's research findings. They said that they knew they should be prepared to hear more distressing information.

Laura started by recounting what they found on water treatment facilities. They took turns laying it out. One discovery that everyone around the table reacted to was that several chemical companies had combined into a single organization to establish Water Works Inc. The women explained that they had developed a summary statement covering the transfer of water departments to the private sector and were playing it safe by running it by board members to see if they thought it might cause the Water Works company to sue. The board members all agreed that the information was well-grounded and written in a straightforward manner, so the women should feel confident about using it. They weren't ready to publish any of their findings yet, but it helped to know that the way they were organizing and presenting their findings was well received by the board.

Dick's comment was, "My reaction to what you're telling us is that the public is losing control over water treatment operations. When a private company takes over, the public has no recourse to a higher authority like the mayor or city council. The owners can't be fired for not doing a good job in response to public concern or dissatisfaction because they are not public employees. The public can demand reports, but doesn't have any recourse if the company doesn't do the testing and make the results available for all to see. Members of the public can try to find an existing consumer support organization willing to sue, but that's an uphill and costly venture. On top of it, it's not like a water department operates in a free market. The public can't go elsewhere to get better or cheaper water."

The other two men registered reactions along the same lines. Adam's comment was, "and the fact that the company that is absorbing a growing number of water treatment facilities is becoming a national corporate entity means that it is further removed from the local scene and has less reason to be responsive to residents served by any one of its local units. It has far less incentive to be responsive because it has less to lose if the local unit fails to deliver a good product. Once such contracts are signed, it takes a major disaster to break them."

"My concern is that the federal agencies that should be monitoring things like water and air quality were captured by big business a decade ago," was Mark's reaction. "Those businesses have armies of lobbyists working to influence politicians to pass legislation that gives license to big corporate entities to act the way they do. The politicians get money to support their campaigns from the very companies whose activities the public expects them to be monitoring. I know that's not news. We've known that all along, but no one is doing anything about it."

Laura and Nikki looked at each other and nodded. Laura asked Nikki if she wanted to tell everyone what they were finding about the sale of public land. She said she would follow up with the fire departments. Nikki outlined what they learned about which agencies are in charge of public land and what authority they have over it. The ongoing problem was that the agencies were leasing the land without requiring payment from the corporations involved. While it was apparent that gas and oil companies were doing the leasing, it was hard to find out how much land was being leased. She explained that one of the latest scandals involved leasing public land to anonymous bidders online. Conservation groups were monitoring the process and going to court to obtain information that was hard to get otherwise. But that was a hit-or-miss operation because they couldn't target all the leasing agreements.

Laura added that environmental groups were involved because the land used for drilling would likely contaminate prime fishing and hunting areas and risk the destruction of archeological sites belonging to Indian tribes.

That brought on more comments from the others, all focusing on the fact that the public was losing control over a growing list of public sector entities. They lamented the fact that responsibility for oversight over water and land resources was being abandoned by the government at both the federal and local levels.

"Moving on," Laura began, "let me tell you what we're finding about fire departments. As everyone here knows, the fire department in our city was leased to a private firm."

"Yes," Jane interjected, "Dick and I watched them in action a while ago. We saw guys with insignia indicating that they were firefighters standing around watching a warehouse fire. One of the older guys was running around telling them to do something. They would just move to a new spot to watch. The guy holding the fire hose couldn't control it. It was waving all over the place. The scene would have been comical if it weren't so serious. Fortunately, no one was hurt. But the warehouse was destroyed. Remember, the city was blamed and was pressed into coming up with the money to provide training for the new recruits. It was supposed to save money, but, in the end, it cost the city money. In fact, that's when the city received the offer to lease the public-school system. I didn't think of it then, but the timing now strikes me as particularly fortuitous to the entity that took over the public schools."

Laura looked taken aback. "I don't know if there is any relationship between the entity that got the public-school lease and the entity that got the fire department lease. The timing suggests that there could have been. That might be worth checking out. It's not unreasonable to assume that while the people behind the big corporations involved in these lease deals may not be best friends, they surely know each other. They meet at fundraising events, museum show openings, private clubs, and so on. An organization named Fire Protection Inc. is emerging as a big player involved in deals in multiple cities. We'll have to do more research on it. Nikki, doesn't the existence of personal connections sound like it might be fun to look into someday?"

Nikki responded with a nod and a grin on her face. "Yes, but right now, we have enough to deal with. The privatization of fire departments across the country is not proceeding in nearly as organized a manner as the leasing of public-school systems or public land, but it is proceeding."

Laura picked it up again from there. "You might be surprised to hear how privatization is proceeding in rural areas. People in some communities who are more conservative and more opposed to taxes are dealing with the problem by turning to subscriptions. Those who want fire protection services sign on with a private company. It's an individual choice. It's voluntary, which makes libertarians happy. That is not a solution that people living in cities are interested in adopting.

Nevertheless, it's clear that people across the country are falling back on the mantra that private companies are more efficient in providing fire protection. And from what we've seen, the private companies in the firefighting business really are more efficient. They run the fire departments like a factory. They've introduced eight-hour shifts, so there is no downtime for the firefighters. There is no downtime because the firefighters are required to engage in profit-producing activities when they are not out on a call. They do fire inspections, sell and install fire alarms, and do fire safety training for schools and companies.

Meanwhile, the private companies have been raising their rates. They calculate the distance and charge accordingly. They charge depending on how many firefighters it takes to deal with the emergency. We'll have to watch how long it takes for the customers to start complaining about rising rates. Then we'll see what they think about the price they are paying for the efficiency they were counting on, which they expected to result in lower prices."

Their friends who had been listening to Laura and Nikki's accounts just sat there. What was there to say? They each said something to the effect that the work the two had been doing was impressive.

Looking serious and dismayed, Dick said, "And to think that you're nowhere near finished tracking these things. You haven't examined anywhere near all the sectors that are moving in the direction of the corporate takeover of services that have traditionally been the responsibility of the public sector."

He asked if others had heard an interesting piece of news regarding the trading of water futures in the market. The media's business sections were reporting that trading of water futures in California, which started at the end of 2020, was turning out to be more successful than anticipated. Investors were eager to put their money into water futures alongside soybean, gold, oil, and Bitcoin futures. The water futures plan was designed to manage the risk of water shortages by creating predictability. It was turning out that putting water into the hands of financial institutions, like the Chicago Mercantile Exchange, was doing what critics warned would happen. The market was working. It was increasing the price of a scarce commodity in response to increased demand. At the same time, a small but growing number of high-profile economists were hitting the media, arguing that water was a basic human need and not a commodity that people could choose to buy or not to buy. The market was the wrong instrument to distribute it.

Laura responded to Dick's remarks with, "We're not going there, at least not for a while. We've been running across references to water rights being sold, water diverted from one region to another, property being bought to gain water rights. It's all going on out west. Living next to Lake Michigan, this is all unfamiliar territory. In fact, it seems that cities and states east of the Mississippi are dealing with the problems brought about by too much water, that is, flooding, while those west of the Mississippi are dealing with water shortages. The idea that water is becoming a scarce commodity is gaining traction in response to population growth in urban areas in the western part of the country, which is happening in areas without water access. Being from the Midwest, I have to admit that I don't understand how water in one place can be sold to someone in another place other than trucking it over there, which doesn't sound like a viable approach. But as I say, we Midwesterners are not facing that problem and are not familiar with how it's being handled. I guess that is part of the reason we're ready to put off work on this topic."

"Besides, we haven't gotten to a whole range of other things that cities and states are transferring to the private sector to stay afloat. No pun intended," was Nikki's contribution. "We haven't looked into the leasing of things like parks, roads, and bridges. Outsourcing various administrative functions is another arena that we haven't looked into, from vehicle registration and inspections to fishing and hunting licenses to collecting real estate taxes. Then there's policing. We've run across some stuff on that, but it's messy. And we certainly haven't done anything on what's happening in the health care delivery sector. That's so convoluted and changing so fast that we're putting it off until we get a lot more done on what we've already started."

Jane was looking totally dejected. "I think I may be more tired and disheartened listening to what you're saying this week than I was last week. I can't help but feel that we, as a society, have abandoned responsibility for the things that were central to the identity of this country. I'm distressed about the fact that people are ready to quit being citizens who have a say in how we deal with community issues and instead become customers standing in line waiting to give their money to big businesses. I'm disheartened to find that people are so eager to relinquish responsibility for addressing shared community service needs to corporations, which are happily turning those needs over to a marketplace where money rules. Who can say that we, as members of society, are happy with what we've brought on ourselves? There is no place to register satisfaction or dissatisfaction with what corporations do. Customer satisfaction surveys are a joke. Their only use is for the company to figure out how to sell us another service. When something goes wrong, corporations let us talk to robots who have a set menu that rarely includes the problem we are trying to have addressed. Boycotting what companies sell is an ineffective solution that only inconveniences the handful of people who sign on to that tactic. And let's face it, some of the people who do sign on admit that they aren't as faithful as they start out to be because it's not an easy path to follow. I'm beginning to think that we're living in a world that would sound like science fiction if we weren't actually experiencing it. If I'm sounding discouraged, it's because I am discouraged."

No one wanted to argue with that assessment or try to cheer each other up. Laura and Nikki apologized for putting their friends in such a dismal frame of mind when they had promised to try to do less of that the last time they met. The others said that they knew that what they were hearing was real, but they found it hard to face up to. They knew they couldn't do much about the direction things were going. They each said they had heard enough for one evening and agreed to come together again, but maybe not next week.

THIRTY-FOUR

This week, Laura and Nikki were looking into what was going on at the state and city levels. The two often overlapped. They knew that there was an enormous amount of information that they would have to uncover in this arena. Instead of examining it all, they planned to develop an outline and fill it in as they came across relevant information. They had run across many interesting case studies documenting the problems that states and cities faced in leasing parts of the built environment to private-sector owners, such as bridges. The leases invariably allowed the private owners to install tolls. That had a negative effect on traffic flow, so city governments had to be careful which bridges they leased.

The same was true of roads when private owners installed tolls. States had been leasing roads out to private sector organizations for years. Nikki and Laura would have to do more investigating to identify the companies involved. The names of the bridges and roads did not change when private owners took over. That made it harder to track who was doing the leasing. They discovered that a foreign company, Infrastruct, Inc., had leased some bridges in the Midwest. They would have to find out if it was the main actor in other states across the country. That would be interesting. Not only was it possible that a single corporation could be in charge of a major portion of the country's infrastructure, but the fact that it was a foreign entity made things more disconcerting. True, the country was operating in a global economy. Still, it was not something that would sit well with many members of the public if they knew that a foreign country had so much control over something as essential as our roads and bridges.

They were not surprised to find a fair amount written on private-public partnerships entered into by the city and the state, primarily editorials and public opinion responses. State and city governments were eager to sign up for such deals when they faced budget shortfalls. In many cases, states were pressed into taking such actions because they had few alternative choices. They have to end up with a balanced budget at the end of every budget year and cannot borrow money to close the gap. The deals have been giving state governments a way of raising money without raising taxes for decades. There was a good deal of patchy history to look at. But there weren't many systematic evaluations. That was attributable to the fact that there was not nearly enough transparency.

It was clear that this was another topic that economists had taken an interest in over recent years. Their involvement produced some technical evaluations and associated commentary. The general assessment by economists was interesting. There seemed to be general agreement, which does not happen very often in their circles. The consensus was that in cases where the private sector ends up making a big profit, the public sector representatives had overestimated risk and undervalued the entity they had let out for lease. Put more simply, the private sector was being overpaid.

Different economists have offered a range of examples of what's wrong with public-private deals. One observation that might not come readily to mind is that the contracts typically require the government to compensate the private entity when it loses money. A number of cases are commonly cited, such as the Indiana toll road story. When the road flooded the area where the toll booths stood, the state allowed cars to go through the toll gates for free to prevent traffic backup. The private company calculated how much money it lost and demanded that the state make up for the loss. The state was forced to pay up because the contract required it. The state hadn't anticipated running into a problem like that. It caused the state to consider suing the company that built the road to see if it could get compensated for the builder's failure to foresee flooding. The state decided not to go forward with the lawsuit against the builder because the outcomes of lawsuits aren't predictable, but they are costly.

Another example comes from Chicago and the parking meter deal. When the city shuts down a street for whatever reason, snow removal, street cleaning, or emergencies, the city ends up having to pay the company for the loss in revenue incurred by the company.

Then there's the state of Virginia story. The state succeeded in its efforts to encourage carpooling to reduce pollution. That had a negative effect on profits anticipated by the company leasing the road and its toll revenue expectations. It required the state to make up the loss.

Laura and Nikki found many examples of instances in which cities and states lost money that they did not expect to lose. States are always eager to sign contracts because the money they get upfront looks good, but the contract details too often turn out to produce problems that the government wasn't prepared for. A non-compete clause sounds reasonable when the government is signing the contract, but it looks very different if the government is not satisfied with the arrangement and wants out of the contract. The non-compete clause prevents the government entity from seeking out a less expensive alternative. Of course, there might not be an alternative private sector company, and the city or state would have to reinstate government employees with all the political falderal that would entail.

There have been more significant problems when something more serious goes wrong. When the bridge over the Mississippi in Missouri collapsed, the courts did get involved in deciding who was legally responsible. The state paid to have the bridge built, but a private construction company built it. And it contracted with another private company to maintain it. There have been some bridge failures across the country in which people lost their lives. In each case, all the parties involved made every effort to avoid accepting responsibility since they knew the penalties would be huge.

Nikki and Laura learned that ports were being leased, something they hadn't thought about before. The one in Miami had attracted some attention. They would have to track how many other ports had been leased and how each of those arrangements worked out. The same story applied to airports. They didn't know much about that either.

They also knew virtually nothing about contracts between the government and the private sector involving Wi-Fi access and anything else to do with software programs used by the government for all kinds of purposes, including surveillance and security. They wouldn't be touching on any of that for a long time until they had developed better control over things they understood better.

Realizing how much more work they had ahead of them was a mixed blessing. It was good to know that there would be no shortage of material to keep their enterprise going. On the other hand, they could see that there was an enormous amount of work ahead.

They were ready to quit for the day and get away from their computers. Laura said, "I'm excited by what we are discovering. And I'm overwhelmed by how much information there is. We are facing a mountain of information."

"No question about it," was Nikki's response. "We have to keep reminding ourselves that there is no deadline. No one is pressuring us to produce something by a certain date. We can do this. We just have to keep things in perspective. Set short-term goals and not expect to develop the complete report anytime soon."

"I'm still not sure whether we should release some of our findings in bits and pieces or wait until we have something far more substantial. I think the rational thing to do is wait. But I'm also eager to get feedback."

"I'm for waiting until we feel more secure about the product we are expecting to produce. Once we have that in place, and I don't mean completed, I think we will be better able to handle the opposition that I'm sure will be forthcoming. I think we need to be prepared for that."

"Yes," Laura said. "I hadn't even considered that aspect. Of course, we'll get opposition. Maybe we should be satisfied, at least for now, with releasing our findings to our board and our discussion group friends. That should be enough to provide a check and tell us whether we're going in the right direction."

They decided to contact Josh and ask if he thought the board would like to meet and hear about some of their most recent findings. He said he thought board members would be very interested. He said he would set it up for the end of the week.

They planned to use the meeting room on their floor, which seated everyone comfortably. They would have coffee and sweet rolls sent in. That worked well the last time the board met.

Laura and Nikki knew they had to get to work on a presentation. They decided that they didn't need to do anything more complicated than putting together a list of topics they covered and a summary outlining what they found, including some things the board had heard already. The statement they created was based on the discussion that they had with the discussion group. They covered public-school transfers, water department leases, fire department transfers, federal, state, and city land leases, plus state and city contracts related to infrastructure like roads and bridges. They would introduce the Fannie Mae and Freddie Mac story, but let Josh handle it. Their summary statement would have to be brief, focused on questions regarding evidence of undervaluing of public goods and services in contracts with private entities; risk of unexpected financial loss; transparency; and legal complications in the event of infrastructure failure.

They outlined a series of issues that required further study. The big topic to which they would be devoting considerable attention was consolidation, to the extent to which a small number of big players were engaged in the public sector to private sector transfers.

They agreed to raise the question of when they could or should be ready to publish their findings. Whether to release some of what they found or wait until they were prepared to release a more complete report. They needed the board's reaction on how to package the findings. What the tone of the presentation should be. And there were still all the other questions that needed answers, such as whether they should charge for access to the findings.

When the board met, the board members were very encouraging. They didn't seem to be nearly as discouraged as their discussion group friends about what the women were reporting. Maybe their presentation wasn't as detailed, or they may have been presenting the material in a more distant and formal manner. The board members said they thought the findings would capture the attention of both the media and politicians. They said they thought the women were going to have a significant impact on society's understanding of the transfer of public goods and services to the private sector.

Nikki and Laura left the meeting pleased with how it went.

*****

That evening, Jane recounted what occurred at the board meeting to Dick. Dick sat there without saying anything until she was finished. Then he said, "We have heard a lot about public entities being transferred to the private sector. But hearing how much is going on, all the sectors that it is affecting is more than I was prepared to hear over the last few times Nikki and Laura reported what they were finding. I presume it's more than the board members were prepared to hear. Finding out that it's a tsunami of privatization ventures is unsettling. I'm sure the public is not aware of how much of that is going on. On the other hand, some members of the public are likely to think this is exactly what should be happening. Did that come up in your discussion with the board?"

"No, it didn't."

"Ever since our last session with our group, I've been thinking about how much society is changing. How much control over the public sector and its functions are people willing to sign away? The more I think about it, the more dejected I become."

"You're right. It is disheartening. But we have to believe that there are enough people out there who will pay attention and understand what's happening. Understand that we are losing control over organizations that ordinary people helped establish to serve shared needs. That there will be enough people who will object to finding that organizations that served to respond to needs expressed by citizens are being absorbed by entities that are more interested in responding to the expectations of investors than to citizens' interests."

"I suggest that we talk about our work to get us off this topic because it does leave us feeling gloomy. Jane, tell me what you've been doing at work."

"I'm not sure that it is a cheerier topic. I've been finding that the rate of deaths from opioid addiction, suicide, and homicide, you know, the deaths of despair, are not declining. They're rising, not a lot, but I'm seeing a steady, slow climb. The solutions that everyone in the public health community embraces are not getting enough support. Lots of happy talk, but no money. The private sector has not been able to figure out ways to make money on things that would help stem the tide of deaths of despair. Things like education, pay for time off to get additional job training, adequate housing, access to healthy food, child care, preventive health care, and, let's face it, an end to racism. Basically, ordinary everyday things but all an uphill battle. In the meantime, the private sector is investing money in developing bigger and better diagnostic equipment, which isn't a solution if there is no cure. The big drug companies are spending more money to develop new versions of existing pharmaceuticals. Few new drugs have come on the scene over the last couple of decades, except for the COVID-19 vaccine. That happened because the government threw lots of money at the problem, but mostly because the potential consumer base was worldwide. Hard to ignore those incentives. I admit that a few wonder drugs did come into existence, but they're not really available because they are being sold at prices that no one can afford. More typically, multiple older drugs are being used in combination, even if that results in an increased risk of side effects. The health care agenda is all mixed up. I wonder if Laura and Nikki will be looking into how much privatization has affected that sector."

"No, let's not get back to talking about the problems associated with private sector control over public sector entities and social institutions created to address society's needs. I'll tell you what's going on in my lab. Of course, that won't take very long because our research findings are slow-moving. I can tell you that the interns have turned into an asset once we figured out how to give them something to do that they could do on their own. They're enjoying the experience. And Adam, Mark, and I feel that we're benefiting from not having to do some of the routine work. Besides, it's fun to watch them learn to master new tasks and learn to interpret findings. We've decided that we'd be willing to take on new interns next semester. The next thing on my agenda is writing a proposal to renew our arthritis research funding. That is due at the end of the month. You know how it goes. We will have to construct an account of what we've been working on, what our findings have revealed so far, and what we plan to do next. It will have to sound like we're making progress to justify the renewal of the contract. I think we have made some progress. We really are learning how to make cartilage grow. But it grows slowly, so we have more to report on what hasn't worked and what we've learned from that. Still, I'm optimistic that we'll get the funding we're counting on to continue to do the research."

"Good. That is good news. I'm glad to hear that you are satisfied with how things are going. Listening to you has had a positive effect on my mood, which I admit was pretty low. Maybe we can plan to do something distracting this weekend. I don't know what, but I'll give it some thought."

THIRTY-FIVE

Adam and Liz had been seeing each other pretty steadily. They had discovered that they enjoyed the same things and had similar views on many topics. They didn't talk about it, but seemed to agree that there was no rush to move things along any faster. The specter of Liz's half-brother continued to hang over her, but he hadn't come up for conversation for a while. That changed when they got together on Saturday.

Liz said that she had been looking at the NEXT website that afternoon and was really upset. She said, "do you know that the people behind NEXT are now recruiting to form a militia? They've been saying crazy things all along, but they were disorganized and running off in different directions, like bribing people in your lab and creating photoshopped campaigns targeting liberal politicians. Some of their efforts did turn dangerous, but they were isolated incidents. Their rhetoric is escalating. Now they are saying that they are getting ready for civil war. They're angry about the fact that liberal politicians continue to talk about the need to raise taxes to preserve public services and address socioeconomic inequality. As to public services, naturally, they want more private-sector control, not less. With regard to inequality, they say that this is a free country, and everybody can succeed if they try. The people who are poor have lost their jobs, been evicted, have to stand in food lines, and so on, just didn't try hard enough. They are vehemently opposed to giving those people any help, which they see as a free ride, especially people born in other countries. They say that they are prepared to defend this country's values by opposing the taxation of good, hard-working people, people like themselves, to support lazy cheats."

"People on the alt-right have been saying things like that for a long time," was Adam's reaction. "I admit that we're hearing more of that now, but what makes you think there's more to worry about this time?"

"I just read an account by someone who got access to the emails of a couple of guys who are most active in heading up NEXT. He found that they are actively recruiting people with military and policing experience. Their reasoning is that they want to recruit people with munitions training who have sworn to uphold the Constitution and to protect it from destruction by forces that are threatening American values. They are out to convince people who have the training to engage in combat that it's time to use their guns to save the country from people who want to destroy it."

"Is there much evidence that this is a growing movement? That kind of thing did happen in 2021 when hundreds of people stormed the capital. So many were arrested that I thought people like that got the message that law enforcement has learned from that experience. That the police were now better trained and the FBI more vigilant. I know there are still some people with police and military backgrounds involved with opposition groups, but I thought they were engaged in a lot of talk and flag-waving without any actual action plan."

"Who knows, maybe so. But the investigator found that the group is getting substantial financial support from unidentified sources. He says that there is good reason to believe that the money is coming via Russian intelligence channels. He's got pretty good evidence. NEXT is saying its funding comes from its huge membership base."

"How huge?" was Adam's reaction. "Is there any way to know how many followers or members there are?"

"I can tell you that the documents the investigator found include lists of people who signed on. The founders wanted to have contact information. Besides, they wanted to know how the new recruits found out about the organization and what skills they brought. No one seems to be sure exactly how many people are on those lists, but there are far more than anyone expected. The investigator said that the numbers are unstable because some of the early recruits have left the organization. That is an interesting story in itself. The people who left all had combat experience. They saw what civil war looked like up close in the Middle East. The investigative reporter writing this is a war correspondent, so he had seen it too. He said the war there is chaotic. People aren't sure who is on which side. They're terrified, ready to lash out, often killing people on their own side. When the reporter asked those who left NEXT if they would be willing to engage in a civil war, with few exceptions, they said they said no. No matter what the reason was. They said that national debates need to be settled through negotiation. The investigator said that the people in the Middle East who were fighting with each other said the same thing. They told him that they wished the war had never started. They said that no one who experiences war up close thinks that it is a good way to handle anything."

"In other words, the people who are staying in the organization that NEXT is establishing are trained to use weapons of destruction but haven't had experience using them in an active military operation."

"Yes. The investigator says that the people who are actively involved now got their ideas about what a civil war would look like in this country from movies and historical accounts that make participants look like heroes. That's the kind of civil war they are envisioning with themselves in starring roles as heroes saving the country."

"Oh boy. It's like kids dressing up for Halloween or a school play or getting into video game action. Only they're really armed. And the Russians are laughing their asses off. I'm not sure that Russians have a sense of humor, but they are certainly enjoying the trouble they are creating."

Liz was nodding and looking defeated. "That's it. I can't see how anything anyone says will change what some people in this country have come to believe. But that's not all. What has me really frightened is that there's someone on the website campaigning to become a new leader. He's saying that nothing will change unless they take bold action. His idea is to coordinate bombing state capitals on a set date, all at the same time. Do you think that it's just scare tactics, or could that really happen?"

"Liz, I don't know. I can't imagine that there will be enough people to sign on to bombing state capitals. They can't be that well organized. There will be people who won't want to go that far. Maybe there will be disagreement in the ranks, and nothing will come of the bombing idea. The only thing we can do is try to make sure that more people know about the militia and what its aims are. Besides, friends and relatives have been turning the zealots in. That is likely to happen with this plot too. I believe, and I hope I'm right, that most people in this country would turn away from something that extreme."

"Adam, I'm not certain of that as you are. Just look at what governments at every level are doing, selling off public entities to corporations to raise enough money to address basic government functions that people in this country are not interested in and not willing to support. People are so opposed to taxation that they think that is exactly what should be happening. The belief that government is useless has become so firmly ingrained that they are ready to take drastic steps to get rid of it."

"Funny you should bring that up. Two women, who are part of a discussion group I belong to, are tracking that very thing. They are just getting their nonprofit organization off the ground. They're dedicated to finding out who out there in the private sector is doing all the buying and leasing of public service entities. One of the findings that they've been following up on is that many of the private sector organizations involved are subsidiaries of major corporations. In other words, it turns out that it's not only privatization but a growing degree of monopolization."

"Wow. Great." Liz was suddenly acting like she'd made an exciting discovery. "Can you introduce me to them? I would be willing to help in any way I can. I don't expect to be paid. I just want to be part of a project like that. It sounds like something that would get me out of my doldrums, make me feel that I'm not sitting around complaining and letting other people do the work."

"Okay. I'll try to set it up. They're kind of overwhelmed right now, but I think I can convince them to take a break and have lunch with us. I think I have some influence there, given that one of the women is my sister." Adam was chuckling while saying that. "I know they'll be happy to talk about what they're doing. They certainly want as many people as possible to get the message. The organization is so new that they don't have a website yet."

Adam called Laura and told her about Liz. He told her that she wanted to help in any way she could. Laura said she was sure that Nikki would be happy to meet with her and talk about what they were doing, but wasn't sure how Liz could participate. She would speak with Nikki, and they would think about it. The lunch was set for two days later.

Liz knew it would be good to come prepared with something concrete that she could offer. Her work gave her a lot of experience designing software programs. She thought she could apply that experience to designing The Public Report's website.

Liz was enthusiastic about what Laura and Nikki were doing based on what she heard from Adam. Once she met them and heard them talk about their work, she was even more enthusiastic. Adam was pleased to see that. Liz said she was prepared to present her idea about what she could contribute to avoid awkwardness in figuring that out. She said, "I'm sure there are a lot of things that you could use assistance with because you've taken on an enormous challenge. I've thought about what I could do that would be helpful. I'd like to volunteer to be your webmaster."

She went to talk about her background and her work. She said she knew she was contributing to society's health in what she was doing. Still, she felt that she would be making a much more personally rewarding contribution to society by participating in Nikki and Laura's project.

Laura and Nikki didn't need to do more than look at each other to see that they were in agreement. Laura said, "Welcome to the team. We definitely could use help with the website. We've been thinking about it, but it's not the kind of thing that we've had any experience doing. We could definitely use your help. We'll have to talk to our board members about it to offer you a real job."

"Don't worry about that for now. I'll be a volunteer. Once the website is set up and needs to be monitored regularly, we can talk about a job then," Liz said. "There's a lot to decide about what function the website will play. Will you use it to solicit funding? To disseminate information? To offer products that you develop based on your research?"

"You're right," was Nikki's reaction. "We haven't settled any of those things. We talked about it with our board of directors during previous meetings. They said they would think about it. We've been putting off making any decisions because that's hard. We keep falling back on doing research because that's what we know how to do. We are not managers. Neither of us likes to make organizational decisions. We do it when we are forced to do it, but as you can see, we put that kind of thing off as long as we can. I think you'll have a good effect on us, forcing us to confront questions like that."

Adam hadn't said anything for a while. He now had a big grin on his face and said, "I'm glad this is working out so well. Liz, I just knew you would find a way to contribute to the work that Laura and Nikki are doing. I knew you'd get along just fine with each other."

THIRTY-SIX

The two women were true to their word about what they wanted to do with their time – more research. They got right back to it. They had already done a lot on federal public land use, but knew there was a lot more that they hadn't gotten to. They continued to be surprised to find how much debate there had been about it over the years. They realized that the debates had taken place in outlets that they didn't usually access. They agreed that the majority of people weren't being exposed to those discussions.

"I've run across some information that puts a new twist on who's buying the land and for what purpose, but we need to do a lot more work confirming what I've found." Laura was looking pretty pleased with herself for coming up with the new twist. "Here's what I've come across. It seems that the three big auto companies in the country have gotten together to form a corporation over the past year that expects to engage in mining. It's called OreExplore, Inc. It will do some oil and gas exploration, but intends to lease the land to oil companies to carry that out. Its primary purpose is ore exploration. They agreed to get together because one of the minerals they need in building cars is rare and is severely depleted. The companies decided that it would be in their interests to cooperate to avoid a shortage that would be devastating. The ore is a mineral known as palladium. It's thirty times rarer than gold. It is an essential component of auto exhaust systems. It turns toxic pollutants into less harmful carbon dioxide and water vapor."

"But aren't they producing more electric cars now so that they won't need to be concerned about building cars with pollution control features anymore?"

"Yes, but they won't be completely abandoning gas engines for another decade or so. They can't afford to drop the production of gas engine-powered cars and trucks all of a sudden. They need to ease away from it," was Laura's answer. "Besides, they will be the beneficiaries of the sale of the by-products of their mining venture. That includes platinum, nickel, copper, uranium, and even gold, which are all in short supply. The new consortium won't be abandoning mining palladium after they no longer need it in building automobiles. The ore is used in electronics, dentistry, and jewelry. It's a win-win deal."

Nikki was looking troubled. "That means that this new organization formed by the car companies will be leasing a large portion of land to mine it for ore. That, plus the fact that the oil and gas companies will be leasing more public land to do gas and oil exploration. Does anyone know how much public land has been leased to these corporations already? And, is anyone interested in finding out whether this is likely to produce much income for the federal government? From everything we've seen, it looks like the federal government is giving away the rights to public land and not getting nearly as much income as it could be getting. That's something corporations have managed to attain through intensive lobbying efforts."

"I'm not sure I can verify this. But I ran across something suggesting that the Koch Brothers enterprises and Exxon-Mobile are engaged in talks to combine efforts to gain greater access to public land for gas and oil exploration. They've been doing it separately, but combining their enormous fortunes would give them a huge advantage in convincing conservative lawmakers of the benefits of that kind of deal. They argue that they are interested in reducing dependence on oil and gas resources from outside the country. They're right. That would happen. It's just that they would then be able to monopolize the industry, which would allow them to increase their prices to unforeseen levels. And they would have an even greater reason to lobby against green energy."

"Laura, we're finally moving to where we were hoping to get. We're finding that the private sector is easing its way into dividing up the wealth found in the country's natural resources. There seems to be a "live and let live" consensus developing among the private-sector investors. The biggest corporations are comfortable dividing up the territory amongst themselves, becoming monopolies, and pressing government to give up more control over public-sector entities with each passing year."

"That's certainly what we're finding, isn't it?" was Laura's answer. "That's what we thought we'd find, but it is shocking to actually see the evidence."

They talked about whether they should move on to another topic or continue to work on the privatization of land. They decided to explore some alternative issues, but not abandon land privatization if they ran across more information.

They talked about the challenges involved in turning to the health care sector. They knew that it was a huge topic to take on with a long and labyrinthine history. They would have to decide how much history to go into. It was essential to understand the history to understand how the system came to look the way it does, but they were afraid that people would find the twists and turns too complicated to follow.

"Maybe we could start with some basic facts," said Nikki. "The most common observation is that we pay so much more for health care in this country, but don't live as long. And we die from preventable causes at a far greater rate than people do in other countries. We could start there."

"That's good. We could also use graphs to illustrate the increase in the percentage of GDP going for health care over the last half-century in this country, compared to other countries, which got their costs under control decades ago. I know that's what everyone who focuses on this topic does. How we connect this country's expenditures to the fact that our country relies to a far greater degree on the private sector compared to other countries is the challenge. No matter what leading health economists have said on this subject, there are still so many people who are convinced that the government is simply not as efficient as the private sector—what a joke. Inefficiency is the name of the game for health insurance companies. Only they get away with presenting it as a matter of consumer choice. In actuality, it is a matter of high administrative costs, and we know where the profits that are generated go. But getting people to see that is what's nearly impossible."

"There are several glaringly obvious observations that can be made in talking about our health care system," Nikki was raising her voice and getting more animated. "One, that costs go up, not down, when the private sector becomes involved. There's loads of evidence, but people aren't willing to listen because the private sector has been so effective in its messaging about government inefficiency. That brings me to the second point, which is another thing the public is just not ready to accept, namely, that the government is underwriting private sector insurance companies, which is what allows the companies to charge less. That's exactly what's happening in the pharmaceutical industry because of patent law legislation. But that is a separate topic. Health insurance is complicated enough, so we'll have to stick to one health care issue at a time. So, back to health insurance – all those subsidies that politicians like to claim are going to people who need help paying for health insurance are going into the insurance company's coffers. The subsidies do not come anywhere near the wallets of people buying the insurance. I'm not sure what it will take to get the idea across that the government is bankrolling private insurance companies and allowing them to pat themselves on the back for being so efficient. This is a prime example of what the essence of corporate welfare looks like. Who said that socialism is good for the corporate sector, but capitalism is good for the public? This is a superb example, isn't it?"

"I'm with you," was Laura's response. "But I still think that it might be better to hold off on this topic since we agreed to put what's happened in the health sector at the end of what we produce. To treat it as an illustration of what privatization holds for other sectors. That, along with the Fannie Mae and Freddie Mac stories. Both of those illustrations should help to show that privatization doesn't do what privatization proponents say it does. It doesn't make things run more efficiently. It makes things more expensive because private companies are responsive to their stockholders, whose sole interest is the company's profitability. Stockholders have no loyalty to organizations that do not produce a profit, a short-term profit at that. And those profits have to come from somewhere. Health care companies have been able to conceal the fact, through their never-ending messaging, that their earnings are not really due to their extraordinary efficiency efforts since those earnings are actually underwritten by the government, which gets its money from taxpayers. Then there's the whole issue of fraud. I think we'd need a heck of a lot more time to document that. For example, there are loads of data comparing nursing homes owned by nonprofits as opposed to those operated by private-sector owners, indicating an enormous amount of fraud is taking place. There's also a record of private-sector hospitals doing unnecessary tests and, worse, unnecessary surgeries. Like at Tenet hospitals in California. That is well documented. The numbers are spectacular, and the data is out there in the public realm. The hospitals paid out a colossal amount of money in fines when they were brought to court. But those fines were minor compared to the profits they were raking in. Fines are treated as the cost of doing business. It's hard to watch that happening and still not see the public registering a negative reaction."

"I agree. But people pay attention to what they experience directly, not so much what is outside their personal experience. They're upset about how much their insurance premiums and out-of-pocket cost have increased. Remember that the premiums have been increasing by about 4 percent a year, and economic growth has not risen above 2 percent per year since the recession set in as of 2020. The 2020 twenty-two-thousand-dollar family premium is now well over thirty thousand."

"True, as we both well know, given how much we're paying."

"People are upset about how much more they have to pay, but they don't seem to care about how much more the government is handing over to for-profit corporations. Those who argue for reducing the role of private companies continue to be labeled socialists. The insurance companies have been spending a lot more on promoting their message, and they're getting their money's worth. Just look at the ads that clutter up TV programs, and our cell phone feeds. The messaging is non-stop. And as all those social psychologists keep telling us, when something is repeated often enough, it takes on the mantle of truth."

"Okay." Laura was frowning. "I know that what you're saying is distressing, and we need to pay attention to it. But you're convincing me that we should leave discussion of the health care sector for later because it is so complex. Maybe identifying some other sectors that people haven't been paying attention to would provide a bigger, more complete picture of how much of the country's infrastructure and the public service agencies are being whisked away. What can we work on next that's a little less complicated? There are so many possibilities."

"True, but before we move on, let's review what we know about the whole health care enterprise so when we get back to it, we'll know where to start. We know that it was hit hard by the pandemic. It has been undergoing a tremendous amount of reorganization. We can see how rapidly the hospital sector consolidated. The big hospital chains now own most hospitals in the country and employ the majority of doctors. Small hospitals that were not lucky enough to be absorbed by the big chains have been disappearing. Rural hospitals are nearly all gone. Pharmaceutical companies are still raking in enormous profits as they continue successful efforts to fight all attempts to reduce the length of time allotted for monopolization by patent law. Health insurance is still central to debates about socialized medicine. What's particularly interesting is that the health sector continues in its role as a provider of jobs while serving as the ideological battlefield between those who say health care is a human right and those who say it's a commodity like any other that should go to the highest bidder. Did I miss anything?"

"No, I would say that's a pretty complete picture," was Laura's response. "Let's get back to what else we should be working on. I'm leaning toward doing a more thorough job of documenting the fallout of not just the leasing but the selling off of public land. I'm interested in who the buyers are. You know that is an area that I didn't think would be very interesting, but it is."

"I'll go with that. Tacking down who the buyers are is certainly satisfying, isn't it? Let's see how far we can get with that. We can compare notes at the end of the day. Maybe there's more information on this buried in government documents, which most people wouldn't bother to access, and the people doing the buying and leasing do their best to keep it buried."

After spending the day doing what they said they would do, Nikki and Laura had determined that the way the federal government was dealing with public land was even more daunting than what they already knew. The material they had gathered was certainly interesting, but they could see that the task they had taken on was enormous. They told each other that it was also a highly rewarding uphill climb.

Nikki was concentrating on fracking, which had risen to the top of the list of issues that environmentalists had been targeting for the last couple of decades. There was extensive debate on the pros and cons, and a growing body of evidence documenting the dangers it posed. Nikki directed Laura to the review of the literature she was looking at. The review stated that increasing reliance on natural gas and reducing coal dependence reduced the emission of toxic gases and improved air quality. But that natural gas was still vastly inferior to green energy sources like wind and solar energy. A large body of evidence had accumulated indicating that greenhouse gases emitted in fracking erased any benefit that the switch from coal to natural gas was producing. The emission of methane was said to be of particular concern. It's colorless and odorless, so people aren't likely to notice it until they experience symptoms, including headaches, loss of coordination, and vomiting. Another finding was that because fracking is a water-intensive process, the water supply in communities near fracking operations was being affected.

Given that fracking operations are being built near established communities, millions of Americans are being exposed to the risk of contaminated water. The review ended with a warning about the dangers of fracking that still hadn't been fully explored, most notably the potential of changing geology that drilling thousands of feet into the earth was causing. The increasing rate of earthquakes in regions where fracking had been going on was evidence of that.

The two women looked at each other for a minute or two before saying anything. Then Laura said, "Reading the findings in that report was scary. I knew that environmentalists were opposed to fracking, but I didn't know how much of a health risk it posed. It's scarier still because this is a relatively new process that still doesn't have a long enough track record to reveal all the other yet-to-be-discovered risks."

"I agree. Reading that makes me want to run out and join the nearest environmentalist group. Maybe we can figure out a way to help, like letter writing or something. But I also think getting further into the environmental risks is a big distraction. For example, all the attention going to methane and animal husbandry is compelling, but we can't let ourselves become too involved in that. It's not the work we've committed ourselves to."

But they just couldn't stop themselves. They kept running into new eye-opening findings. "By the way," Laura began, "did you run across the New York Times discussion about the electricity industry building new plants to run on natural gas? The energy companies are patting themselves on the back for switching from coal to cleaner energy. The issue is that there is no need for more plants. With the growth of clean energy, the plants will be obsolete in no time, and the customers will be left paying for the construction of those plants for years. I like the observation made by the journalist writing the story who said that the electric companies are behaving like smokers who truly want to quit, as soon as they finish off the carton of cigarettes they just bought."

"Nice imagery. The debate about energy sources is never-ending, isn't it?" was Nikki's response. "The idea that consumers have any say in what products the market offers is a fairy tale that too many people, including a whole contingent of older economists, had bought into. This case is a perfect illustration. There's so much disagreement among economists about basic mainstream economic tenets these days, like rational choice, that it may develop into a big enough crack to let everyone begin to question the assumptions having to do with consumer choice that the old guard used to build its economic models."

"You're absolutely right. But we keep getting into hugely distracting discussions. Let's go back to the main thing we said we'd work on. On that point, I wanted to mention that earlier today. I found some interesting information on how much money the government is getting from its land dealings. But I'm kind of worn out by reading about all the environmental risks that the government is ignoring in its land management. Let's start fresh tomorrow."

"Okay, but wait before we quit. I want to tell you what else I ran into that's pretty remarkable." Nikki just couldn't get over what they were finding on fracking, which she knew so little about before they started looking into it. "This is also too much of a distraction but, as I say, very interesting. It seems that there is a shortage of helium looming. The Russians apparently have the biggest supply. It's a by-product of fracking. I thought its main use was for filling balloons, but that's sure not the case. You know why? It's lighter than air. I wouldn't have thought of that. Of course, I had no reason to think of it. It's used to make high-speed computer components, space shuttles, nuclear reactors, fiber optics, semiconductor chips, and MRI operations. Who knew?"

"As interesting as that is, I repeat, I've had enough for today. I hope I don't end up thinking about the dangers related to fracking and helium uses in the middle of the night."

THIRTY-SEVEN

Over the next few days, Laura and Nikki continued to work on issues surrounding public land use. They continued to be surprised by how volatile the debates were about topics other than oil and gas extraction. They knew about the stand-off between the Bundy family, who insisted that they should have access to public land for livestock grazing. They claimed that the federal government was not a legitimate owner. But they hadn't paid much attention to the details in the story. The ranchers took the stand that the land belongs to the people, which meant they shouldn't be charged for using it for grazing. The government's position was that there were laws governing grazing fees. They said the fees, set in 2007, were used for land maintenance purposes. Maintenance, including, for example, the killing of carnivores that were a threat to the livestock. Road maintenance and monitoring the quality of the groundwater in the area were other costs.

In reading about the Bundys, the women were surprised to find that the ranchers had been paying grazing fees since 1954. But they suddenly stopped. It took another forty years before the Bureau of Land Management canceled the family's grazing rights. Nothing happened for another twenty years. The Bundys weren't paying for using the land, and the BLM wasn't doing anything other than writing letters telling them how much they owed in grazing fees. Finally, the BLM came in to herd the cattle off the land, telling the family that it had accumulated a debt of one million dollars in unpaid grazing fees. The Bundys called in every right-wing militia group they could to participate in a protest. The Bundys, father and two sons, were arrested for threatening the lives of the federal agents. But the courts dismissed the charges. Other court cases have not been settled. That includes the case of a protester who died during one of the confrontations. His wife and each of his twelve children sued the government. In the meantime, the whole grazing issue seems to have died down.

"The public just isn't interested enough in animals grazing on public land for the media to continue focusing on the story. The stand-off was pretty attention-getting, but after that died down, interest in the federal land issue died with it," was Laura's observation.

"Let's face it," said Nikki, "most Americans who are city dwellers, us included, have no idea where and how the food we buy in grocery stores is produced. There have been stories about taking little kids to farms to show them where milk comes from, where eggs come from, and where the chicken nuggets they eat come from. Adults laugh when children act surprised. Most people probably think of cattle grazing on the land with nostalgia and prefer to imagine that rather than giving any thought to the fact that most of our meat comes from industrial farms. I bet most adults in the country don't have much of an idea how industrial farms operate to get them the hamburgers and chicken nuggets they eat – and don't want to know. If they did, most people would probably become vegetarians. Increasing numbers are doing that."

"Then there's logging," said Laura. "The government took steps during the Trump administration to reduce the impact of the Endangered Species Act and the Clean Water Act by reducing the review period before allowing projects to go forward. It ignored research outlining best practices aimed at attaining sustainable timber harvesting. That would have been bad enough, but in responding to the lumber industry's bidding, it manages to spend a whole lot more to subsidize the industry. The industry continues to benefit in various ways. The government has been building logging roads used by the industry and no one else. It administers timber sales for lumber companies. The government spends more than it gets in return for the support it offers lumber companies in large part because it has not attempted to evaluate the worth of the lumber. Even without that, it's obvious that it should be demanding a bigger cut of the profits."

Nikki's response was, "Okay, so we've established that the government is not being responsive enough to environmentalists' concerns about public land use. It isn't getting a fair share of the profits from logging, grazing, and oil and gas extraction. And, that the public isn't invested in such issues, at least not invested enough."

What interested Nikki and Laura about the Bundy story was that the ranchers would have had to pay a much higher fee if they had had to pay for grazing rights to private-sector landowners. According to some estimates, they would have to have paid over twice as much.

"It seems that the federal government is engaged in leasing land for grazing and saying that it is making money doing so, but it is paying more to maintain the land than it is getting back in fees. Do I have that right?" Laura said to Nikki.

"Yeah, I don't understand why that is. Private-sector owners of similar land plots are charging ranchers much more for the right to graze and charging extra for water access for the animals. Ranchers are forced to rely on private land if there is no public land nearby. They seem to be ready to pay a higher fee. They're not going out of business because of it."

"We'll need to do a lot more work on this, but I think that the ranchers who pay more for grazing rights can still make a profit because the beef industry is subsidized. In other words, ranchers out west get two kinds of government subsidies. I sure don't understand why that's happening. Is it a matter of effective lobbying? The ranchers raise a very small proportion of the beef that Americans consume. Most of the beef comes from industrial farms. The industrial farms use enclosed feedlots. They use hay and grain to feed the cattle and antibiotics to allow them to crowd all those animals together."

Laura was looking unsettled. "Alright, maybe we've done enough on federal land use for now. Let's go over what we have. I think it's time for a review of where we've been and another review of where we're going next. Do you want to do that? I feel buried in facts. I know we've come up with a lot of attention-grabbing information, and I don't want to get it muddled up. I want to create an outline so that we can separate what we are finding in each arena. I'm especially concerned about tracking down who is doing the leasing and buying of so many of the goods and services we've looked into."

"You're right. Let's take a break for lunch and start on that when we get back. We can think about running the list of corporate buyers we come up with past our discussion group. I'm not sure we should go back to the board just yet. What do you think?"

"I'm all for getting some feedback from our friends first," was Nikki's reaction. "I think we need something more fully developed before we go back to the board. Maybe when Liz has done more work on the website, we can have her present it to the board and go back to the question of what they think about how we should use it. We can get back to the whole question of what we do with the information we are collecting at that time, whether we go for membership, or simply the sale of the product for a fixed price, or donations. Stuff like that, that neither of us wants to think about."

*****

The two women decided to call Liz. They needed to get away from their research for a bit. They were feeling like they were getting a lot done, but at the same time, they were beginning to feel overwhelmed. Talking about the website might be a good antidote. Liz said she had been doing some work on the website and was happy to meet to discuss it. They agreed to meet at the end of the day for dinner.

Liz had done a great deal more than think about the website. She brought her laptop and opened up a slide show of options for the design of the website. She came up with several logos that she thought might be good symbols. She arranged all the things that had to go on the page, filling in what would be script about the organization and its purpose, with a repetition of a phrase over and over: "It's the economy, stupid."

Laura and Nikki got a laugh seeing the phrase. They liked all the examples of possible logos. They agreed that they should choose one and get the website up. They agreed on the symbol of an open book. Liz had created a space for signing up for whatever they decided – membership? Liz suggested that they include a section up front highlighting new findings that would be integrated into the body of the text after a week or so. Nikki and Laura liked that idea. They told Liz to keep coming up with suggestions since her contribution was proving very valuable.

All three women were in great spirits. Nikki and Laura told Liz that they were happy to take a break from their labors. That, as much as they enjoyed doing the research, what they were finding was so vast that they needed to keep taking breaks to think about how to organize it all. Liz said she could understand that from what she had heard about their work. They all knew what writing a report on findings was about. But this report was much more extensive and would need to be continually updated. Some of the transfers of public entities would run into problems, just as was true with various past transfers. Those kinds of things would have to be included in an ever-evolving document. They hadn't thought about how to handle that.

The three women went on to talk about how they each got into the work they were doing. The evening ended on a very positive note and with the promise of getting together soon.

*****

Laura and Nikki were eager to share the latest development with the group. Nikki called Jane and said that they wanted to celebrate deciding on a website. They told Jane that Liz had created it, so they wanted to give her credit. Would it be okay to invite her to the celebration? Jane said she was pleased to hear about this new step and would be glad to include Liz.

Laura said that the guys had come up with such a great potluck dinner last time that they would have trouble coming up with something equally interesting, but that they would bring something. They agreed on Friday night. Jane said she would contact everyone and tell them to be prepared to celebrate yet another stage in the development of The Public Record.

The women decided on Thai food. Who doesn't like Pad Thai? They would add green curry and some other noodle dishes that they both liked. The group welcomed them and their food selections.

Nikki and Laura said they were eager to tell the others about the prototype of the website that Liz had created. They asked her to talk about it. Liz laid out the basic plan and added that she had suggested using an open book as the Public Record symbol. Everyone agreed that it was the perfect image. They all congratulated Liz on what she had produced. They said they were eager to see the text that would replace the "it's the economy, stupid" paragraph that Nikki mentioned. Laura and Nikki promised to work on the paragraph and run it by the group soon. They said that they would be working closely with Liz to get the website in shape because they were excited about how it was turning out.

Laura and Nikki went on to say that they were eager to get feedback from the group about what to say about the country's readiness to transfer public goods and services to the private sector. They went on to outline what they were thinking regarding how to end the document they were creating. They said they knew that it was premature to think about that, but it was what was on their minds, and they were eager to get the group's reaction.

They began by telling the others that they had been tossing around ideas about how the country got to the point of being so opposed to taxation. "Here's what I've been running across," said Laura. "A lot of respected scholars and well-known public opinion columnists have been offering explanations. They are largely in agreement about the idea that the mid to late 1970s stand as a turning point. The idea is that Americans left the excesses of the 1960s behind and were suddenly ready to embrace new ideas that would shape public policy well into the twenty-first century. These were ideas grounded in Milton Friedman's economic theorizing, starting with the notion that human beings are rational; therefore, they should be permitted to choose without government interference – choose to act in ways that benefit them or not. That reinforced the growing commitment to individualism, justifying a "me-first" attitude, where everyone would get what they wanted as a result of self-interest and that, in turn, would make for a booming economy."

"Exactly." Mark jumped in to say, "As far as I can see, taxes became defined as an instrument being employed by the government to expand government control, which some pundits turned into the claim that taxes constitute a restriction of individual rights. That claim became firmly entrenched in the conservative playbook. How that happened is hard to pin down. Variations on that theme are even harder to comprehend fully. For example, I don't think anyone has a good understanding of why masks during the pandemic became so symbolic of government control. Decades ago, government agencies started prohibiting smoking in public places. There were no public protests. People simply went along with that directive. Maybe it was just a different era. You could look into the debates among libertarians about when government regulation is justified over a range of things like drug safety, air and water quality, and car safety. Airbags in the front seat of cars were mandated in 1998 without much protest. How about the more recent issue of whether disinformation presented via social media should be monitored? That might be fun to do. But I realize that it would also be highly distracting."

"You're right. That would be interesting to explore and totally distracting," said Laura. "Even more scary is the fact that private media companies, no, make that private individuals, like the heads of Facebook and Twitter, are taking control over who gets to say what. Pundits are encouraging private companies to withdraw advertising from media outlets that support disinformation. While I'm in favor of the goal, I'm not at all comfortable with the idea that we are shifting responsibility for such things to a small number of very rich and powerful individuals."

The others were nodding. But the discussion moved ahead before anyone could respond.

"Let us tell you what we're thinking of saying," Nikki was eager to get back to the main topic. "Fascination with the promise of efficiency, when added to the aversion to taxation, goes a long way in explaining where we are today. Handing over public sector entities to the private sector is invariably accompanied by the promise of greater efficiency. That proponents of privatization say it will cause the price of the goods and services involved to fall, which simply doesn't happen. And more importantly, when it does happen, it's because the government is subsidizing the private-sector entity to which the public goods and services have been transferred. Health insurance is the prime example. If health insurance premiums have not skyrocketed, it's not because health insurance companies are more efficient than government agencies. It's because the government is handing over money to the insurance companies, which, we should note, they pass on to their stockholders. Those are tax dollars the government is handing over. Paying the middleman is not unreasonable if the government puts some controls on how much it is prepared to pay. That would require regulation, and just the thought of that makes health insurance companies cry "socialism."

"You've touched on a huge topic," was Dick's contribution. "The socialism scare works every time. I don't think people understand what it means. Like that Rand Paul book we talked about a few weeks ago, the most vocal critics of socialism start talking about dictators right away. Why don't they realize that socialism is how our ancestors survived in small towns here and wherever they immigrated from? People had to cooperate, or they wouldn't have survived. They built institutions together, contributing the skills and money that the projects required. Co-ops were common. Anyone growing wheat knew that. Each farmer wasn't going to build his own mill. They built a single mill that everyone used and earned money based on the weight of the grain they brought in. They elected the person doing the weighing and trusted that person. That's certainly the way Native American tribes operated."

"As an aside," Jane jumped in, "as I told Dick the other day, I just learned that Indians don't want to be called Native Americans. They want to be recognized as members of nations of their own, not as Americans. They consider their tribes to be nations. I bet everyone else here was well aware of that. Okay, okay, I know we can't debate the implications that go along with that. I know we're concentrating on something else entirely."

"This is also not on topic, was Adam's contribution. "But I can't help feeling the need to go back to the idea that so many people have this crazy notion that they are in complete control in making choices that determine the course of their lives. It's obvious that some people are seriously disadvantaged from the beginning of their lives. Saying that those people have a choice about how they will lead their lives is nonsense. That belief is behind the idea that government shouldn't intervene, shouldn't tax people who have more to help people who have less. And that the private sector allows people to make their own choices about the services, and some goods like food and housing, they want, and the government somehow restricts choice – is absolute nonsense." Adam looked around to see if anyone wanted to add to his observation. He could see that everyone in the room was ready to add their bit. Jane was the first to jump in.

"It's hard to miss the fact that the private sector is perfectly willing to take over tasks that the government has been responsible for in the past if it can charge for it. Even if it charges the government, I notice that the private sector is not establishing companies to carry out work that it sees no way to profit from. Taking care of the disabled and elderly who need assistance with daily living is a good example. Private companies aren't rushing into that market unless it is to bid on a government contract for doing it. They aren't rushing in to deal with all kinds of social problems, like runaway youth, the homeless population, and addiction. Problems like that aren't moneymakers. When for-profit organizations attempt to get into this kind of thing in response to government incentives, they don't do it well. Besides that, too many of them are found to be engaged in fraud. The responsibility for dealing with society's most vulnerable falls on public agencies and nonprofit organizations, which require funding. And the source of funding is the government, which does make money on its own. The money to deal with socially problematic issues comes from taxes."

"So, where are we?" Laura was looking somewhat impatient. She was eager to come up with a clear statement. While she enjoyed the long and wide-ranging discussions they were used to having, right now, she wanted something else. "What I want to pin down is what are we going to say is responsible for the state of affairs this society finds itself in. Saying that people in this country have been sold a bill of goods involving the glories of efficiency would not be popular. But I think that we need to figure out a way to present that idea. I think our data indicating that the takeover of public entities by private sector organizations that go on to become monopolies and oligopolies in the name of efficiency would be eye-opening to people who have not been paying attention to the fact that is exactly what's going on."

Nikki was having trouble sitting still. She was even more energized than Laura. "Good, good. You're right. We're back to what we were thinking when we started doing this research. Corporatization decreases the choices people have available to them. Individual rights suddenly don't look so commanding in the face of powerful organizations that don't have any competitors interested in challenging them. It means that there is little choice, no matter how often the market proponents try to convince us that we are doing the choosing. That raises an interesting question, and I don't think anyone is putting it this way. What it comes down to is the question of whether the promise of efficiency is worth giving up choice. You have to admit that is an attention-getting argument. It leads to the question of whether it would be better to pay taxes to the government and maintain control over the entities that are charged with carrying out public services than to lose control to powerful private sector organizations over which individuals have little influence. Private-sector organizations that are overseen by boards primarily interested in profit and so large that dissatisfaction on the part of consumers doesn't matter much since consumers end up having no alternatives."

"I don't think people realize how true what you are saying is," said Mark. "Just think how much trouble liberal politicians have had passing legislation to increase the minimum wage. Then Amazon decided that raising the minimum wage was a good idea. Even if it was a tactic to forestall unionization of its warehouses, the effect was that the minimum wage was suddenly a reality. Corporate America is not only highly efficient, but it's also highly effective in achieving what the government struggles to accomplish. The chances that it's a good objective are not guaranteed. It could just as well be a damaging objective."

"I just want to throw in another observation." Dick hadn't said too much so far. "This comes from an economics professor at the University of Chicago who is from the new school of thought there, the post-Friedman school. He says that this country has moved from a "market economy" in which the market is a tool used to distribute goods and services to a "market society" where everything is up for sale. He uses the example of the availability of an upgrade in one of the California prisons. Of course, that's if the prisoner can afford it. The prisoner can get a nicer cell, maybe with a room with a view, a better mattress, or a private bathroom. Actually, I don't know what the person gets, but I understand the upgrade costs about $100. The point is, if there is a way to monetize it, to put a price on it, it can be sold. Public-sector organizations are all up for sale to the highest bidder because governments need funding to carry out the tasks that the private sector isn't interested in. This economist says that monetization is exactly what is crowding out the sense of community. And that monetization has become central to this society's values. If you can't afford it, too bad. You don't deserve it. If there is no sense of community, everyone is at each other's throats. And here is the big leap forward in thinking – no sense of community means society can't function. It all collapses."

"That is an overwhelming idea." Jane looked stunned. Everyone else was looking uncomfortable, but no one disagreed. Adam's contribution was, "That's really what it comes down to, isn't it?"

Everyone was quiet for a while, then Laura looked around, looking both serious and sad, and said, "Everything you've all said connects a lot of dots. It's a convoluted, coherent, and terrifying story. All the two of us have to do is add up the list of who in the private sector has been buying up, leasing, or otherwise acquiring public sector entities, and we will have a complete and very formidable document."

"Right. I'll let you write that up," said Nikki, which took the edge off of the serious mood everyone was in.

"Ha, ha. I think that we'll be sitting up nights drafting and re-drafting that statement – together."

Liz hadn't said much during the discussion. She was surprised by how fast ideas and thoughts were being tossed around. She was impressed with everything she heard and was even more pleased to be part of the project now that she was hearing what everyone had to say.

They all agreed that the discussion had gone far enough for the time being. They asked Liz to talk more about herself and her work. About how she learned to develop websites.

The evening ended with a sense of closure about the discussion that had taken place. Everyone in the room was well aware of the fact that the image of society they were watching unfold was not something to cheer about. Even so, there was general agreement that Laura and Nikki were doing something that was very demanding and very much worth applauding.

THIRTY-EIGHT

"For a group of people whose day jobs don't involve analyses of socio-economic and political issues, our friends did a pretty good job of helping us put together the story of how we, as a society, got here, ready and eager to shift public sector entities over to the private sector. They certainly left us with a very discouraging picture of reality, which will not be easy to convey," Laura said as they got back to work that Monday.

"Yes, it was interesting to watch people taking disparate ideas and bringing them together. The result was a fairly complete and explosive explanation for why people have become so opposed to being taxed. It was less of an attack on someone else's ideas than a straightforward account of one set of beliefs after another coming together, ideas largely attributable to the campaigns waged by parties that are clear beneficiaries. And now we know the consequences of those campaigns. The interaction between opposition to taxes and commitment to the idea of private-sector efficiency is perfectly clear."

"Are you ready to work on the rest of it? On developing the outline of private-sector entities that are involved in buying up public sector organizations that we said we would use to fill in as we uncover more material?"

"I guess so," was Nikki's answer. "I can't say I'm eager to get to it because it's such a big step. But I guess that's what we said we would do, and now we're at the point of doing it. So, let's get on with it."

Once they got started, they found that the list of private sector organizations doing the buying and leasing wasn't that long. The buyers were easier to identify in some cases than others. Some public sector entities had become fully privatized, like the U.S. Post Office, with Amazon now in charge. Others, like public school systems and water-treatment plants, were well on their way to being privatized, and ownership was evident if not yet fully consolidated. Ownership of public land, a topic that they had no preparation for tackling, was unfolding in a clear pattern with a small number of corporate entities involved. The health sector had been moving along toward privatization for a longer time and was now well on its way to control by a few clearly identifiable oligopolies. The Freddie Mae and Freddie Mac story was an important addition. Then there were the unsettled cases like fire and police departments, plus utility companies, which were not as far along in the process but getting there.

"There are so many more instances of transfers going on, but I think we've hit some of the biggest ones and can add all the others that we haven't tackled later.

Nikki said, "Are we done yet? I can't think about this anymore."

"Yes, I think we're done with this part. But remember, we have to take what we were talking about with our friends the other night about what we say at the end of what we produce. And we have to turn it all into words on paper, digital paper, of course."

"I knew you'd say that."

"Actually, I think it might not be that hard after the discussion of the other night," Laura was looking pretty smug as she was saying that. Nikki's response was, "You've got to be kidding."

"No. Listen. I think starting with the notion that we are witnessing the collapse of society could be the overall theme of this project. We can cast the transfer of public sector goods and services over to the private sector as one of a number of indicators. The inability of people in this society to cooperate and the readiness to hand over responsibility for handling shared responsibilities for the maintenance of society to a handful of very successful business people is a symptom. I'm appropriating observations here made by the historian from the University of Chicago that Dick mentioned. He said that stressors that would be manageable have now become insurmountable, including epidemics, protests and uprisings, and natural disasters. Just look at how dysfunctional Congress is. Doesn't that sound familiar? People who have wealth and power are committed to protecting it and adding to it. What we are watching alongside that trend is the opposite side of the coin. We are witnessing increasing numbers of people losing the things that gave them a sense of worth and security, starting with their jobs, their savings, their houses, and on and on, up to and including losing their health. Those with wealth and power are reacting to what's happening in society by advocating efficiency. The people with most to lose are accepting that solution because it is so effectively sold to them. The result is the consolidation of control over society's resources by the few and the reduction of benefits to the majority. What do you think?"

"Wait, I have a vivid illustration to add," Laura was already going on. "It's like what happens to a colony of bees when people out to make a profit take advantage of the bees, stressing them out by moving them around to provide pollinating services. The bees become weak and lose the ability to deal with the stress. The result is that the colony collapses. Now, what do you think?"

Nikki was sitting there with her eyes bugging out of her head and her mouth open. "Right, as I said the other night, you write it up."

"And, as I said, we'll do it together." Laura looked upbeat in contrast to Nikki, who looked like she was in a state of psychic overload. "So, do you agree on using society's collapse as our overriding theme in arguing that collapse is the ultimate outcome of privatization of public resources? Aren't you glad we're just focusing on public sector transfers? What if we were crazy enough to try to document what's happening in the private sector too? We know that the consolidation of the private sector entities is growing at an even faster rate. We can see that a small number of billionaires are in a position to buy up any new start-up that looks like it might be profitable. Like what Amazon, Facebook, Google, and Walmart have done. It looks like our billionaires are acting just like the oligarchs in Russia. See, doesn't our task look a lot less formidable now?"

Nikki thought about it for a minute, then said, "Oh my god, don't go there. I'm overwhelmed enough as it is. All I can say is that intellectually I'm with you. Emotionally, I think we are in over our heads. I'm not at all sure I can stand up and say the things you are saying with the confidence that requires. Saying all that to the board for a start. I don't feel that I have the credentials to do that."

"Here's my thinking. I'm not sure who has better credentials than we have. Look at the research we've done, what we've been finding, and what we can provide evidence for. Besides, we're not advocating something revolutionary. We're just laying out facts and providing our interpretations. It's up to those who hear what we have to say to come up with steps to address what we present."

"Okay. That's a good point. You know, I never knew you were so tough. You're really formidable. What you just said makes for a pretty compelling argument. In fact, I think you may succeed in convincing me to stop being a chicken about presenting our conclusions to the rest of the world. I'm ready to follow your lead. Let's write up what you've just said and give it to the board. I'm suddenly having a vision of the board members standing up and cheering. Tell me you agree, or I'll think I'm going crazy."

"I think that is an absolutely stunning image that I am enjoying having in my head. And then, of course, I envision armies of people doing that."

"All I can say is that I would be thrilled if we achieve even a minuscule amount of that kind of reaction."